HOLT'S
ALMANAC

HOLT'S ALMANAC

L.C. HUFFMAN

gatekeeper press
Columbus, Ohio

Holt's Almanac
Published by Gatekeeper Press
2167 Stringtown Rd, Suite 109
Columbus, OH 43123-2989
www.GatekeeperPress.com

The editorial work for this book is entirely the product of the author. Gatekeeper Press did not participate in and is not responsible for any aspect of this work.

Library of Congress Control Number: 2021948746

ISBN (hardcover): 9781662918247
ISBN (paperback): 9781662918254
eISBN: 9781662918261

Contents

v

PROLOGUE

I was on holiday in the United States when the world came to a halt. Being unable to return to my country provided some challenge to occupy my time, until a greater purpose overwhelmed my prior duties. If it were not for the modern day artifacts which fell into my possession, I would be aimless in the dark.

If I could believe in chance, I would have no reservations assembling this collection of experiences. The *voice recording* that I stumbled upon and the *journal* of a character that complements it seem to carry many of the answers we have been seeking. Having transcribed and summarized them, my research on many of the included topics has led to my own supplemental information. My footnotes contain some of this research, which I hope will be a means of clairvoyance for you — or at least inspiration.

If you embark on this journey, you too will see the unfortunate life of the protagonist, who was made to do what no one willed, and who willed a path that resisted his own nature. It has been said that a rising tide lifts all boats, but some men are stones. Evidently a few are destined to live out this struggle. This is the story of a man named Holt Dooley who certainly adheres to this concept. However, I would not categorize his entire journey in a negative light.

Holt was tormented for and by his ability to think. I do not believe others would relate to him, let alone understand him. He might be described as extraordinary, quirky, and sometimes, a bit harsh, but his development throughout the account might surprise you. In my humble opinion, exploring his trials alongside him is our best chance to understand him… and understanding him will be an important key to the future of all people alike.

Although a blunt account of the story is told in the audio log, It was necessary for me to elaborate in the transcription in order to relay the information intelligibly. Without revealing who I believe the narrator to be, I hope that when we reconvene at the story's end, you arrive at the same conclusion that I did. Various hints exist that (whether intentionally or not) lead one to infer that a character from the plot is also the orator. With that statement, I encourage you to pry at the meaning behind every word, and infer any imaginable possibility. For whatever dark closet fosters the dullest parts of this story, when the door is opened and light creeps in, there might just be a skeleton. Without further ado, I give you *Holt's Almanac.*

CHAPTER 1

(The Dark is Never Lonely)

Reflections are easy to see, yet difficult to grasp. It is frightening to think that whatever you can see in a mirror can possibly see you. Holt Dooley was reminded of this truth, as he held a burbling parallel of himself in the water of his cooking pot.

Rotating on its ancient, invisible axis, the portion of the globe Holt sat upon was spotlighted by our sun. He took the pot from his rock oven and savored the rest of his sassafras tea alongside the colors of dawn. That wholesome moment of respite, sandwiched in between two difficult days of traveling on foot, was just as palatable as the tea. Crossing the Carolina-line on the Appalachian trail toward Mount Mitchell, he supplemented himself with a mulberry to every hundredth step. A wayfaring forager such as himself, counts on every ounce of nutrients to propel them on their journey; constantly moving and constantly eating to keep enough energy. Arguably nothing is as valuable as ecological knowledge for this lifestyle, which is why he had been in the process of memorizing every detail of recently purchased Audubon books. An occasional branch would untuck his locks from underneath his cap, but his determined countenance

1

remained unchanged. Every calling bird he counted and every passing plant he named.

The perception of Dooley based on a newspaper description versus a television depiction would portray two drastically different characters. His newly found skillset bore the resemblance of a mountain hermit, while his physical appearance showed a reasonably well kept man suitable for the social world. Although, I suppose his hair had grown to a hockey-cut, and his red flannel jacket was covered in dirt. The Appalachian humidity certainly didn't favor his clothing choice, which was reflected in the fact that the flannel was tied around his waist. He planned on getting more use out of it further down the way on his expedition.

The peak of Mount Mitchell[1] became a well deserved viewpoint, and he took to sketching the scene in his journal to remember its rugged grace. As weeping trees dropped their vermillion splashed leaves, the slow setting was better etched into his memory than his paper.

"6684 elevation...remarkable. Last great peak until the Rockies," Holt thought to himself.

The exercising of his mind was clear by his outward expressions. His fingers would become restless, and twiddling a small piece of driftwood in between them was alleviating and almost involuntary. It was smooth from the natural oil of his skin and the consistent friction it experienced when he would twiddle it. The face of the twig showcased lines of contour like a fingerprint, from its growth patterns when it once lived in the soil. It was a special gift to him, representing an important relationship in his past. Holt always had a lot to think about, even when events around him

---

[1] Mount Mitchell is the tallest Appalachian peak, and the largest peak east of the Mississippi River.

were mundane, his mind was occupied. Yet being twenty-something and on-the-run, jobless and fatigued, he was not worried. No, certainly not worried. Dooley had thought of every possible outcome for any reasonable situation he could find himself in, and consequently rarely encountered regret or even excitement.

His burning calves took him northwestward off of the Appalachian trail to blaze his own. Almost walking into a spider web, he abruptly stopped and examined his hated enemy[2]. It was bright yellow, spiny, and particularly ugly. He decided to traverse around the web rather than destroy it, solely because he was feeling merciful, but it was clear he was no friend to arachnids.

Without alluding too much, I can say that he had mustered a tremendous amount of courage to leave his home in the way that he did, and for weeks he kept it up. For Holt's sake, his origin and all it encompasses will more easily be accepted if one gets to know him first. That is why I don't plan on documenting these events so directly and to the point; the way I'm choosing to elaborate is deliberate. Anyhow.

It was just until entering this hauntingly thick forest, that his confidence wavered. Although he anticipated this personal low would happen at some point, prior knowledge of the event didn't comfort him in the present. It seems anticipation alone gains nothing, but coupled with preparation, it emerges as a powerful tool for one's psyche. In light of this, he had not prepared for what he was witnessing: a forest that grew darker faster than nightfall.

"Under this canopy, I wouldn't even be able to read a map if I had one," he thought.

---

[2] *Gasteracantha cancriformis*

The woods were inescapably dense, wherein branches were tightly gathered, even woven like a basket. In the earlier days of his journey, Holt relied on the sky and its stars for direction. Yet, being dusk, and incapable of seeing a full-picture view of the heavens anyway, he began to guess his way around. He hoped that "his way" wouldn't actually turn out to be "round". Oftentimes this happens to wanderers. Having one's left leg undetectably shorter than their right, or maybe even using one side of your brain more than the other, could make them eventually walk in circles. But having measured his legs before taking on this expedition, he figured this was one problem he wouldn't have to worry about. Not because his feet met the ground at simultaneously perfect lengths, but because he knew his dimensions, and calculated his steps accordingly. As you will ascertain by the end of this account, knowing your dimensions[3] is very, very important.

At the start of the seemingly enchanted, ink-blotched forest, light leaked through the treetops as rays, like tiny streams of water through a beaver dam. He would, on occasion, stop and stare through the opening to remind himself what the sky looked like. Unfortunately, where Holt found himself further, whatever leaked through the analogous dam that existed previously, had been patched up. He could not see rays, but only mere photons clinging to the rough surface of tree bark and the tips of pine needles. The bright specks resembled what he imagined fairies to look like, their wings somewhere hidden in the blurry light bubble that surrounded them. His slight astigmatism made the creature's detail much more amorphous.

---

[3] When I first listened to this audiolog, I didn't give this sentence as much attention as it deserved.

If Dooley wished to continue, it was clear that the only solution was to create his own light. He gently felt across the deeply cracked and furrowed bark searching for spots where the trees were injured. His fingers, like a king's signet ring, met a tar like substance and sealed their prints into its wax. He broke a cedar branch and gathered the resin on its end. The nearly empty lighter rested in his bag, which he used to place a small flame on his branch. After a few attempts to get it started, the fire did take, and his pine resin torch was a success. The war on darkness had begun, and he was brutally disadvantaged, but content with his standing.

Holt walked with his torch until his muscles ached and pleaded with him to rest. As far as the fire's light could reach, he searched for a suitable spot to make camp. Moss laid the foundation for the visible portion of every tree trunk, however, it assuredly lay on more than just the north facing side[4]. Finding a boulder outcropping for shelter, he arranged a bed of the moss to rest on. He then converted the torch into a campfire, by whittling its own cedar handle into kindling.

Apparently, like bugs to a lamp post, the fairies had returned, sparking around the campfire in all directions[5]. He counted them, as one counts sheep when nodding off. Coupling this hazy visual with a whiff of Eastern Red Cedar would coerce nearly anyone into coziness. The sound of it crackling into embers is akin to story-time whispers...for some at least. Others find the whispering to be unsettling.

---

[4] In the Northern Hemisphere, moss grows mostly on the north facing side. The setting that Holt had stumbled upon apparently didn't follow this natural suggestion.

[5] Possibly firebrands, floating embers

"At least I'll sleep well tonight." He mumbled to himself, as some Appalachian natives have the habit of doing. His subtle blend of a rural southern and mountain accent was apparent in a few words, but not most.

Having great self-awareness, he conjured a comical mental image of himself talking in his loneliness, and laughed. Realizing that he had then also laughed to himself, he decided to cut his losses, and go to sleep. It is widely accepted in the circles of wayfaring people, that extended periods of isolation puts immense strain on the mind -- as truth, in all its viscosity, is mainly established through consensus. Oftentimes, when one has been alone for long, they speak to themselves because they *are* sane.

Waking to less light than when he fell asleep, Dooley saw that the canopy was too thick to notice if the sun had risen. He wielded the fire's remaining glowing embers by a new torch and trudged through the now peculiar feeling forest. For a moment he thought he saw a face with a red mustache embossed into one of the thick trunks that surrounded him, but upon further inspection, the fire's light revealed the contorted surface of an oak's knots and knobs. A maroon mushroom[6] fixed above a small crater in the tree explained the mustache. Increasingly, the feeling that something was stalking him, crawled out of his mind, tingling his neck just before leaping to fallen twigs and the noisy dry leaves. Holt had goosebumps. The sounds of a forest when you are alone are enough to make one paranoid, but in a scenario such as this, the worries are exponentially greater.

Holt's nostrils flared in response to a new scent, not one that he himself had been harboring. The fragrance of burning herbs wrapped around him and murmured that he was not the only one

---

[6] Perhaps a Red-Belted Polypore or a Beefsteak Mushroom?

occupying the area. Instead of being wary as most humans would, Holt decided the apothecary would have direction for him and followed the source downwind.

The fragrance[7] he was following now took a visibly sentient form and continued cantering with its back turned. It was an entity composed of pure white smoke, with no intention other than movement. Just as one exhales in the cold pushing their breath ahead of them, so the being appeared, stacking fume upon fume in a puzzling propulsion. Detailed footprints of finely powdered ash wisped upwards, defining the feet and calves of the fragrance, yet the knee upward was considerably less structured.

"Where are you leading me?" Holt inquired

"Baba[8] Unaka[9] summons you," it answered.

"Oh. Well, do *you* have a name or something to be called?"

The being sped up to Holt's jogging pace, refusing to reply. He figured its sole purpose was to fetch, and according to its anatomical make-up, must have a short lifespan. In which case, it would have no need for a name; that would be an unnecessary accessory to its prompt purpose. This intrigued Dooley and brought up new questions he would contemplate for the rest of this trek. "Does the smoke-being believe its lifespan to be long or quick? I wonder what the trees think about their lives, and what

---

[7] Here is where the story becomes considerably more difficult to relate.

[8] "Baba" is the first name of the witch in the Russian folktale, *Baba Yaga. Yubaba* is the name of the witch in the Japanese movie *Spirited Away,* and vaguely similar is the name "Elphaba" from the novel called "Wicked".

[9] "Unaka" was the name of a national forest in North Carolina, Tennessee, and Virginia, that made up over 840,000 acres.

they think that I think about mine." He briefly observed the trees, and how their branches followed the fire of his torch, hungry for any bit of light. A half of an hour passed, along with all of this speculation flooding his mind, but he didn't speak to the smoke any longer.

As the torch burned brightly, it cast to the ground an occasional silhouette of a feeding bat, distracting Holt and almost causing him to bump into the being he was following. His abrupt stop was in front of a particularly eerie home sight. The vapor-like being walked forth and dissolved over top of a mixed burn-pile of goldenrod, black walnuts, and an assortment of strange fungi.

The house was constructed into a small hill where it existed cohesively with the surrounding nature. Similar to the Incan homes of the Andes, rocks were painstakingly placed like a jigsaw puzzle to act as a frame. The entrance lacked a door, but vines hung from the rocks so that privacy was easily kept. Contorted trees were in pairs of three and the branches held an assortment of trinkets and ornaments. Mossy pebbles formed intricate mosaic patterns around the patio, but the light struck them so faintly that Holt could not make out any full shape[10]. Though perplexed, he was not troubled, choosing to make his way down the meandering path toward the threshold.

He peered through the hanging vines and saw a room with no occupants other than an odd collection of objects, scattered bones, and miscellaneous ingredients from plant cuttings to mineral powders.

"Baba Unaka?" He murmured softly.

---

[10] Intriguingly, the house is described in detail, despite Holt not being able to ascertain the details very well in the darkness.

Hearing no answer, Dooley spared the time to wait out front. The goal of his journey required some amount of punctuality, but his need for direction overshadowed any urgency. He sat on the bedewed grass, and began to write poems[11] in his journal to pass the time. These are my two favorite of the ones he wrote:

A bat without sight
Sees even more than I night;
But do they know why?
A bear with his paws
Bears little weight with no flaws
A bare land's bairies[2]

Holt tuned his ear to the hooting of nearby owls and practiced his own call back. Great effort yielded him poor results and slight embarrassment, but he listened to see if a response would be made. Out of the silence, he heard the maneuvering of an aviator cutting the air and whistling toward him.

Seeking out the figure, which grew lighter by the second, he beheld the image of a woman riding a broom. "Classic," He thought to himself. The pilot flew within feet of him and threw herself off in walking pace as if her agenda owned no time to stop. She looked familiar. Her hair was luminous and as red as fresh cinders. With

---

[11] These two poems are actually rhyming haikus, displaying the 5-7-5 syllable structure.

[12] It can be difficult to discern the true meaning behind anyone's poetry, but one can at least more easily ascertain its literary elements. This naturally themed haiku contains 4 homophones: "bear" as a noun, then "bear" as a verb, the adjective "bare", and finally the made up word "Bairies". "Bairies" is not a meaningless word though, in fact it is a homophone pun on the words "Berries" and "Bair", both pertaining to food.

her appearance and demeanor, she held at bay more than a few suitors, toying like a cat with a ball of yarn.

"Sorry I'm late, an egregious man in Georgia was in a fiddle standoff[13] with some important friends," said the witch jokingly, "I'm..."

"Baba Unaka, I know who you are," interrupted Holt.

"Hmm, I was planning to say that to you... a bit full of yourself maybe?" she mumbled. "Well, Baba Unaka is just a title. My real name is Rosaline, but you can call me Rosie. How did you find yourself in this place, Holt Dooley?"

"Your knowledge is tangential to my purpose, isn't it? Let's get on with it. I imagine your rules resemble the Baba Yaga I once read about?"

"Strictly business with you, isn't it?" She smiled. Holt remained stone cold with his expressions despite her charm and beauty. "Yes, there are similarities between witches, of course. Come inside so we can discuss out of earshot of the trees."

He pushed the vines out of his way and followed her in. Rosaline took her mortar and pestle, crushing herbs while she talked. He inspected her shelves and poked around with his piece of driftwood. Her back was turned as she multi-tasked, and he hid any sign of emotion to the witch when she would look back on occasion. He figured the less she knew of him, the better.

"So, what is it you desire?" Her grin widened.

"I would like direction out of these murky woods and northbound toward Kentucky."

---

[13] A possible allusion to the song "Devil Went down to Georgia"

"Is that all? How about the ability to fly out of these woods? Or maybe an elk skin map that can get you to places even the most brilliant cartographers can't comprehend?" She glanced at the shelf behind her, revealing its location to Holt.

"Elk skin, huh? No, I'll be fine with just the directions," he replied.

"Well, as per the rules, I can't give you much for free, even though your request is so small. I'll give you the directions in exchange for this: tell the green-eyed head[14] when you pass it, that it can find a body with the headless train conductor of Chapel Hill[15] that the locals complain about. That will save me some annoying socialization."

Casually strolling toward the elk skin map for further inspection, he made a half circle around the witch, and questioned her to repress any suspicion.

"Hypothetically, if you give me those directions, and I cross paths with a mischievous band of goblins, or maybe a hungry ogre, what will be the use of your service since I didn't make it to my destination?" he inquired.

"Ah, so you desire insurance additionally? The creatures who roam about this realm don't act according to any fiction book you might have read, so it might also require skill in bartering. I can either give you an object of value, or lend you the ability to speak with sly persuasion. Which will it be?"

A raspy voice yelled from outside, "Baba Unaka? Let me in." Holt looked across the room and saw a green-eyed head, sitting at the entrance. The witch turned and gave her attention to him, while

---

[14] "Old Green Eyes," is a character in a local folktale about a Civil War soldier. Maybe this is a connection?

[15] Joe Baldwin, from the "Maco Light" folktale

Holt quickly snuck his hand to the top shelf and felt for the elk hide.

"Hmm... jar of something, bowl of squishies, pointy rocks...Ah, the map!" he thought. "Stealing isn't morally wrong if a witch is the victim. Imagine what she would do with this anyway."

Holt justified his actions, and swiftly pulled it down, consequently dislodging the "jar of something" as well. "She doesn't need this either."

He stuffed both items in his rucksack, and turned his head to the witch walking toward him. Barely sparing the time to appear innocent, Holt assumed the witch did not notice anything out of place yet.

"You managed to get away without having to track the green-eyed head down, that was him," she said with a sigh.

"Couldn't have guessed it." He replied in a sarcastic tone.

"Ah! So you could indeed see him? Interesting."

"Of course, I could see him. Who would miss a head rolling around with glowing green eyes?"

"Yes, well back to business. You wanted persuasion, that will cost you. I'll have that piece of wood you twiddle in between your fingers...as it must mean something to you."

"Nope, I don't want persuasion." He deliberately interrupted again. "What if I make it through the woods on your direction, and don't encounter any dangerous beast? Then I will have to pay for the persuasive speech without my gain."

"So, you want an object of value then because you may profit whether the demons question you or not," she said, starting to feel a hint of annoyance. "Tell me, what is it exactly you are looking for?" Her informal words rolled off of her tongue breathily, as she commonly talked, like a purring cat.

After Rosaline teasingly pushed him backwards by his chest, Holt rudely rejected any physical interaction with the witch. Not because he wasn't attracted to her, but simply due to the fact that he had places to be and things to do.

"I have decided that I simply will have the directions."

Now the witch had not met such a human that perplexed her like this. Although his prideful nature annoyed her, she was also captivated by a certain aspect of his character. However, her cheeks grew flushed with embarrassment after he refused to reciprocate her flirtatious gesture. Consequently, she ordered a gust of wind to throw him further into the dark forest. She proceeded to watch him through a crystal ball -- though it looked more like a reptile's scale[16] than the traditional sphere type.

Dooley hit the forest floor with great force. He was relieved the witch spared him, for he knew acting in disrespect was a gamble, but having her flustered would produce this outcome, and this outcome was more profitable. He sat up and regained his breath, pulling out his jar and new map to guide him north. His content expression fell briefly to confusion, when he realized the jar was empty and his map was more of a conundrum than he had planned for. He would turn, and lines would suddenly appear on the elk hide, with a script he was not literate in. He pointed in the direction he thought likely to be north and attempted to follow the lines on the map as they were drawn.

---

[16] An interesting parallel: The great horned snake from native american folklore has scales that can aid in divination.

Hours passed and the forest remained as dark and dense as it was at Rosie's home. His stomach spoke to him in grumbles, complaining over the lack of attention. Stumbling upon a few berries in the brush, he ravished the branches, making the area around him desolate. Furthermore, the last fluid of his antiquated *Zippo* lighter was emptied while creating his next fire, solidifying his need to get out of the forest and re-stock.

———

A leaflet, soaked from the morning mist, danced through the wind and clung to Holt's face. His eyes opened, and his pupils were still heavy from the dark. Though sight proved to be difficult, his hearing remained acute; but from what he just faintly heard, it wasn't clear whether his mind and ears were working as a team anymore.

In between the moon and you, angels get a better view, of the crumbling difference between wrong and right

A torn voice, accompanied by guitars, drums and accordion shouted to Holt through the woods. "Counting Crows?" He thought, "Such an unusually dissonant sound to the natural environment, but I'm not going to complain," He hurried toward the music, seeking the source[17].

Round here we all look the same. Round here, something radiates.

Hopping over the brush and dodging, well, almost every tree and branch, he made his way to the music. A razorback boar stood

---

[17] These particular lines mentioned from *Counting Crows* do not seem accidental, nor do the other lines that the source plays throughout the rest of the story.

there staring, with a solar powered radio among his tusks. It was blaring the static filled sound of an FM station.

"Hello there," Holt said. "What exactly are you doing over here?"

"You don't like it? I can change the station...just gotta ram it against one of these old tree trunks," replied the boar.

"No, the music is great. I suppose I just have questions of why you are here playing it."

"I'll be leaving soon, I need to get back to the sun to recharge the radio. It's solar powered," replied the boar, as if to brag.

"I noticed, but why did you come here in the first place?" Holt patiently asked.

"Well, it's a little less erie here because of it, don't you think? How about you show some gratitude?"

"Yes, thank you. Do you mind if I follow you to a lighter area? I've been stuck in these woods for quite some time."

"Sure, I'll get you outa here. I'm Hamlet -- it's a character from one of Shakespeare's stories. And what's your name, traveler?"

"Though this be madness, yet there is method in't." Holt nodded assuredly.

"I don't get it."

"No? It's from *Hamlet*..." He paused for a second. "Holt, my name is Holt."

"Well, Holt, how do you like 90s hits?" the pig asked.

He followed as the boar trotted rhythmically to the music. He was offset by his acquaintance's blissful nature, but considered it more of an artistically enraptured trait than one of ignorance. Of course, this may have been a result of the radio accompaniment. The boar on occasion would backtrack, having his sense of smell enlightened by differing mushrooms and fungi, but Holt was caught up enough in deciphering his elk hide that he didn't suffer from absolute impatience just yet. Even so, as time passed, and realizing he was not used to the constant jabbering of the boar, his liability of succumbing to hunger-driven thoughts increased.

"When's the last time I had pork chops?" he asked himself. "No, I couldn't kill such a reasonable pig, guilt would be inevitable here seeing I know his name...regardless I need to utilize its guidance before I could eat it." Looking up and seeing the animal pressing its snout against the soil, Holt had an idea.

"Hamlet, why don't you sniff out some truffles for us to eat?" he asked.

"Nope. There isn't any chocolate just laying here beneath the trees." The pig snorted in its laughter, directed toward Holt.

"Not chocolate, edible fungi. But it doesn't have to be truffles, I'd gladly settle for mushrooms. I am just getting desperately hungry and I don't have the capability of smelling fungi like you do." [18]

The pig nodded and started east. After mere minutes, they found themselves surrounded by mushrooms. The forest floor was characterized by scattering color, some tall and skinny, some globular with no stalk; the diversity was remarkable. It was a dream-like setting, since Holt had neither seen such abundance, nor so many new species to him. He knew the risks of consuming

---

[18] Pigs are often used in the business of truffle hunting.

unidentified mushrooms, but decided he might be able to determine the least likely to be poisonous and satisfy his stomach.

"Hamlet, which of these do you find appetizing?"

"Well my favorite color is yellow, so I'll eat those first."

The boar gobbled up the food like a vacuum, while Dooley picked a yellowish brown mushroom and decided to give it a try. Having a nutty, somewhat recognizable smell, he trusted the species and ate a few. Directly afterward, his senses heightened, and he felt the wind pressing forcefully against him. Acting as a knife, his body separated the wind into two fierce currents, enveloping him. Suddenly he saw clouds around him and the earth coming toward him at an incredible rate.

"That's just great, psychedelics..." he said to himself, "at least it may buy me some time to figure out how to get out of this forest before I starve to death."

He heard a familiar Tom Petty tune[19], and looked beside him to see the boar swimming through the air after his radio. Were they sharing the same experience, or was the boar a doppelganger, built by his mind? He wished to know, but before he could ask, he watched the earth open up and swallow him. Finding himself parachuting through a remarkable cavern, he experienced an adrenaline dump, despite consciously comprehending that the experience was fabricated. Quartz crystals and irregularly constructed limestone formations flew past him, gradually trading the light of the sun for the blue-tinted light of bioluminescence. Eventually touching down on the underground landscape, Holt didn't see the pig or hear the radio. He wondered how the texture of the ground was so intricately recreated from his mind and

---

[19] Referring to *Free Falling*

projected into his psychedelic surroundings, and decided to explore. He noticed more masses of light emitting from around a sharp turn and dug in his pocket for the driftwood to help himself think.

"Surely Hamlet, or my copy of him, has an idea how to get out of this dream. Wouldn't that be odd, another replicated mind functioning inside my own?"

He came around the corner to find a cave-village, mimicking the Jordanian city of Petra. Houses were built into the cavern wall, and the city infrastructure was lined with a variety of plants that seemingly didn't undergo photosynthesis. The plants were grey and didn't adhere to the same physiological structure commonly attributed to the plant kingdom, but there were other sources of color. Plentiful minerals displayed a color spectrum from blue to green. Unfortunately they didn't contrast well enough with the dark atmosphere to paint this village as beautiful as it truly was, but Holt would have been unimpressed regardless; seeing as the image was, to him, figmentive.

He stepped through a puddle made by a dripping stalactite, and felt his socks soak up the water. "Pseudo-tactile," he whispered to himself. He assumed the feeling of water was too realistic for his mind to conjure, so he must be actually feeling some form of water outside of his illusionary trip. The driftwood once again emerged from his pocket and found itself useful in Holt's restless hand.

"Does anyone live in this village?" he yelled jokingly, "You know, I created it."

He looked up and saw movement from inside one of the houses. He was now very curious as to what life his subconscious may have developed, and if they had any purpose. To his knowledge, his created cave dwellers could be a testament to the complexity of the human brain, just as he felt his own purpose was to point to something greater. The entry frames of the domiciles appeared strangely ornate, with organic branch-like patterns carved into the foundation. He pressed his fingers against the pattern as he entered, and searched the square room corner to corner, noticing nothing. The next two appeared to be empty as well, until he caught a glimpse of motion up in the centerpoint of the architecture, resembling a town-square. He hurried up an extensive set of open stairs, and noted that the dimensions were a broad 9x14 rather than 7x11. From this, Holt gathered that creatures might be on a grander scale than he originally imagined. He hoped to find out if the ghost town he had created would reveal something entertaining, be it nail-biting, or wonderous.

Reaching the top of the stairs, he entered onto a plateau and gazed at the various geologic structures that decorated the village's inner workings. A steady trickle of dripping water from a stalactite, collected in the center of its downward facing summit and filtered around stalagmites on the floor below it. It seemed this was akin to a fountain in the village's town-square. He walked to the dripping water and cupped his hands as if he were to drink from it. Paltry was the time between each drop, almost to an undetectable point; but Holt didn't struggle deciphering that it was uniquely nonrhythmic. From this fact he further concluded that its unevenness yet still resolved to a pattern, and one vaguely comparable to what might be caused by biotic locomotion. He jotted all of these thoughts and more down in his journal. Dooley wondered if there was a second floor above the cave's ceiling, in which something was stepping so heavily, that it was disrupting the stream. He decided not to drink from it anyway, as evident in his writing; he was afraid of contracting giardia or cryptosporidium.[20]

The main stalactite then began to reform, as a creature of stone appearance emerged from inside limb by limb. As it descended, like a gorilla hanging by a branch, it fell toward Holt. He inspected the pure-white hyphae[21] acting as ligaments by connecting pebble to stone and stone to boulder. The being resembled a human, but Holt believed it to be only attempting to take a form similar to his own, as its anatomy surely had the ability to replicate whatever image might suit its need.

"The fine strands of vegetative fungi...the mycelium acting as your joints. Are you a fungal life form? Or maybe a golem[22], living with it symbiotically?"

It didn't reply.

"I guess the closest relatable sense to a human's, might be some sort of detection through vibration...and that could, in a roundabout way, allow for a similar feeling to hearing, sight, and touch. It should at least know that I am speaking to it," he thought.

"Can you understand me?"

With no response, it turned and led Dooley through the dimly lit grotto. The silence broke as noise comparable to a train on its tracks accompanied the multitude of rock based life-forms that

---

[20] Microorganisms common in the whole planet's untreated water bodies, spread out as far as the east is from the west.

[21] The branching filaments of fungi, making up the main vegetative growth

[22] A being of Jewish folklore, oftentimes made of mineral material. The Hebrew translation of psalms references how God may have made humans in a golem form before giving them life. (*Psalms 139:16*)

were emerging from the geological structures. They all appeared in a similar shape to the one leading, except some were more heavily colonized by fungi than others. He quickly developed a theory that the clear hierarchy among the beings was established according to a factor in relation to this. They ventured deeper into the cave, and the golems walked in a line behind, and some in front of Holt. Occasionally, he would stop to sketch a picture of some mushrooms, noting that some bore striking resemblance to the supposedly psychedelic one he consumed. His short stops and inspections of the new world would cause all the golems to stand and wait for him, but on more than one occasion he would stop to make them wait just for his own satisfaction. He guessed that they didn't pay much mind though, as he again figured they were all just part of his subconscious. When they finally came to a stop out of their own volition, he peered around the golem in front of him and beheld a hair-raising sight; he was surprised and disgusted, for the first time in quite a while.

"NO!" he yelled. "I hate spiders!"

He proceeded in a dancelike martial-arts-esque motion, where he eliminated the threat and its home, shaking off any trace of a web left on him. Then standing stiff and gracelessly next to his speechless rock acquaintance, he could feel the tension in the air. The scene was chucklesome in its own right, aside from the fact that Holt had stumbled into the throne hall, where the sovereign ruler of the golems sat reigning. Fortunately, it was entertained by what it presumed was a dance offering. An enormous throne engulfed an intimidating organism, mostly covered by fungi. As a peculiar means of communication, it commanded the cave floor in front of Holt to re-form into English letters, just as if a talented engraver chiseled away each grapheme with ornate care. It appeared instantaneously in a full-paragraph form, rather than word by word.

"I am pleased by the dance you offer. Unfortunately our bodies are not agile enough to move reciprocally. However, It is not often we receive visitors, so we would like to extend an invitation to stay as long as you need. I am called Armillaria[23], and I have lived here for thousands of years, providing communication as well as other amenities to the forest above. My hyphae is connected to the root systems, and information is passed on to many different species[24]. Anything you are searching for here, I certainly can point you in the right direction."

By this time Holt had noticed there was something strange happening. His subconscious couldn't have produced this magnitude of imaginative data. He immediately ascertained that by consuming that mushroom he opened up the ability to speak with its source.

Holt began to speak in a formal tone. "I would take you up on that offer, since clearly it's not everyday you get to experience this kind of thing...but I am on a minor time constraint. My purpose in these woods is only that of a traveler. However, it would be nice to acquire sustenance when I wake up, as I am both hungry and thirsty."

"And to where are you traveling?" Armillaria wrote back

"I'm planning on meeting someone on the west coast."

"Conveniently, I owe a favor to a friend who also aspires to see the western side of the continent, but unfortunately is unable to travel

---

[23] A genus of fungi that includes the largest living organism in the world, as well as some of the longest living specimens. Supposedly, some have reported evaluations of over 9500 years.

[24] As Armillaria reported, many species in an ecosystem rely on hyphae for communicative signals from one to another.

alone. If I lead you out of this forest and feed you, I trust that you could adjust your route to accommodate the favor?"

Where can I find your 'friend?'" he asked.

"A horse-farm city in Kentucky named Lexington."

"I was born in Lexington," Holt said.

"Then you will have no trouble finding the doughnut and coffee shop *North Lime*. If you ask around there, you will surely meet." Armillaria's disposition had not changed, it seemed to be characteristic of a statue, built into its throne.

"One more thing, have you seen a pig carrying around a radio recently?" Dooley inquired.

"... pigs are not native to these woods."

"Well I understand that, but in some places in the U.S. they have been naturalized..." One of the hyphae golems nudged Holt on his shoulder and shut him up.

"Have you heard the story of Grandfather Mountain?" Armillaria asked.

"Ah, I'd rather just be on my way," responded Holt, cheekily turning to what he assumed would be an exit. "Is the dining hall through here?" he asked, before the golems forcibly directed him to a sitting position.

"Long before the Europeans settled our land, there was a highly respected mountain in the same direction you came from. He was named 'Grandfather Mountain'[25] as the first nations thought his face resembled an elderly man pondering the stars. He spent his

---

[25] Coordinates: 36.10411141191302, -81.81811032924544

ically just as humans do, sleeping for years and waking ents. He had grown accustomed to the practice of various tribes making the journey to speak with him, waking him happily to stories of their lives as they asked for his wisdom. He became close friends with many humans and would relay experiences from their ancestors; sometimes with sorrow as he hated seeing them pass on. This practice went on for millennia, until new settlers came with greedy hearts.

For the first time in ages, the Grandfather had woken up by himself without visitors. He kept his eyes facing the sky and sat as still as the other mountains, but his mind was racing uncomfortably. He had high hopes his friends would return and inquire with him, but as time slipped on, he became weary as he maintained consciousness for his longest time yet. At his feet he felt the trimming of forests and mining of stones. He knew something was wrong as resources used to be shared among the wild, and aggression such as this was a new concept to him.

He struggled to look across his home, seeing it quickly shaped into an unrecognizable setting. The new settlers joyfully struck his heart with their pickaxes. 'Where have my friends gone? Have they forgotten me and my love for them?' He asked with his last minutes of life.'"

"I don't understand, why are you telling me this?" Holt asked.

"You will find that some Native American history is especially pertinent to your future. I am showing you your destiny. You are not the settlers in the story, but the old mountain. *Up on a pedestal for all to see, your last waking weeks will bring you a shock you will not believe. Your time on this earth will come to a peaceful halt[26], but your love will live on."*

"Is this a literal fortune or more of a metaphorical one, because I seriously doubt my time will end in a peaceful death. Do those even exist?"

Jotting this down in his journal, he was shoved onward in the direction of a narrow tunnel. It opened to another cavern endlessly large, where much of the floor was covered by an underground lake. He could see bioluminescent fish periodically lighting up the water. Holt pondered whether the fish did this for breeding purposes or as a hunting mechanism, but rested in the conclusion that it was a refreshing aesthetic either way. The glowing pool was clear and otherworldly. He watched as another golem crushed a substance and threw it to the lake. The once sporadic lights then became less of a display, as fish rose limply to the water's surface. It was as if gravity changed direction; they were buoyantly suspended, waiting to be collected by the golem.

A deep, rock-tumbling sound preceded the formation of a limestone bridge, which came up from the cave floor. Foot by foot, it developed deeper toward the center of the lake. Holt knew he was supposed to follow that path, but decided to take one last up close glance at the golem who led him there. He looked for where the white hyphae connected the rocks and pressed it with his pointer finger. The being morphed its appearance for a second and reformed back to its original shape.

"Please, do not touch!" it wrote with an aggressive font.

---

[26] Important wording to pay attention to, in anticipation for the story's end. Hearing it the second time is much more meaningful.

25

Holt snickered and walked the bridge about fifty meters out. When a newly placed stone began to rise in elevation, the golems stood back and motioned him to proceed. Almost as if he were in a platforming video game, he rose higher for a moment, until the rock he was standing on formed into an unmistakable high-dive. He stood at the top viewing the abyss. He had confidently taken his previous steps, but now felt as though he had taken them for granted. The next bit of tread crumbled beneath him as the bridge gave out, throwing him to the lake.

He smacked the water in the same manner a book would slap the floor if it were dropped. In a daze, he oriented himself by using his arms for propulsion, and then his legs.

"Must've fallen into a pond or something in real life," he thought to himself as he swam toward the surface. The water was drastically lighter and the sun could be seen greeting him. He reached the surface, and sprawled out like a cold-blooded reptile soaking in the rays. He believed that by proxy, Armillaria truly did lead him out of the enchanted forest, and furthermore would be supplied with food.

"I hope it's Dim Sum," he said, patting his growling stomach.[27] His head swivelled around getting his grip on the situation. He had fallen from a limestone arch into a pool of water made by an eroded hillside and a rushing spring. Lucky not to have broken an ankle or leg, he immediately went to the spring headwaters and cupped his hands to drink. The water was so refreshing in appearance, he forgot his healthy respect for microorganisms. Directly afterwards, the rattle of a squirrel piling nutshells grabbed his attention. Inspecting the walnuts and their tree, he noticed

---

[27] Traditionally dim sum is a Cantonese array of food dishes

there were no other plants in the small vicinity around it. This was due to the poison it gives off to the competing plant life.

"The serial killer of plants.." he said to himself. He peered at the black walnut shells and flashbacked to the golem, throwing a substance to the fish. "The juglone compound in black walnut husks will bring to surface any fish in this water-hole!"[28]

He crushed them, and tossed them into the water. While waiting for the poison to take effect, he made a small fire. Three small fish floated to the surface and he gathered them to cook.

"Hmm I should've checked to see if these fish could talk, considering the whole pig ordeal...you can't right?" He lightly squeezed the fish and released in intervals, causing the mandible to mimic speech, while inserting words for it. "Yes I can," he replied to himself in a squeamish voice, "but I would much rather die this way than from the excessive buildup of algae on the water surface, blocking light and photosynthesis to the plants underwater, killing off the insects which once acted as my food source. Eutrophication[29] is common here."

"Consarn it![30] I am becoming psychotic." He chuckled.

He savored the fish, and tried to forget what just took place. Moving his belongings by the fire to dry, he noticed the clear sky. When the stars came out, and it was a good time to configure his route, he connected them in the air with his piece of driftwood, and pointed toward Lexington. He decided that it was then an

---

[28] Using jugalone as a toxin to fish is an old, little-known Appalachian fishing technique.

[29] The process of nutrient build up, wherein animals often die from lack of oxygen. Poor agricultural practices are sometimes the culprit.

[30] old expletive that might come from the word "consternation"

optimal time to decipher the elk skin map he stole from the witch, since some directions have at least been laid out. Unraveling it like a scroll, lines could be seen autonomously etching symbols and pictures of unknown sites. One drawing resembled a hill with a small sun on it, so Holt assumed it either to be relating the time of day, or a lit up residence on a hill. "Well, if I see something like this on my path, I guess I can briefly stop by."

The lines started to reform on a small portion of the hide, and a previous image was replaced with the likes of a walking boar. Holt focused his ear past his immediate environment, and sure enough the radio could be heard blaring out "Universal Sound" by Tyler Childers. He swiftly took off to the pig and caught him blissfully singing along.

"Oh, Holt! I thought you were a goner. You were tripping pretty hard on those mushrooms and I couldn't get you up. I even tried peeing on your feet, but you just whispered something like "pseudo-tactile" and kept going."

Dooley looked disgusted and frantically stripped off his socks and discarded them. He wasn't one for littering, but he also wasn't one for pee socks.

"Idiot, why would urinating on me wake me up? I wasn't even asleep technically!"

"Okay, okay! I was just trying to help. Where are you going now that you're out in the light?"

Ignoring the pig, he turned and began walking northwest. It wasn't ten steps before the inquisitive boar liberally strung a few words out accidentally forming another question.

"So, why then, and how long have you been going, to where?" The pig's eyes rolled to the left[31], contemplating if his question made sense, and then nodded in affirmation to himself.

Provoked by these questions, Holt took to journaling his thoughts as he walked.

Ideas, moral and hopeful, in the course of impact, are too often shaken by the opinions of those in power--those who are fortunate enough to own only the slightest bit of empathy. No matter the relevance or beauty of the idea, credentials enjoy hindering their fruition and allotting it to those who live in stagnant states. Though I would like to imagine my steps as the stimulus for new action... I know internally they are merely from the shoes of a poet. Nonetheless I will continue.

"To save my missing wife," he replied.

"Well, how do you know where to find her? Are you being chased by bad people?"

"How about you tell me why you are so mindlessly accompanying me?"

"I asked first."

"Hmm. Alright. I can find her because I created an algorithm that would detect patterns involving her, and tracked it through a series of technological devices that you would not understand. As for the people, I'm not sure if they are good or bad. Your turn."

"I have nothing better to do." the pig confidently replied.

---

[31] I haven't quite connected why this detail was included, but close attention seems to be paid to minute details of the boar as the story goes on.

"I don't buy it. You said that with too much certainty, as if you rehearsed it," Dooley sighed, "Ah, well. I suppose I'll find out sooner or later."

CHAPTER 2

(Chase of Fate)

An important integrant in Holt Dooley's journey helps to explain a lot of issues encountered along his travels, as antagonists do. However, though certainly antagonistic, he was not necessarily a "bad guy" at the time. I could embellish and attribute to him some more villainous characteristics, but that simply isn't how the story goes. He was a twenty-seven year old average Joe, except his name wasn't Joe, it was Chase Griffith. But everyone called him by his family name. Griffith's most distinguishable features are found in his uncanny good luck.[32] He was born healthy and wealthy, and seemed to rely on everything falling directly into his lap. This is a seemingly deficient background for his job, as private investigators are typically resourceful, intelligent, and hard working. Yet, Griff had a mysteriously well-alcolaged track record. While others may have perceived him as a man of great talent, full-picture evidence reflects that he is consistently and accidentally, I might add, in the right place at the right time.

---

[32] This is another important detail with a deeper meaning you will gather later on.

31

He once "solved" a homicide case, wherein the perpetrator threw a crucial piece of evidence, in an attempt to hide it on top of a building, but instead overshot it and landed directly on the cafe table Griffith happened to be dining at. Claiming he had staked out the most likely spot for an interaction with the suspect in question, he was highly praised in the workplace. However, I happen to know that it was half-priced doughnut Tuesdays, and Griff had a stereotypical weakness for doughnuts.

He first caught wind of Holt Dooley at the beginning of his trek out west. Griffith was based out of Charleston, South Carolina, where he wore button up shirts with floral patterns or sea novelties. The day they met he was wearing one with palm trees. Holt was sketching the Cooper River Bridge and whispering dimensions and other numbers to himself, and Griff was relaxing on a park bench. Overhearing Holt's murmuring, the sly-feeling investigator decided to confront him.

"Everything alright here, Sir?" he asked Holt.

Picking up his pencil from his unfinished drawing, our beloved main character's head swiveled toward Griff. "It was. You are not the best detective are you?"

Griffith was shocked that Holt almost guessed his occupation and responded accordingly. "Well, um.. what's your name there, pal?" Griff didn't bother delineating that he was not a detective, but a private investigator. [33]

---

[33] Sometimes, withholding the full truth, can lead to a snowballing effect of lies. It is notable that Griff was not in a governmental position of authority, as an actual detective would be.

"Are you wearing that shirt because you think it fits the South Carolina ambiance? Cause it doesn't. We don't even have that species of palm in here."

"I know that! It was a gift." Griff said confidently.

The investigator's phone dinged with an alert stating that a 6', athletic, caucasian male with shaggy hair was on the run. He glimpsed at it, and didn't piece together that Dooley fit the bill, as he sure didn't seem to be on the run.

"Welp, I gotta go. Stay safe out there."

"On the lookout for something?" Holt asked.

Turning to his car he said "Some escaped fugitive is out and about. Another day, another dollar, right?"

"Hey, I don't know how you do it, brother. Keep on keeping on," Holt said, in a heavier rural accent, raising three fingers in a boy scout salute.

Griff squinted his eyes, and couldn't tell if he was being made fun of, or if the stranger was actually just plain strange. As they made their separate ways, Holt ascertained that the "fugitive" was himself. He hastily left Charleston, heading north.

Griff took a call from the police, requesting his help on the case. He often worked in tandem with them, when their cases had fallen cold. Despite having some occupational success, Chase Griffith seemed to harbor an inferiority complex, which defined a lot of his decisions. He rendezvoused at the station and saw pictures of the escapee, realizing it was the same man he was talking to earlier that day. He was told that Holt was wanted everywhere, not just in Charleston. He accidentally spoke too soon, telling his comrades that he had encountered Holt sketching the bridge. They thought it funny that such a reputable P.I. was obliviously chatting with Holt without recognizing anything suspicious, but he deflected their comments, and saved his good name, by stating that it was purposeful. He said that he actually knew who Dooley was, and that he was part of a large crime syndicate. He stated that he is letting the perpetrator lead them straight to the 'head honchos' as he called them. This didn't fit Holt's background, but why would they question Griff's motives? He had done his fair share for them after all. Griffith unraveled a handful of fibs over the next few minutes, escalating the importance of Holt Dooley's capture, and further solidifying his own role in doing so. His phone rang multiple times while he was there, and after many times of declining, he decided to finally excuse himself and take it.

A confident feminine voice asked if she was speaking with the investigator. She told him about her concern for a friend who she thought was wanted for arrest, and how corruption among authorities might be involved. She refused to share her personal details with him yet, but offered to pay him a hefty sum to track Holt Dooley and gather as much information before the government officials and police did. He scratched his head as he spoke to her, and wiped his forehead as one does when they get nervous. Being that he was standing in a police station hallway, he told her he would think about it and talk to her later. That evening, arriving at his apartment, he swiftly kicked off his shoes, ran into his room and dove into his bed accompanied only by the echoed sound of a slammed door. He then pulled the blankets over his head and turned on a flashlight in preparation to call his mysterious client. The phone rang, and rang again.

"Hello?"

"This is Chase Griffith, with whom you were speaking earlier."

"Thank goodness. Listen, I'm sure you are partially aware of the situation involving Holt Dooley. But what you've been told is just not the full story." She could barely speak in between her shuffling and sniffling.

"Calm down ma'am, everything is alright. I'm listening," he said, as he sat on his hand to keep it from trembling.

The two hashed out the details and Chase Griffith was convinced to discreetly help out. Though he was scared of the situation he was putting himself in, money is a good motivator, and to him, so was helping a young woman in need. The next morning, he set off on the race to find Holt. However, now that the suspect was aware that people were looking for him, Dooley acted cautiously, trying to leave no trace of his travel. Inspired by Holt's detective accusation, Griff ended up purchasing a fake detective badge and taser, figuring it may come in handy. However, the only chance anyone would have to catch him, was to rely on chance itself. That is exactly what the lucky Griff, unwittingly did.

———

Quite some time later, Griffith had found many leads, none of which were real or aiding in the pursuit of Holt Dooley. To his great fortune, the witch, Rosie, had whimsically decided to seek out the enemies of Holt. She had found great amusement in keeping tabs on him, and for lack of a better phrase, wanted to spice up the plot a little bit.

Dressed as a commoner of Charleston, she tailed the unknowing investigator through varying coffee and doughnut shops as he halfheartedly looked for Dooley. She took great interest in how lazily confused he was and how assuredly unaware. The witch decided to further intervene in this game of cat and mouse, to make it a little more entertaining.

As swift and destructively as a dust devil, she gathered some materials (and by gathered I mean stole) from the local businesses to set up a faux street vendor shop in the same line of traffic that Griff would walk. A sign that read "free beignets with purchase of voodoo" was placed on an ornate wooden table, with a variety of trinkets. She eyeballed him as he walked near, and it was clear that after reading the sign he wanted to chat.

"Hello Miss, I was just curious about what kind of beignets we are talking here…"

"Well, I can quite literally provide whatever kind your heart desires." She said with a sly smile.

Raising his brow, he realized that the vendor was just the type of person he was attracted to. "Here's an idea for ya. Rather than paying you to predict my fortune, I am going to predict yours. And if you're impressed, I'll be taking one of those beignets off of your hands," he said with a flirtatious glance.

"I'm listening," she replied

"Your favorite Disney movie is *Princess and the Frog*," Griff said confidently.

"Well.. that is not at all where I thought you were going with the bit you were doing, nor is that a fortune, but yes I do admit that one would be my favorite if I were to choose."

He held up his fake detective badge and said, "It's what I do for a living ma'am."

Acting impressed she gave him a beignet. "Oh, wow. A real-life detective. Are you out on a special mission to find some fugitive?"

"Why yes, I am, and though entirely top secret, I will say that this particular felon is quite the snake. But you know what preys on snakes?" he said with a wink, "Bald eagles. Which happens to be the national bird. See, it's on my logo right here."

"Well, if you're interested, Mr. Detective, I could put you right on his trail, no questions asked."

Peaking his curiosity, Griff continued conversing and made a deal with her. Not necessarily a believer in the supernatural, he wasn't spooked at the thought of selling off his soul when she demanded it. Just to be sure though, he signed a childhood bully's name on her contract rather than his own. She gave him a small elk figurine that was carved out of an antler, telling him that the figurine would tug his hand forward, with the force of a bull elk in the direction he needed to go to find his target. This voodoo was based on the fact that Holt's stolen map was made from the hide of this same elk.

Griffith was satisfied with this transaction.

CHAPTER 3

(Tightly Fastened Bible Belt)

Autumn is a particularly beautiful time for the commonwealth of Kentucky. Even at dusk one can detect the dimly glowing hues of a painter's warmest palette. Edvard Munch's own painting[34] may be remembered when indulging in these surroundings. The dark hills, silhouetted against the increasing opacity of the sky, emphasized the light that was hiding behind densely treed foliage. I've always thought that it is a spectacular moment in time, when one can watch the sky become translucent, exchanging a blue atmosphere for the details of the stars and satellites that exist beyond it. Fog rested perpendicular to the mountains, and rolled like a river through the creek hollers[35], where it originated. And this "fog" is made of the same grit and turmoil that makes up the smoky mountains down south. I've heard locals talk of it as if it were a congregation of their ancestors' ghosts. After living a difficult life, some ghosts have unfinished business, and hover around their mountains looking for peace. That being said, if one

---

[34]This is likely a reference to *Der Schrei der Natur* (The Scream of Nature).

[35] "Holler" is the pronunciation of the geological term "Hollow" in Appalachia.

could see through the fog and forest, the serenity of the scenery might be broken.

At one time, it was common in the Appalachian foothills to live self-sustainably, due to the rugged lay of the land and distance from any local grocery. Foraging in the temperate deciduous flora provided more than enough for families, and there was no lack of hunting either. Now with this semi-isolation, a family would be tightly knit and woven to their land, making it almost sacred to them. Trespassing onto another's property, or even crossing their claimed territory could very well translate to target practice to the owner.

However, there were times when passing through seemed necessary. If for example a natural swale in the land brought a considerable amount of animal traffic, and your family hasn't had luck with hunting recently, that spot might be your best chance for food, even if it means fighting people for it. Over time, run-ins occur and accidents happen, causing groups to hate each other. And family feuds, such as the infamous *Hatfield and McCoy* dispute[36], could spring from a series of vengeful actions leaving both families for the worse.

Generally for the people of the hills, it seemed best to keep to themselves; only communicating for the occasional sale of mountain dew[37] here and there to a townsperson, as well as their local delivery boy. This distributor would often consume some of the product as payment, and take to his automobile with the speed

---

[36] Brutal and well-known feud between two families over land in Kentucky and West Virginia (1863-1891)

[37] "Mountain dew" is an old term for moonshine. The soda brand later trademarked the name in light of this.

and maneuvering of a *NASCAR*[38] driver to escape the hand of the local sheriff. Now sometimes the policeman would chase, in hopes of catching not the boy, but to secretly steal a sip from the mason jars; while paradoxically appearing as the regulator of safety to the morally inclined citizens. Oftentimes, these moral citizens went to church every Sunday, not because they thought highly of themselves, but because they figured they were just as bad as the criminals who's moonshine stills[39] lit up the hillsides. And so it goes with the confusion of the "Bible Belt" region, as it is coined. They spend their time working to do good, despite the fact that their religion is maybe the only one that doesn't claim works-based salvation. Anyway, those are some dynamics of a bootlegging community, which Dooley was likely familiarized with by stories in his upbringing. Dooley[40] is a bootlegger's name, after all.

Holt looked up from his elk-hide map which seemed to be directing him toward a glowing light on the hillside. He wasn't quite adept at reading the map yet, but it was clear that something strange was afoot. The lines would reform as he walked, as a gps would, but furthermore would show icons and write in a script unfamiliar to him. The icon in the direction of the light looked like a minimalist drawing of smoke, and became alluring to him. Similar to the way that it is difficult for some people to break away from a new movie, Holt had to see through to the "ending" of

---

[38] The origins of NASCAR were found in the sport of moonshiners evading police during car chases

[39] "Still" is a term referring to structure and the distillery process involving moonshine.

[40] "Dooley" is a bluegrass/folk song by *The Dillards* about a bootlegger's life.

sorts, of all the build up he had been following with the map for the past few hours.

"Keep moving, swine!" he joked, while prodding the boar with a stick, to spur it forth and break the spider webs.

"You know that human saying, 'Sticks and stones may break my bones but words will never hurt me?'" the pig replied.

"I don't know if your high-podge content would allow a stick to break your bones."

"Do you want me to leave?"

"You won't. You stick around because you are desperate for socialization, no matter how rude."

"I'm accompanying you out of my own will. Maybe I'll sink my tusks into your gut on my way out, how would you like that?"

It seemed Holt was actually the one desperate for socialization. He constantly entertained philosophical ideas and debated with himself in his head, so he was looking for a way to bring his ideas before another. This was a little more stimulating for him than writing in his journal. I guess you could say he was sometimes... confrontational.

Holt laughed to himself. "If you intended to do that you certainly wouldn't have told me, in fear that I might react outside of your favor. But since you brought up your will, I don't believe you have that either. As a man of science, I believe in destiny. You can only reach the potential given by your genetics, and your environment fills any possible gap in choice structure that genetics would leave."

The boar began to trot faster and slower to demonstrate his choice in doing so. "See this? I'm doing that. Nobody is making me go fast or slow."

"Sure, illusively it appears that way from your perspective, but let's break it down. Your genetics are responsible for your ability to move, and the speed to which you are limited -- even the ability to think that you can do so anyway. As far as your environment, you never would have changed your speed unless there was a stimulus to do so. Indirectly, I influenced you to take that action by telling you I believed in destiny. So, obviously you could choose to leave, but even that decision is based on if you like my own 'decisions' or not, and then the next thing that enslaves your attention will be your captor," said Holt.

The pig wasn't ready to respond, so Dooley just started back up and explained further. For him, this was a meaningful way to pass the time as they traveled.

"And on a related note, for you specifically, it is odd that you speak, but do you realize the majority of your species is limited to instinct? Whether complex instinct or simple, they still lack the cognitive power that humans have. Don't get me wrong, I don't sympathize with Descartes[41] and his immoral experiments, but I do think there were elements of truth to them. Where do we see a decent example of animals' speculating like we are now? Anyway I believe I'm chasing rabbits now."

"Elephants carry around the bones of their dead friends and family, and dolphins have a bigger brain than humans," the pig haughtily responded.

---

[41] René Descartes is responsible for the highly challenged notion that animals are like machines, unable to think in the same way humans do.

"That should only prove my point. I don't see these big brained dolphins driving around cars, creating music, or even cognitively trying to further their species. As for the elephants, it doesn't matter if they have the ability to remember their loved ones. That is easily trackable when looking at the brain from most species. Do you not think that it is odd to have to stoop so low, that their bragging point is solely being able to feel sad for a herd member who died? I can break it down really simply for you if you'd like."

"No," the pig replied, walking through the webs and clearing the way for Holt. "I expect an apology soon or I *am* leaving."

"And if you do leave it will be because I made you want to leave," Holt said to himself, shrugging his shoulders.

As they approached the light, the crackling radio tuned in and started playing "Pig in a Pen" by Ricky Skaggs. The pig only added to the noise, trying to change the station by ramming nearby trees. Holt smiled, thinking the radio was on his side of the argument. Among the racket, he realized that if anyone was remotely nearby, they would surely know he was passing through their woods. In light of this, to divert suspicion of being a lurking robber, he assumed a direct route to the light would resonate best with the locals. However, the people living in the woods are not typically the type to reason, so in case confrontation were to come about, he began to question whether to rely on his brain as usual, or brawn.

"Ay!" A firm voice shouted from the trees behind them. "You're so dumb, you're just gonna try'n walk straight to the house without sneakin'? You think I waddn't gonna have no gun?"

"No, I just thought you wouldn't shoot," replied Dooley.

"And why's that?"

"Well, you haven't yet, right? It's because you recognize we aren't from around here and don't have any ill intention."

"I hope you're itendin' to give back my hog."

"Is he talking about me?" The pig grunted as Holt nudged it quiet.

"Oh, Hamlet? Yeah, you can have him, he's plagued with the disease of illiteracy." The pig shifted his weight onto Holt's pinky toe.

"A-lit-er-ossy? Sounds like something I can catch."

"No sir!" He shouted, pulling his foot from the pig, "not contagious, but definitely something the owners of the coal mines up here want you to have[42], and I'm not going to let them do that to you. That's why I've taken the Hamlet burden as my own."

A skinny old man hobbled out of the brush with his barrel facing the sky and grinned as if he just made new friends.

"We don't like mining coal in my family, ya know. It gave me bad lungs, and they ne'er gave us nuff of their mining dollars to buy food for the family. Then they'd tell us we're in the debt, and are lawfully obliged to work for 'em."

"Dusty old bag of bones." the pig whispered to Holt.

"I understand that. My family is from a little bit west of here. It's not the oppressed people's burden to fix all the poverty-filled

---

[42] Holt seems very intentional with his words, wanting to tug the strings of a person who likely did not like coal mine officials. The Harlan County War (1931-1939) and many other tensions over time have left many Appalachian people to dislike authorities over coal mines, even though they were often dependent on the mines for steady work.

45

backlash, the commonwealth needs to incentivise the educated population from leaving, so wealth can cycle through the system."

"He's so wrinkly," the pig continued.

"Ya darn right, that's why me and the nephew are in our own business. And you wouldn't believe if the government is tryna tell us we'd go to jail for doin' it."

"So what exactly do you do then?" Snorted the pig.

"C'mon up I'll show ya! But step lightly, I got my traps set out for the enemy." His voice squeaked as he made his way back up the hill.

Leaves crumbled under Holt's feet and rustled around the pig's, but the old man seemed to glide through the woods undisturbed by the thicket. Holt gathered that the man's jargon was a bit out of place, as the accent seemed to resemble film rather than present-day lingo; yet he decided not to question it outside of his own head. Trusting the path set for him by the old man, Holt was caught off guard by a web-spinning arachnid hovering in alignment with his two eyes. Stopping in his tracks, he reversed his steps and shivered for a full 5 seconds -- a record time. As his eyes switched focus from the tiny monster to the swift old man, he found it hard to conceive that he had somehow left the spider untouched. He altered his course slightly around the web, placing his fear for the spider above any worry of the traps. Even still, he progressed, fiddling with his piece of driftwood.

The denim overall pockets of the old man concealed an object of rectangular shape (about 4 inches by 3). Differing marginally from present day's typical circular item[43] of choice to fill a back pocket,

---

[43] Dip cans fill the back pockets of many rural Appalachian residents, making a small circle imprint in pants' pockets.

the desire to investigate fell upon Holt with such force, he nearly dropped his driftwood.

"Is that a can of snuff I see in your pocket? I haven't had any of that since my older brother used to sneak it to me in highschool. What brand are you carrying?"

"Oh, this?" Two fingers untucked the can from his pocket. "It's empty, I must have forgotten to throw it away." He said, tossing the can to a structure of leaves that somehow remained stable.

Holt had a brief look before the can disappeared into thin air. It was labeled "Velvet" [44]with red coloring, advertising a pipe for aged Owensboro tobacco. His brow raised and he let some distance grow between them so he could converse with the pig comfortably.

"Hamlet, what do you think?"

"My feet hurt and I'm ready for a rest."

"First off, you don't have feet, secondly, I meant about the old man! I can't decide if I should tell him he is a ghost."

"What do you mean?"

"He's a ghost, he doesn't know he is, and he is leading us through the woods to a cabin probably now occupied by some bootlegger or sociopath."

"It sounds like you just mixed the plot of the 'Sixth Sense' with the 'Blair Witch Project,'" the pig joked.

---

[44] Velvet is an obsolete brand of American tobacco, made from sun dried Kentucky burley.

Hiding his chuckle by coughing and clearing his throat, Dooley elaborated on the matter.

"The guy's got a pipe from the late 1800's in his chest pocket, probably from his father, which he uses to smoke an early 1900's can of tobacco. His index finger is stained with oil and it's clear he's been hauling copper. He uses vernacular out of his time and..." he said, gasping for breath, "Well, just look at him up there literally just phasing through those trees."

"Well even if he is a ghost, why do you think he doesn't know he is?"

"He thinks he owns a moonshine business, while people nowadays buy liquor from a building in the shape of a barn. It cost less than he could offer it for, even with the taxes."

"Look at your deer map, maybe it will tell you what to do."

"Ah, not a bad idea. I wonder how he'll take it when I tell him this hide can detect paranormal activity erupting from him?" he said, staring at the pig and shaking his head. "I guess we'll just see where he leads us."

An old cabin rested atop a pine covered hill, harboring the faintest whimper of held breath from the group approaching in the distance. Of course, Holt could not hear someone listening to them, but he was sure the cabin would be occupied. They inched forward accompanied by the fog often associated with that region of the Appalachians.

"When was the last time you were here, old man?"

"A few hours or so, I reckon. Why?"

"Do you not get cold at night with the windows broken out and all?"

"Windows? Which'n are you lookin' at? They look fine to me!" The old voice faded like the ripple of water. He reached for a non-existent knob and pulled backward, then phased through the door which remained unmoved. Passing through an unseen threshold, the apparition was no more.

"He must be seeing the world in a different timeline.." Holt said, twiddling his driftwood.

Dooley closed his hand and gently knocked the door, which resonated with instability. He listened to what seemed to be a quiet conversation and decided it best to confront them with words.

"I'm just looking for a place to rest my head."

He heard one say to the other something to the point of "I'll put 'em to rest alright!" Tipping him off to take evasive action. Holt flattened to the ground as a shotgun spread punched out the wood above him. "Consarn it!" Holt yelled, as he army-crawled swiftly away. He began to roll as if he would accelerate and catch the pig already halfway down the hill. Swiftly increasing the distance between the occasional gunfire and themselves, Holt was running in an unorthodox manner, possibly to shake off spiders. After some time, his legs grew tired and he motioned to take a rest.

"Think we lost them?" the pig asked.

"Of course, they probably stayed within a couple acres or so of their cabin," he said, gasping for breath.

"Then why did we run so far?" Its voice trembled with agitation.

"I have somewhere to be, don't you remember?"

The boar grunted in confusion and tried to catch its breath.

"Who are you really trying to get away from? You know, like in the big picture of things?"

"I'm not trying to get away from anyone, they just happen to be following me and I am not letting them find me."

"And why are they chasing you again?"

"Because I made a bad impression. We are probably getting close to Harlan, maybe we can stay there for the night."

Holt pieced together the recent events and determined that the current occupants of the cabin were bootlegging some drug, just as the ghost had been bootlegging alcohol in time past. He believed it was possible that the ghost's nephew, that he spoke of being in business with, was one of the occupants. This event confirmed to Holt that the elk hide acted as a map to the supernatural, in addition to giving regular direction.

———

Nestled in between two old shrunken mountains, rests the beautifully tired city of Harlan, Kentucky. All too often towns of such character are thought of as dead, when in reality they are just peacefully sleeping off the hard times. Martin's Fork Tributary meanders ever so gently adjacent to the population, allowing for the creation of bridges to act as a pleasing contrast to the abundant plant life. In fact north of this area is known for its swinging bridges along the trails of the Appalachian foothills. The height of beautiful scenery to me, is when human structures noninvasively interweave with the structures of nature.

Holt emerged from a frozen yogurt shop with an armful of sample cups, and shared with the boar.

"I heard some kids talking about a haunted school around here, sounds like something you're into." The pig said.

"I think they should call Bill Murray." [45]

The pig squinted, as if the reference was unclear.

Holt continued, "Anyway, we have something else on our plate. Before we make it all the way to Lexington, we should look for some agates to sell at one of these town's farmers markets or something."

Dooley pulled out his journal and began to draw what faintly resembled Pine Mountain, which overlooks Harlan. However each passing step undulated his pencil to create unsteady scribbles.

"What's an agate?"

"Cryptocrystalline silica and granular quartz come together and make some desirable features that prove to be ornamental. Think semi-precious jewelry."

"Sometimes you sound like a robot."

The two emerged from Harlan in a slightly better mood than they had been accustomed to earlier in their travels. Even so, Holt felt physical strain as they quickly overtook the ridge separating the town from Straight Creek. Searching on eroded banks proved unlucky, as no agate was found. However, advancing a bit in the woods they happened upon a couple of persimmon trees. He grabbed one of the tiny orange fruits from the ground and ripped it open to find that insects had devoured a portion. He attentively searched for a more perfect specimen, and took a bite. Finding them sweeter than honey, he pulled out the empty jar he had taken

---

[45] The *Ghostbusters* movies reference

from Rosaline and began to fill it. A few minutes passed, and it seemed the jar was special, as the fruit never reached the brim. He snatched up a large portion, but still left some for the bugs. Heading northward through the thick forest, leaves dropped and the boar played a game of catching them on his snout. The landscape appeared serenely untouched. As the developing world around it constantly laid new pavement, parts of Eastern Kentucky remained similar to how it was when Daniel Boone[46] was exploring it.

"It is amazing there is still so much forest left after people have settled right, Holt?"

"Yeah it's nice, but I don't know how close to their original state these forests are... just like down in the valleys there used to be a biome in the Southern Appalachians consisting of widespread sugarcane called 'canebrakes'. With the rise of agriculture, we decimated those along with some bug and animal species."

"Like what?"

"Well, the cougar for one was thought to have been impacted, but there is a type of bird, the Bachman's Warbler that might have gone extinct because of it. Some butterflies too."

"Well, at least there aren't as many cougars in the world."

Holt turned to the pig and scrunched his brow, "Just because it preys on other animals doesn't mean it's evil. For a chicken to kill another chicken, yes, maybe it's wrong; but for an opossum to kill a chicken is right. Otherwise, there would be overpopulation and

---

[46] One of the most famous American frontiersmen, blazing a trail into Kentucky through the Cumberland Gap

disease. What I'm saying is that one act may be wrong for someone, but not wrong for another...make sense?"

As they moved northwest along the highway, Holt threw his thumb[47] in the air to occasional passing cars. A small pick-up truck with corroded exterior pulled off to the side and waited for them. As they approached it, Holt remembered what his father told him years ago concerning hitchhiking and safety.

"You know, my dad used to tell me not to pick up hitchhikers because a high percentage of them are crazy...I think a lot of people who pick them up probably are too," Holt said.

"Do you think he'll let me control the radio?" The pig asked.

"Yeah, I'm sure he won't be able to hear it from the truck bed anyway," he replied, winking his eye.

Holt opened the back and threw his pack in, thanking the man for stopping. The driver resembled a classic hillbilly, with a long beard and hair, but he was dressed in Sunday clothes, tipping Holt off that he must be on his way to church.

"Who were you talking with back there, that hog?" The driver asked. [48]

Holt ignored the question, "What do you do for a living, make duck calls?" [49]

---

[47] The old signal of "hitchhikers" as they were called

[48] One of the first notions that many other people can't rightly hear Hamlet speaking in the same way Holt can

[49] Holt's witty jab at the driver's appearance was a reference to the show *Duck Dynasty*.

"Son, are you crazy or something? You look like you need some faith." He replied.

"And what do you have faith in?"

"Well, the Lord God of course! If you don't then you will burn in the pit of hell for eternity. It's in your best interest to come to the church with me."

"Coincidentally, I believe in God as well. So actually it is probably not in my best interest to waste any time, as I am on a long journey to the West."

"Well after this service you will know if you are saved or not! It's better to be safe while you're on that journey right, Sonny?

"Sure, we'll go with you if you drive us farther afterwards to make up for my lost time. But Hamlet's gotta come in too, I don't want him to turn into eternal bacon if you know what I mean."

They pulled up to a secluded property, with cars around the old wooden steepled building. "No trespassing" signs scattered about the premise, and tire heaps aided in the resemblance of a slipshod barnyard. As he cracked the car door, he could already hear the faint sound of rowdy worshipers. The boar hopped out and looked at Holt with confusion, but followed him regardless. Some people were standing on their chairs dancing and some people were chanting unknown words to each other, and Holt didn't attempt to bridle his skeptical grin. The pastor yelled out at the newcomers and called him to the front of the congregation.

"Do you have faith, my boy?"

"Yes, but I think our operational definition of faith is quite different."

"Do you know how to have assurance if you are in the right?" the pastor asked, with the voice of an opera singer.

"Do you think he always speaks like that?" the pig whispered.

"The Lord God will show you!" The pastor continued. He turned around and opened a box full of rattlesnakes[50], reaching for one with great confidence, and placing it around his neck. "Mark 16:17-18 tells us '*And these signs shall follow them that believe; In my name shall they cast out devils; they shall speak with new tongues; They shall take up serpents; and if they drink any deadly thing, it shall not hurt them; they shall lay hands on the sick, and they shall recover.*' So we can know if you are in the Lord's favor if you are not inflicted with the poison! Are you ready to receive a new testimony, young man?" The congregation swelled with "amens" and other words of affirmation as they clapped loudly.

"The snake is rattling, you're going to let it bite you?" Holt said.

The pastor rolled his sleeve to expose a few bite marks.

"You must have milked the venom out of it, then."

The snake launched off of the pastor toward Holt, as he nimbly dogged and crushed its head between his heel and the wooden floor. "Well it didn't poison him!" one member shouted. The pastor looked shocked and claimed that God allowed him to do that as a symbol of Genesis 3:15. Holt, tired of the shenanigans, left with the boar and began to walk on the highway again.

---

[50] Snake-handling 'churches' illegally practice in some areas of the rural south. Many of the leaders were known to cite the bible out of context, and use snakes to convince others to join their cult.

"Hamlet, Do you remember talking about the canebrakes? It brought up a fond memory I forgot about."

"Tell me about it!" the pig said.

"I was going to," he chuckled. "It obviously wasn't too monumental as this is my first time recalling it, but it was pleasant. I was running around exploring with my brothers outside of our home, when we came across those river canes for the first time. It was dusk, and the lightning bugs were out. We watched as they weaved through the reeds, signaling neon-yellow in unison. I liked to freeze when they flashed, and continue moving when it was dark. As for discovering the new plants, in my mind, the reason they were so thin proportionally, was because they were stretched too far to the sky. I bent one down and created tension to cut it more easily with my knife so I could show my dad. I remember seeing the faint sunlight leaving Lake Cumberland, and thinking the canes really accentuated it."

Around the Goose Creek area, the two made it to their first swinging bridge. The archetypal image of a rope bridge with wooden tread held true to the ambiance of this one. Of course, it creaked and wobbled with movement, with the racket of instability.

Holt told the pig he had business to attend to in the woods and to go on ahead, as it would only be a minute. The boar was high-stepping as a trotting horse would, in full faith of the creaky bridge. Through the cracks of the boards below his cloven hooves, the pig didn't notice the flagrant movement below it. Reaching above the bridge, was a forearm and hand resembling a tree trunk and branches. It plucked the boar like a fruit, and brought it down below to get a better look.

Now Holt had finished his business and was making his way across the bridge when he witnessed the grimy hand rise from the depths placing the pig back up at the end of the posts. The pig winked at him, as Holt twiddled the driftwood between his fingers. A quick shrug and a couple more steps, and the hand reemerged to grab him. Its sandpaper skin was stained with blood and odor. Dooley flew through the air like an amusement park ride at Dollywood[51], legs dangling and torso clenched. Holding Holt up in front of its mouth, the monster revealed its numerous serrated teeth and opened its yellow eyes. Its nose was rather large, but other than that it resembled an unhygienic human. It yawned and rubbed its eyes as if it had recently woken up from a lengthy slumber.

"Did Hamlet tell you to hold your appetite because I was coming?" Holt asked.

"He made you seem bigger." The bridge above quivered from the mere sound the beast projected.

"And I suppose people call you a troll?" he asked, as he was placed in its mouth. It mumbled something that Holt didn't understand, but he responded anyway. "But you're a Nephilim[52] aren't you?"

It spit Holt into its palm, and stared at him for an interesting half-minute. He and the beast accidentally began to speak at the same time.

---

[51] Amusement park named after Dolly Parton in Pigeon Forge, Tennessee

[52] The exact Hebrew translation of the word "nephilim" remains unclear. Some believe it to mean fallen angels, giants, men born from angels, or giant men. Cross check *Genesis 6:4* for a common reference of the word.

"How do you know that word?"

"I've read the Bible, and other uncanonical works. How are you so undiscovered in our modern world if you still exist?"

"I may not divulge things of this nature to you. You live in the age of ignorance, it is effortless with this world's new distractions."

"We call it the age of information."

They sat in another short time of inelegant silence before he decided to let Holt go.

"You know it is not much different in these times. Your people disbelieve the past in the same way their ancestors would disbelieve their future, and your present. Time on this earth is broken into a few periods regarding mankind: you were formed to glorify your creator, but instead began to worship lesser spiritual beings, and now you are centered around idolizing technology," said the Nephilim.

"So, where are the 'beings' of the olden days now? And why do you hide under this bridge?"

"We have been instructed to wait. Soon the era will be when the realms are mixed."

"I'm sorry, I still don't quite understand.." Dooley started.

"Nor am I allowed to make you understand. For good reason. You are not a worthy vessel to carry many of the questions your species ask. Even if I wanted to exchange information of this sort with you, they could have my life...or worse."

"Who's 'they'?"

"Do you not understand social cues? Get out of here." The Nephilim flicked Holt in the back angrily.

Holt tumbled up the hill to the base of the bridge and faced the pig who was kicking dirt, stirring with guilt. It claimed to have known Holt would find a way out, and that he had a better chance of survival in that situation than itself. He patted the boar on the head and turned on its radio, continuing their journey to pick up Armillaria's friend in Lexington -- in a roundabout way.

"Hard Livin" by Railroad Earth was playing, and their countenance was that of happy travelers. The sweet mandolin tones flew through the air and landed perfectly in the leaves of the temperate Kentucky Forest.

"I heard this band only travels by train," Dooley said.

"The signs say we are headed to London, and we just came from Manchester. Those are English cities too, right?" the boar randomly asked.

"There were a lot of settlers of English, Irish, and Scottish origin here."

After much conversation, Holt surprisingly seemed less annoyed with the boar than when they first began traveling together. Eventually, they reached Laurel County, the home to the first Colonel Sanders' Kentucky Fried Chicken.[53] More than eighty percent of the town claims a conservative political stance, and the economy is largely built on the highway cutting through it. Most of the citizens are known for the southern hospitality, but Holt always has a way of unforeseeably impacting others.

---

[53] At the time it was called *Sanders Court & Café*.

Now, the last of the year's farmer's markets had begun and Holt was excited to see what he could sell and swindle. Funnily enough, he exhibited goosebumps like a musician might get before taking the stage. Even so, compared to the canopy tents, his cardboard table was a shabby set up. A couple of drawings from his journal, his jar of persimmons, and rocks he had been collecting were priced for sale. Some of the vendors were talking and had become upset that Holt was making their establishment appear gaudy.

"Are you gonna try to sell that toothpick in your fingers or what?" one of them asked. This particular vendor seemed out of place. He was broad shouldered and had a notable mustache, the color of a fox.

"Um, sir, a toothpick has a diameter of about two millimeters.. this is a whopping twice its size." He said.

"Well, what about all that other horse crap you brought?" another vendor asked.

Holt squinted his eyes to express his disdain for the speaker. Mumbling insults and using an assortment of gestures, he took a piece of paper and set up a sort of sign up sheet. When a citizen of London began questioning him about the price of his boar, he was busy developing a plan, and mindlessly sold it to her. She put the money on the box and the pig wandered away with her as she lured it with food from another vendor.

"Watch this Hamlet. Hamlet? Ah well."

Holt yelled to the crowds asking them to gather around. He said that if anyone could guess how many persimmons in the jar within five, he would give them 100 dollars. He set it up so that each guess would cost 5 dollars. Everyone lined up and started buying guesses, as they all believed the "give or take five fruit" had made it easy. He asked if everyone had finished, and said he would pull the fruit out one by one counting them in front of everyone. As he got to number thirty, the crowd had already diminished, seeing that there were only a couple guesses that high anyway. When he made it to the last one at seventy-three, nobody was standing around anymore. He laughed and counted his money, while reading the guesses on the sign up sheet. The vast majority were in the twenties, with one large exception at 70. His eyes widened in disbelief, as he swore under his breath. The name adjacent to it said "Mis Vinela". He was surprised for the first time in a long while.

"What kind of name is...WHO IS MIS VINELA?" he yelled.

A young girl holding a doll raised her hand.

"Young girl, how are you so good at spelling? You're going places." he said after her shoulder-shrug.

He handed her a hundred dollars in fives, and began counting his left over money. "Hmm, how do I still have forty-five bucks... and two twenties? He didn't bother finding the source of the money, but pocketed it and looked for the pig.

"Let's get going."

"This lady thinks she bought me from you. Should we run?"

"Oh, that makes more sense...yeah, I'm not about to give up our money."

They took off with great speed, and of course drawing attention to themselves. The lady screamed that her pig was being stolen, and one of the wisenheimer vendors happened to bravely step in Dooley's path as he was in full sprint. Leaping like a cat, he pulled his fist back and his back leg up, enacting the infamous "superman punch"[54] and dropping the victim to the dirt. Unfortunately for him, he lost the jar in the process, breaking it upon a rock. He kept moving without much regret.

While traveling west, after a few rotations of the earth, Holt had another stop before making it to Lexington. He told the boar they were going to see Lake Cumberland. However, scenery wasn't the primary reason for traveling to Somerset, as his family had moved there when he was young, and he intended on seeing them. After all, it had been a great deal of time since they had even heard from him.

They arrived at a large Baptist church that his family regularly attended, and the pig waited outside. Dooley sat in the back so as not to draw any attention in case it was possible to recognize his older self through his facial hair. A challenge of equal caliber, he was concerned with recognizing the back of all of their heads, trying to pick out his mother. He wasn't surprised as his childhood best friend took the stage and began to preach, but he did sketch a picture of it into his journal. As the pastor began to pray with the congregation, a toddler resting on her mother's shoulder was staring at Holt relentlessly. The toddler tattled in a yelp to her mom, that the man behind her had not been closing his eyes during the prayer. The mother hushed her child, and Holt felt uncomfortable. After the service it seemed that his family was not there, and keeping interaction at a minimum, he decided to go to his old home.

---

[54] Muay Thai style punch

They made it back to his family's farm late in the evening, and the mile-long driveway felt the same underfoot as it did when his bike tires scattered grooves into the gravel. The house could be seen from the majority of the road's distance, and the light inside of the kitchen could be seen from two farms over. He lurked behind his old car, a Mini Cooper, and peered into the house. The car seemed to have not been moved from its original spot on the pavement, as if he would come back to use it someday. The night was navy blue, and the window illuminated starry yellow with the occasional blotting-out from a passerby. He thought he'd see both of his brothers and their families enjoying time with his parents testing combinations of pies and ice creams. Instead, he witnessed something else. He rubbed his cold and nervous arms, hoping to alleviate his goosebumps. [55]

The two men speaking to his parents were not his brothers, but men he didn't know. Both were muscular and one with a red mustache appeared to be packing a handgun. They were dressed formally, and by their body movements, Holt inferred that they were looking for something, which he presumed was him. The boar believed Holt was feeling excluded or forgotten, but really he was experiencing a burst of adrenaline.

"Well, what are you waiting for, Holt?"

"A train," he replied.

He limboed under the garage door, which was cracked open for the ancient dog to move as it pleased, and grabbed a screwdriver and hammer. Fortunately, when he came back out he heard a train

---

[55] Holt's goosebumps are mentioned often. I wonder what the connotations are.

sounding off and took the opportunity to break into his old car, punching the screwdriver into the ignition to start it.

"What are you doing? Why would you come so close and not speak to them?" the boar asked.

"Distance is not solely measured physically. My family might as well be on the moon right now, as my words would reach them just the same."

They pulled out and raced north toward Lexington. After all, there were places to be and tasks to fulfill. After an hour and a half, they made it to their destination, and parked close to the North Lime doughnut shop that Armillaria had mentioned. Sleeping in the car was a luxury as opposed to the woods and landscape they had grown accustomed to.

Waking to Dooley writing in his journal, the pig peered into his writing before his consciousness was realized.

The sequacious grumphie still follows, as a premonition does when one can't keep the annoying past from handling in to the present.

"What does that mean?"

Holt slammed his journal shut and closed his eyes. "A grumphie is a term for your species, derived from the act of grunting you often perform, first coined in Scotland.."

"You were writing about me? You are so weird."

"Weird compared to what? You don't even know any other humans."

He opened the car door and they walked toward North Lime doughnut shop. The shop's exterior displayed a hue like a scarlet

64

cardinal, whose wings were slightly worn with time. The interior was typical of a rustic coffee house, and hosted a group of people who seemed to be setting trends in fashion, on the smallest scale. He placed his flat hand on his brow to block any view of the city folk, as they made him feel uncomfortable. With his head leaned down and his eyes watching the feet in front of him, he successfully made it to the ordering counter. With a smirk, the worker asked what he would like to order.

"I'm looking for a friend of a friend.. and I sure hope it isn't one of those people. Especially not the one wearing suspenders along with his belt," he said, as he peered through a gap in his index and middle finger.

"Well, do you want to buy a doughnut and go ask them, or..."

"No."

He peered around at every readable object to deduce some sort of clue like Sherlock Holmes would, except the lack of substantial information Armillaria left him with, was not a promising foundation. Holt briefly recalled its words:

"*If you ask around there, you will meet my friend.* Quite uninformative for a hint.." he whispered.

He noticed a tip jar with the name "Carl" on it, a punch card for frequent doughnut eaters, and a flyer from a local musician. The musician briefly crossed his mind as the possible target, but Dooley was distracted by the Carl jar, as he was trying to decide who the proceeds of the tip were going to. He couldn't determine if it was for a sickly child in the community, or perhaps a fictional character with a story crafted to generate extra income to the workers.

"Who is Carl?" he asked.

"Me," Carl said, tapping the register impatiently.

"What?! Why would you label the jar with your name, you could have left it blank and everyone would have already assumed it was for you!" Holt was pointing aggressively, as Carl shrugged. "Anyway does the name Armillaria sound familiar to you?"

"No...man, we are pretty busy, and if you're not gonna get anything you should let the other people order."

"Busy?" he said, under his breath. Turning around he did deduce that a rather large line had formed.

At nearly the same time, a young man barged through the entrance with some supplies for the store. He mentioned finding a potted plant in the company car and asked where to bring it. The storekeeper had no knowledge of the plant and said it wasn't theirs. Upon seeing it, Holt's face lit up as if there was something special about it. The "plant" was a bonsai tree in a classic terra cotta pot, but at the base of the tree sat decorative aquamarine minerals that he recognized. Over-hearing that the workers were unfamiliar with it, doubly sparked his interest. The tree was a giant sequoia by species, although by its looks one might call it a tiny sequoia, since the pot had obviously restricted growth. However, it was obvious that the tree was ancient, as the trunk girth was considerable. As it was being carried to one of the tables, presumably to determine further action, the main trunk was solid as a statue and the foliage bobbed with the steps of the worker.

Holt hurried over to the bonsai, spinning his piece of driftwood in between his fingers, and leaning in so closely to the tree to inspect it, that the customers took notice, and felt uneasy. He mumbled a few words to himself, and smiled mischievously at the people looking at him, with full knowledge of them thinking he was crazy. He then created a scenario in his head out of humor, wherein he picked up the tree and quite literally waltzed out of the shop, answering nobody. Contemplating the consequences, that is just what he did.

"Umm, stop," said Carl, "Don't umm.." Being rather shocked at Holt's audacity, his words disintegrated to the point of stupidity. Holt made some interesting facial expressions as he danced out the door, knowing the people in line would be less likely to hinder, or even fault a crazy person. Just as he suspected, nobody followed him out the door.

"Holt, why did you steal that plant?"

"Are you so ridiculously unobservant that you couldn't tell this was the "friend" Armillaria was talking about?"

"Well, for one, you never really filled me in on what he said, or what we were supposed to be doing.."

"I'm repaying my debt by doing what he asked me," he stated, "bringing this little guy across the country with us."

"Oh, so the talking rock wanted you to bring a plant across the country as a favor?" the pig sarcastically retorted.

"Why don't you just ask him yourself? Private Sherman, this is Hamlet. Hamlet, this is Private Sherman."

"I'm not talking to a plant, Holt."

"Why not? Everything communicates, it's just a matter of being able to translate those signals into some form of understanding. Just how you refraining to verbally communicate with Private Sherman is actually signaling a negative response toward him."

"Why did you name it 'Private Sherman'?"

"Don't you know who General Sherman[56] is?" Dooley answered. "It's the biggest tree on the planet. Ironically, it is the same species as this little guy. It's a good name."

The two continued their journey to the west, with the additional passenger, Sherman, now strapped into the front seat. The last stop that they made in Kentucky was at the Comfy Cow shop in Louisville, where Holt carried out an ice cream robbery that he claimed "rivalled the *Oceans* movies." He swerved through city lines, eating ice cream by the pint and listening to "Take the Money and Run" by the Steve Miller Band on the pig's radio.

---

[56] General Sherman is the largest single-stemmed tree in the world, located in California, and named after a Union Army Civil War general.

CHAPTER 4

(The Deciduous Detective)

Chase Griffith waited in line with a visible amount of jitters, as one would when going through withdrawals. He edged closer to the counter slowly, almost breathing on the neck of the customer in front of him. Somewhat audibly, he read through a sign with the headings "North Lime" and "Specials" and decided to order the pumpkin pie filled doughnut, along with many other kinds. Most everyone watched as he fidgeted in his chair, waiting for his order. His head appeared as a swelling, red balloon, ready to pop; and once his name was called, all the air squeezed out of him with a sigh of relief and excitement. Rather ungracefully, he ravished through the doughnuts, consuming five in a matter of minutes.

Since he had obtained a somewhat magical item from Rosaline in order to discover Holt Dooley's location, his search finally had direction, though he didn't know where exactly. The elk figurine had tugged his arm nearly out of socket and into North Carolina, and then over through Tennessee, to Kentucky as a result of Holt using his elk hide map. However, Holt actually hadn't used the map near the North Lime doughnut shop, Griff merely appeared there out of his own volition.

The investigator had now done some research and understood that he was in the state where Dooley was born, and decided to pay a visit to his family to find some leads. He traveled down to Pulaski County, where he talked to Holt's concerned parents, who alluded that they already talked to government officials. They discussed the recent car theft from their driveway, and decided that the thief must actually have been Holt himself. His parents furthermore tipped Griffith off to the fact that Holt used to spend a considerable amount of time hiking through the woods of McCreary County, and inspired him to continue his search down there.

He considered the possibility that Holt would travel south to a land that was familiar, but also entertained the notion that Holt could be fleeing to a new part of the country. He had in fact seen in the news that a strange man had stolen copious amounts of ice cream from a shop in Louisville, and decided on a whim that he would search that area first, and then McCreary county if he had no luck.

The darkness of midnight came upon Griff with surprise, as he seemed to waste time all too easily. Like a fish out of water, he wandered aimlessly, in hopes a lead would fall into his lap, as had luckily happened with his past cases. It is unclear why he wandered out of the metropolitan area, and unfortunately for him, luck works both ways. For what he had stumbled upon at this time of night, he must have certainly been defying probability, though not for his own benefit.

He wasn't sure of what he had just heard. At night, in the thick of shadows and gloom, one's ears can sometimes deceive them. Griffith's hearing never had any issues in the past, which reassured him to continue further into the trees. The continued dull sound of a voice he remembered was haughtily spouting off facts somewhere at the end of the woods. He recognized it easily, as he was shamed by the voice's owner before, and he swiftly trudged on to find the source. He climbed a fence that urged trespassers to keep out, and threatened them with arrest. His flashlight, along with his close ties with multiple governmental entities gave him the courage to move onward.

Walking with a slight hop, from the spaces in between train track logs, he found himself on the top of a trestle bridge over Pope Lick Creek. Griff was not aware of the wildly infamous folklore that surrounded the Pope Lick Monster,[57] nor would he have strategized a different method of entry if he was aware. "Flying by the seat of his pants" was the foundation of his preferred methodology.

He believed he saw Holt at the base of the opposite side of the railroad trestle, doodling the bridge into his journal, just the same as when they met. He listened as his target loudly spoke the dimensions to himself.

"Hey, Holt! Have anything to say for yourself? I just caught you trespassing." Griff shouted. The reason he shouted was specifically to test the waters. Subconsciously, he was picking up on plenty of hints that he was entering a scene from a horror movie.

Holt continued drawing as if he didn't hear. Griff was feeling uneasy, but allured by the ease of his situation, he picked up the pace. When he was nearly halfway across the trestle, He thought he heard Holt's voice change as he kept mumbling to himself. He stopped for a second to watch Holt's figure dimly wavering with the wind, almost like smoke. For a minute, he confused his

---

[57] Legendary goat humanoid, also commonly referred to as "Goat Man". Many locals believe the monster is responsible for the deaths that have occurred around the train trestle.

appearance with some sort of animal. Wiping his eyes, he started to walk again.

"You don't want to play games with me, Holt Dooley."

In between the railroad ties, he noticed the glimmer of two eyes below the trestle. Pointing his flashlight in its direction didn't reveal much but the rusty frame with chipped paint holding up the train bridge. He pivoted on his stance and quickly brought the light behind him, to make sure someone had not followed. His courage was depleting. He could not seem to find Holt with the small amount of light he wielded.

"Maybe you should have brought a lantern." Said a voice, eerily similar to Holt's.

Griff pointed the flashlight directly above him, in the direction of the noise. Nothing sat on the top of the trestle's frame, but he swore he heard it climbing around him.

"That's the problem with a flashlight, it only illuminates the direction you point it in." It continued.

Again, Griffith spun around, in a panic, doing his best to find Holt.

"But then again, look at me, I can use flashlights pretty well." It taunted him, pulling Griff's flashlight straight out of his hand and shining it directly in the investigator's face.

"I will shoot you, Holt, don't provoke me!"

Two flashlights from ahead seemed to be approaching him at an amazing speed. He felt the bridge shaking and pointed his gun toward it. He shot two bullets toward the beast, but instead of hearing the loud snap of a pistol, he heard the horn and squealing brakes of a train. Realizing he would be obliterated if he stayed still, he leaped from the train bridge into the creek. By his great luck, he had survived the jump without sustaining injury. He looked back up at the trestle, murkily revealing the beast who had been toying with him. He could make out a bipedal, standing upon two hooves, hanging with strong arms from the beams of the trestle as the train passed. Eyes glowed on a head with horns, shaped like that of a goat.

He ran the fastest his feet have ever traveled, back to his car, and drove out of Louisville, to clear his head. He coped with the memory by telling himself that he had eaten too many doughnuts, and sugar does crazy things to your mind.

———

A few days passed and Griffith found no new information, spurring him to travel back to Mcreary county as planned. He pulled into the Natural Arch Scenic Area, and sat on a ridge overlooking the Daniel Boone National Forest. Bringing out his enchanted elk figurine, he traced the carved grooves with his finger.

"C'mon baby give me somethin," he whispered, "Show me where this guy's hiding."

After hours of nothing, he became angry and tried to break the figurine by throwing it on the ground beside where he was sitting. It remained unfractured, but seemed to move a bit on its own. Griff extended his arm out to pick it back up and inspect it. Instead of him grabbing the figurine, it evidently had a hold on him, yanking his arm forth and pulling him directly off the ledge of the bluff he was sitting on.

He crashed through the treetops like a ragdoll, breaking branches and bringing leaves down with him. He became deciduous,[58] like the trees around him, and it was a blast of autumn color. A dark red liquid contributed resentfully to the yellow and orange leaf bed he fell upon, and was further spread among the forest floor as the figurine dragged him arm-first over logs, rocks, and anything else it wanted. He was the red paint on the end of a paint brush, and the forest floor was the canvas.

It must be said, allegorically, Griffith wasn't the most substantial leaf to fall. That one would come soon enough.

---

[58] "Deciduous" in botany means "tending to fall off," and is the category of plants that lose their leaves in autumn, as opposed to evergreen.

CHAPTER 5

(An Outlaw Among Villains)

Holt, the boar, and Private Sherman were taking in the enormity of the great Ohio River along the Indiana shoreline, when the topic of water pollution came up. The Ohio is one of the most polluted waterways in the United States, due to the bad industrial practices throughout the course of history. As recorded in Holt's journal: *"at one point the river was so acidic that the pH consistently measured less than 1"*. Yet, sometimes this is the sort of atmosphere that breeds adventure. Catfish the size of cars are rumored to be radioactive, while sharks and octopuses[59] sometimes find their way here unexpectedly. Lost watches, phones, and articles of clothing are abundant, and treasure hunters for some reason are not.

"I triple-dog-dare you to jump in," said the boar.

"Consarn it, Hamlet! I just told you how the river was adulterated by toxic chemicals to both of us physiologically. Why on earth would I do that?" Holt said laughingly.

"Because the map is showing some suspicious activity over there."

---

[59] No, the plural is not "octopi".

"Put that back in my bag! We really should get a move on soon."

"Oh, come on, I know how much you like to investigate this thing."

Holt was not yet aware how much of a hold the map had on him. It was constantly compelling him to action, distracting him from his journey's end goal. Holt contemplated for a minute, and abruptly stripped to his boxers, bolted toward the river, and dove in. The pig called out directions from the shore, and Holt swam accordingly. His countenance changed, and it was clear that what started as a fun act of leisure, quickly turned to serious interest.

Believing he saw an old sunken ship down below him, he told the pig that he was going to see if he could dive down and explore it. He made it to around 24 feet deep, when it seemed the muddy and murky sediments resolved around a large bubble, which completely encased the sunken steamboat. Holt swam into it from the side, rather than the top, so as not to fall to the ground inside of it. He found that he was able to walk around just as you would on land.

He read the name "H.K. Bedford" [60] on the siding of the steamboat, and proceeded to climb up the old paddle wheel that used to propel it. A small band of gleaming light refracted downwards to Holt Dooley's eyeline. From the broken glass sitting in a sill that used to belong to it when it was a window, nobody would have guessed the activity taking place within the boat's old bones. Holt peered in, just his eyes, forehead, and hair visible, and spied on a certain civilized meeting.

The reason I describe it as "civilized" is not to indicate the meeting's normality, but rather to emphasize its peculiarity. These

---

[60] A trade ship built in the late 19th century, and sunk in the early 20th

particular folk were intentionally meeting under the cover of darkness, as villains do. Well, it wasn't literally dark, but their assembly room resembled some unholy sanctuary. It was lit by muddy old flashlights, which dimly gave way to the piles of gizmos and gadgets presumably gathered from the bottom of the river. The figures who gathered them were sitting in furnishings that spanned many decades and styles. There were maybe twenty members in total, most of them sitting silent and watching the speaker at the forefront. Each member was certainly distinct, except that a few of them shared the likeness of some cold blooded creatures, some with amphibian appearance, some possibly reptilian.

Holt shifted to a more covert mindset, and attempted to get a little closer to hear what was being said without disrupting them. The one speaking, had a theatrical voice. It was indistinguishable from the sounds and inflection of a human, and it spoke English just -fine with a knowledgeable vocabulary. Being dressed like a human in the clothes of a 1950s air force colonel, It had two arms, two legs, and pale human looking skin. Maybe he was, in fact, just a regular human -- sorry for the build up. Oh, but he did have yellow eyes with a skinny black line as a pupil, rather than a circular one.

"Let's make sure we all get here on time at the next meeting, so I don't have to call roll at the end anymore, alright everyone?" said the Colonel. "I'm looking at you, Loveland Frog." [61]

Some mumbled and laughed quietly, others snickered. Holt saw an empty chair at the front that wasn't necessarily nice, but in the hierarchy of chairs that they had collected from the bottom of the river, it would be a king's seat. On it there was attached a piece of

---

[61] The *Loveland Frog* is an Ohio folklore monster, described as a 4ft tall, intelligent humanoid

paper sitting on the torn upholstery that read "Mothman." [62] He laughed at the thought of possibly discovering a league of folklore villains and continued watching the roll-call, fully entertained.

"Pope Lick Monster?" the Colonel asked. "Not here today? That's odd...ah well, how about the Hopkinsville Goblin?" [63]

"Present."

"The supposed 'Indescribable' Octoman?" [64]

"Here."

"Yes, but you're not really all there, are ya, airhead? Thetis Lake Monster?" [65]

"My name is Kevin." the monster retorted.

"We don't care. No talking please. Green Clawed Beast?" [66]

"Here." it said, raising its claw.

"Of course you are. Always hungry for attention, aren't ya?" The Colonel continued, "Mothman?"

---

[62] One of the most famous folklore beings in America, Mothman is reported to haunt the people of Point Pleasant, West Virginia.

[63] The Kelly-Hopkinsville encounter is one of the most well-documented UFO cases in America, maybe having some relation to this goblin.

[64] Another amphibious folklore monster from the Ohio River

[65] Folklore beast from the movie *Creature of the Black Lagoon*, supposedly from Canada

[66] Cryptid from the Ohio river that has been reported multiple times, but never fully seen

"Why do you keep insisting on this? He doesn't even live in our district," one complained.

A grimy looking humanoid with thickly matted fur stood and exclaimed to the others that it smelled something strange. They conferred and looked around the room at each other as suspicion grew. Holt, detecting that he would soon be caught, decided to be proactive about the matter, and introduce himself.

"Hello, everyone. It is good to see all of you! Goblin, Octoman, Kevin." He said, addressing some of the names he heard from the roll-call, in order to relieve their tensions.

"And who exactly are you?" the Colonel asked, looking directly at Holt.

"I am the one and only "Evil Shapeshifter," as the locals in my region refer to me."

"Is that why you look and smell so much like a human?" The Colonel's brow raised as if he didn't quite believe Holt.

"Why yes, it is exactly what Mothman suggested I should do," he wittingly replied.

There were gasps amongst the crowd as some edged toward the end of their seats. "You know The Mothman?"

"Of course I do! I guess you could say he is my sidekick." Dooley said.

"Liar!" shouted the Colonel. "You know nothing of The Mothman! Thetis Lake Monster, apprehend him this instant!"

"Hold it there, Kevin. I say we ask Octoman, I can detect that he would be a wise candidate for deciding my authenticity or not, what do you all say?

79

A few nodded and it was clear Dooley had won over the hearts of some, with his charming words. In his speech, he included the names that he heard the Colonel use to insult some of the members, and instead, associated their name with a compliment. The Colonel was disgusted and astounded, and the monsters were tuned in to Holt's charisma. Holt inquired about the ambitions of the group and discovered that their primary motive was two-fold: to haunt the residents of their area as a means of revenge for the pollution of the Ohio River, and to clean up litter that recreationists lose in the waterbody. Their litter pile was full of valuables, none of which the group were concerned with. Holt ended up convincing them that he would recycle some of the materials, although his true motive was monetary. Octoman agreed that this was a great idea.

"As a sentiment from Mothman and myself, I will take some of these materials off your hands and recycle them. I hope to be invited to future meetings." He picked up a muddy coat and put it on, and put some watches, rings and other accessories he could sell in his new pockets. "With all that, I will take my leave. Nice seeing you gentlemen. You should think about demoting this one though." He pointed with his thumb back toward the snarling Colonel and slipped out of the doorway.

Leaving them all mostly in a state of confusion, he traveled from the safe confines of the dry air bubble back into the river's current. As he swam to the surface, he emerged a long way downstream from where he had left the pig. He ran up to them dressed in his new coat, unstuffing his pocket and revealing the loot he had procured.

"Were you two not worried that I was drowning? I was down there for a good while," Holt asked. "I expected as much from Hamlet, but you, Private Sherman? I'm disappointed."

"I figured you had found something magical or something, and were doing something... I don't know."

"Eloquently put," replied Dooley.

Now, Indiana was not a favorite state of Holt Dooley's. The Southern region of the state had been nicknamed "Kentuckiana" due to cultural similarity with Kentucky, but the university basketball teams were enough to make sure comradery was not felt across the border. He grew up disliking the Hoosiers, but his present critique fell more in the theme of poor environmental planning. However, the congenial city of Evansville boasted a redeeming urban ecosystem, the Howell Wetlands. Consequently, he scheduled to spend some time walking through it, bringing him once again to act as a philosopher, writing questions and attempting to answer them in his journal.

"When is it acceptable to conserve nature? My initial thought would be 100% of the time, since globally we have impacted such a significant amount of nature, to the point where some might say that there are no virgin forests, and virtually no landscape that has gone completely unaffected... but is this just the way of the world? The earth cyclically destroys and repairs itself, and human work is a factor in this, but it is hard to determine when we have gone too far or when we are moving appropriately. What if we looked at this analogously: Would you look at the land allocated to the Center for Disease Control and Prevention, and make the point that the cost of building on the landscape, killing that ecosystem and everything in it, is outweighed by the good they have done to humans? Most certainly. Hence, value can be attributed to not conserving land, if it is for the greater good.

On the other hand, there is a place for the argument of incorporating more conservation into our urbanization, since without flora and fauna altogether, humans would die regardless of the CDC being around. There is a balance to be found, and it probably weighed too heavily on the side of urban sprawl, since we could be building in harmony with nature, having more city parks, and more streetside and rooftop greenery, or even changing our building materials to be less environmentally impactful. I think this would ultimately yield a higher quality of life for us."

They spent no more than a few hours passing through Indiana, to Illinois where they would spend the night in the Shawnee National Forest. Southern Illinois is often referred to as Little Egypt, possibly due to the resemblance of fertility between the Mississippi and the Nile.

"Garden of the Gods," Holt started, "the 'gods' must not have cared about this garden as much as the one in Colorado, they barely decorated it!" His comment was ignored, to discourage his attempt at humor. After exploring the area, Holt made a minor discovery of some rock art, which he said was possibly indigenous petroglyphs.[67] They appeared to be quickly carved into the stone, without much detail. Dooley could discern what bore resemblance to an engraved human, standing between two beasts. One, possibly an eagle, descended from the sky, whilst a horned snake-like creature ascended from waters below to meet the stick-figured man in the middle. He replicated it in his journal, and speculated on the meaning.

The pig, now saddled by the bonsai called "Private Sherman", took a majestic stance on a sandstone bluff overlooking the warm

---

[67] Already, Holt encounters Native American lore, just as predicted by Armillaria.

colored canopy, with the radio still sitting in his tusks. The setting sun shone strongly against their silhouette, eliminating color and detail to Dooley's focused eyes. His mind was always so analytic, with thoughts that the light waves were undulating at a desirable frequency to his retina's photoreceptors, rather than the typical human who might just perceive the color contrast as enjoyable.

A dark cutout of the pig and bonsai lay on top of the trees, and quite visibly, mimicked their movements. Holt's head swiveled from the pig and the bonsai to the shadow they cast, and determined that the bonsai tree was in contemplation. He drew the elongated shadow in comparison to the small bonsai tree who made it.

Private Sherman must believe he is as tall as the other trees. I think his shadow at the moment is misleading him.

Holt went back to the car and slept with the windows down, comforted by the wind's whistling, and the rustle of harvest colored leaves.

Abruptly waking to the sound of commotion outside, he sleepily stumbled out of the cozy car, looking for the source. It was still dark outside, and the sun was about an hour from rising. Dooley was surprised to find that the source of the commotion was the clearly flustered pig, who had cornered someone to the edge of one of the sandstone bluffs.

"Woah, woah, Hamlet... what are you doing?" Holt shouted. "Sir, are you alright?"

The man behind the boar's razor edged tusks proceeded to grunt and growl in response to Holt, revealing that something was irregular about him.

"It's a zombie, Holt! I found him wandering around aimlessly, probably looking to eat us with his rotten teeth!"

Dooley began to piece together the actual scenario, when he noticed a torn piece of gauze-like paper laying on one of Sherman's tiny branches. Upon closer inspection, Dooley claimed Private Sherman identified it as a mummy, not a zombie. The crucial difference here being that the undead person in question wasn't trying to eat anyone.

"Nice work, Private!" Holt exclaimed. "You keep this up, and you're getting a promotion."

He led the mummy to safer ground and inspected it, as it continued to murmur incomprehensible sounds. Looking at its clenched fist, he ascertained that it was holding something. Holt pried the mummy's stiff fingers open to find what appeared to be a display label containing a few hardly legible words in cursive. One important word, "Wichita," led Holt to believe it must have escaped a museum there. He was rather good at deducing answers from observation.

"Luckily for you, my friend, we are headed in that direction anyway. We'll give you a ride. You can huddle down in the back there." he said, pointing to the Mini Cooper.

The sunrise gently placed Illinois in the rearview mirror, and welcomed the eclectic crew to Mark Twain National Forest in Missouri. Private Sheman, allegedly in contemplation, was wondering about why his leaves were green, while the trees around them were exhibiting yellows, oranges, and reds. Holt Dooley anticipated his questioning and went ahead and told him why.

"There are a couple types of trees, Private. You are a conifer, which typically is called an evergreen, since you keep your leaves through the winter. They, however," he said, pointing out the window to the foliage surrounding them, "are deciduous trees, meaning they lose their leaves. As the leaflets go through senescence, the chlorophyll (green pigment) is broken down, and the carotenoids (warm colors) are visibly left. The hormones that allow for this activity in plants are ethylenes, which happen to be the same culprit that allow bananas to help other fruit ripen faster. I'm sure you've heard someone tell you that a banana can make an apple ripen more quickly...well it's true and it's neat."

"Who is Mark Twain?" the pig asked from the back seat.

"Hamlet, did you pay attention to anything I said?"

"No."

Dooley sighed and began to tell the boar of Mark Twain's literature, and even included a recitation of some of his quotes. Twain supposedly said that the two most important days in your life are the day you are born, and the day you find out why. This resonated with Holt, but he stated that he didn't fully agree with it. They enjoyed hearing Holt's take on different poems and natural themes; Sherman sat happily in the front seat, his foliage bobbing with the bumps in the road, and the mummy grunted, somewhat intelligently.

As they made it into the city limits of Springfield, one of the most distinguishable icons of the town came into view. A two story statue of a person holding a gigantic doughnut, with the words "lard" and "lad" conspicuously rested off of the highway next to a comparatively inconspicuous diner. Sparking Holt's interest, of course, they decided to make a pitstop in the quaint place. Holt's passengers gave him their breakfast orders, as he took some of the loot from the Ohio River in to barter with.

85

Holt didn't notice the police car outside, but he stood in line behind a lazily shaped officer, who's demeanor slightly reminded him of his encounter with Griff. At such an ironic timing, as the world often enjoys doing, a picture of Griff's face appeared on the news. It stated that he had been missing, and now presumed dead. The anchorwoman further revealed that the major suspect involved in this possible case of murder, was none other than the criminal he was chasing, Holt Dooley. A picture of Holt's face, when he was short-haired and more cleanly groomed was then displayed. The program further elaborated that he often exclaims the profanity "Consarn it!"

"Strange. Good picture of me though," he said to himself as he continued to wait in line.

"Uh, what did you say? the cop in front of him turned around and asked, thinking Holt was talking to him.

"I said that's a good picture of me," he replied, pointing at the screen.

Wondering if Holt was crazy and possibly homeless, the cop asked if he was new in town and introduced himself as "Chief Clarence Wiggum." Holt introduced himself and then ordered a coffee. It wasn't his name and face plastered on the television that made the Chief question his character, but thinking it was unusual that he was twiddling a small piece of driftwood.

"Uh...Chief?" said his second in command, pointing back and forth between the TV and Holt.

Finally making the connection, the Chief confidently spoke up, saying "Cuff 'em". With a victorious cackle.

Soon realizing that his sergeant had speedily retreated to the restroom, The Chief then addressed Holt directly and told him that they were going to need to take a "nice little" trip to the station. After asking why, Dooley pulled out a diamond ring he found in the steamboat and attempted to bribe the officer. The chief replied "Read the badge, criminal!" and Dooley read the small print, "cash only bribes". Holt walked out the door, and The Chief, having to make a fast decision, decided to wait for his food that he ordered before attempting to go after Holt. The Chief then proceeded to eat his meal and doughnut, justifying that working on an empty stomach was less efficient.

Holt Dooley was then more fully aware he was "at large".

CHAPTER 6

(The Storm Chase)

Various law enforcement entities had been alerted to Holt Dooley's escape and alleged murder. He had become somewhat of a priority, with news lines describing him as a "dangerous fugitive" who could be anywhere in the U.S. His brush up with the chief of police in Springfield, however, connected some dots as to his current direction. The authorities in Missouri's border states were waiting and ready for Holt's next appearance, especially those in Oklahoma, Kansas, and Arkansas. They had gathered that he was traveling westward, though his destination was still unknown.

With his friends at his side, Holt pulled out his journal and sketched a scene of the Great Plains in Kansas. The radio between the pig's tusks turned on again, and played the song "Plain to See Plainsman" by Colter Wall. Private Sherman purportedly swayed along. Dooley drew the mummy as it walked aimlessly through the fields unraveling its body wrap as it tripped upon the brush.

"You've gone a little too far, come back this way!" Holt yelled toward his new and ancient companion.

"Why are you calling that pile of rags back? He smells so bad," the boar sighed.

"Frankly, my friend, we all do..except little Sherman over there. We're almost to Doo-Dah, I just wanted to document this in my journal before we drop him off at the museum."

"Doo-Dah?"

"It's always so many questions with you. Do you know anything? Doo-Dah is an endearing nickname for Wichita, of course."

Holt had been waiting for nightfall to deliver the mummy, as he didn't want the Egyptian hitchhiker to draw too much attention to himself. Alas, sometimes it seems that when one is trying to deflect attention, they end up gathering more of it. Holt regrettably fell into this trap by driving through the city with his headlights off. Parking directly adjacent to the museum, they planned out how they would break the mummy back into its home. Well, Dooley did all the planning. He drew out an insanely elaborate blueprint, and initiated "Phase 1: The Approach." As they proceeded toward the building, the security recognized the missing mummy and immediately dispatched the police. The guard didn't have a chance to notice much movement originating from the mummy, but assumed Holt was in fact the one moving it. Sprinting out of the building with shaking hands on his taser, the guard demanded the mummy be brought back to the museum immediately.

"Sir, I realize you are anxious, maybe even afraid. I know museum security guards don't get very much action. However, I am here to *return* the mummy, not steal it!" Holt exclaimed.

After a short exchange of pronouns, Holt learned that the mummy was in fact female, and the crew halted for a second, mumbling phrases such as "how 'bout that." The guard attempted to shoot a taser at him, but instead shot the mummy, incapacitating her further. Dooley laid her rigid body to the ground, as they rushed back to their car to get out of the city limits.

"Welp, I definitely felt some secondhand shock there, but that's fine. C'mon gang let's roll."

As they rushed back to their escape car, the boar yelled out, "Bye mummy! Sorry we confused you for a stinky man!"

Sirens wailed through the streets, and Holt calmly made it through the lights and turns that lead to Highway 135 northward. It was then, in the stench of his Mini Cooper, that Holt decided it was time for a shower. So, they made the Cheney Reservoir their next stop, on the way to Garden City.

"Forty-seven degrees, Hamlet. It's getting a bit too cold to bathe outside," he said, drying off his boxers with a beach towel."

"Well, since we are here, we better check that map and see what's going on in the area, right?" [68]

"This all feels so cyclical. We keep relaxing, looking for supernatural things, almost getting caught by the cops, and then relaxing again. I'm thinking maybe we should just carry on with the rest of our journey."

"Well if the cops come in a swarm, you're going to need some help." said the pig pulling out the map. "You always seem to find interesting things, let's just see if we can find something to help us."

"I suppose you're right. Can't hurt just to check."

---

[68] The pig does seem to entice Holt to the supernatural workings of the elk-hide map.

91

Dooley complained about still not being able to translate the script on the map, but trudged blindly onward anyway. He could at least guess from its depiction of an "X" on the ground, that some buried treasure might be up for grabs. They were led to a contorted oak tree above a tombstone shaped rock, wherein the roots crossed over each other making the "X" they were looking for. Oddly enough, the phalanges of a skeleton were grasping the root, and holding a key. Holt assumed it went to some container buried around the area, and shamelessly snatched it up. The pig and Sherman aided in digging past the skeleton, to a wooden chest nearly six foot-deep.[69] The chest was large enough to fit a body inside, and was cracked slightly. This left Holt with no answer regarding the skeleton's key, which he discarded on the remains, saying he wasn't willing to dig another hole and find out what it went to. Their digging wasn't in vain though, since In the bottom of the chest was a note with a musical score on the back page, and on the front it was labeled as an incantation for the "Flying Head". [70]

The note had instructions that urged him to build a fire and have roasted acorns ready to eat. They read that when a flying head is summoned, it is necessary to let it see you consuming the charred acorns, as it will be tricked into thinking you are eating the coals from the fire. This will warn the beast that you are not to be trifled with, it continued. On one portion of the note, the writer had attempted to draw a picture of the being, and while it was not the best, it still communicated some sort of evil to the viewer.

---

[69] probably a correlation to the euphemism regarding six-foot deep graves

[70] The Flying Head is a spirit from Iriqois and Wyandot mythology, often exhibiting cannibalistic behavior.

After thoroughly reading the instructions, Holt started the incantation, but only loosely followed the suggestions. He thought about starting a fire, but instead decided to just skip that step and pick up some acorns. He thought that it would be intimidating enough eating them without roasting them, because...well, who does that? He started to whistle the song on the back of the note, and then, not enjoying the tone color, started over and switched to a hum. The tune was in a minor key, and the note choice was adorned with intermittent rests, which Holt embellished to make it even more unsettling. It was then that he met what I might describe as the creepiest individual in all of his travels.

She was there in a flash. Leaves swirled around her in a fury at her appearance, then all at once rocked back and forth until they reached the earth. She was cloaked in blinding white light, and whirlwinds made up the tail of her coat. She looked radiantly kind and attractive, as an angler fish's light does to its prey. She stared directly into Holt, and saw that he had the chills.

"What are you eating?" In a high register, she breathed out her words like a piano key stuck in a sunken position, when just a little of its noise is expressed. Holt's eyes glanced at his hand and back to her. "Is that the fruit of an oak tree?" she continued.

His plan immediately expired. He thought to himself that if she called acorns "the fruit of an oak" then she must not be intimidated by it, and decided he would just attempt to scavenge up the hot-coal-bit he read from the instructions. "It's a hot coal," he said.

"I don't see a fire nearby. Are you lying to me?" she questioned, leaning in toward his ear. Her voice fell cold as ice on his skin and greatly discomforted him, with her close proximity to his ear tickling his spine. He jerked his head away from her.

"What's wrong? I know you didn't happen to hum those notes earlier by chance did you? No, that can't be. You see, I think you were led to the last person who summoned me, and read the note he was given. After I was through with him, I tried to bury the note with his skeleton, you know, but his bones were stubborn." she said, pointing to the skeleton's remnants. Her words decadently became less infatuating, and her presence less flirtatious. In lightning quick movements, she appeared at his other side and breathed in his scent. Holt's head swiveled toward her widening grin, as light began to leave her face replaced by the darkest shades of silver.

The blinding light that shrouded her figure settled to the ground and he was finally able to ascertain her image. A giant's head was covered in thick hair past her chin, where her legs existed. She had talons like an eagle, sitting upon the paws of a bear. She had sedan sized leathery wings like a bat, that when stationary, wrapped the sides of her head like ear muffs. In the most respectful way possible, I tell you that her face was hideous. Deep wrinkles held the misty, beady eyes of a cadaver in her skull. With abnormalities too many to count, it looked as if a wax figure was melting. Her teeth were sharp as needles, and nearly as thin.

"Why did you call me here?" Her voice was now lower and gravely, and with a mournful tone.

She showed her teeth to him as if to brag, and then re-wrapped herself in light and reverted to how she appeared when he first saw her. Holt glanced at the boar to see if he was okay, and saw him a hundred yards off, running with great speed, and great fear.

"Truthfully, it is just to escape those who are trying to stop me from going to where I need to be. I thought you might be able to give me an advantage, where I have none."

She shifted her image again to frighten him, and began to speak. "Do you know that I eat your kind?"

Holt, with a straight face, decided to bite into the acorn as if there was still a chance of intimidating her. "I have heard rumors that flying heads, like yourself, are just humans who have been transformed into malicious beings after committing acts of cannibalism. Is this true?" He chomped the hard acorn shell loudly.

The acorn seemed to have no effect on the monster as it continued to talk with countenance unchanged. "Not at all," she said, laughingly. "It is in my nature to eat humans as it is in yours to eat plants and animals. And it is equally moral."

"What you fail to realize, Miss, is that these acorn husks I'm devouring are indigestible. So I am feasting on something contrary to my nature. Does that make you afraid of me?" he said, as if pulling off a checkmate.

"Uh, no, it does not…" she said, dispirited. "You're a strange one. Not like the other humans. I think you are right that you are disadvantaged." She stopped attempting to frighten Holt. "Hold out your hand, I'm going to give you something."

Holt reached forth and received a hair she plucked from her head. She said that dipping her hair in water and letting a drop run off of it would bring about the heaviest rains imaginable. Holt, stowed it away in his pocket, and watched as she slowly faded from view.

"Wait, what's your name?" he asked curiously.

"Dagwanoenyent,"[71] she responded. "Daughter of the Wind."

---

[71] Considered a dangerous witch by the Native American Seneca Tribe

It wasn't long until Holt had to use the gift he had gotten from the flying head, as forecasted by the goosebumps he had the entire day. Late in the evening, Holt had just pulled into Garden City, where the pig had convinced him to reluctantly agree to go to an indoor water park. It was closed, but they managed to break in and enjoy an hour or so of splashing, diving, and wading. As they were leaving, they were met by a couple of people dressed [72] as state troopers, eagerly waiting by the Mini Cooper they had been traveling in. Holt, not expecting to have to use the hair from Dagwanoenyent so soon, had left the strand in his jacket pocket in the car. He didn't see much of a solution to his current predicament other than to meet them with utter surprise. In a drastic move, he assaulted the officer nearest to him with a spinning backfist to the chin. Meanwhile, the boar rammed the other trooper in the leg, almost causing Sherman to fall off of his back. "Keep the Car Running" [73]blared on the radio, as Holt was finally able to pull that magical hair out of the car, and sprinted back toward the waterpark. The trooper was hot on his trail, but Holt ran with wild unpredictability. He dipped the hair into the water as he slipped past the pool's regulation "no running" sign, and let a drop slide off of the strand just as the flying head had told him.

He skipped two stairs with each leap as he ascended to the top of the waterslide. With both troopers directly behind him, and the pig behind them, he thought he might be able to lose one down the slide and fight the other one off. He leaped for the metal bar above the circular entrance of the slide, and the first trooper dove

[72] The wording here, "dressed as" seems to imply fraudulent activity.
[73] Song by Arcade Fire

after him, landing onto the waterslide's current just as Dooley had so cleverly predicted.

The fire-control sprinkler system suddenly began raining inside of the building, setting the perfect stage for a dramatic final battle. The entire building began to shake, as if they were experiencing an earthquake. Holt looked the officer in the eyes at the top of the waterslide and readied his boxing stance. Possibly, out of respect for Holt being unarmed, or maybe due to the fact that he wanted a revenge-punch, the officer drew his hands rather than his gun or baton. The first trooper must have been tumbling in quite the awkward manner down the slide, as a gunshot reverberated through its crooks and crannies and sounded out the top, signaling the start of the boxing match.

Dooley was a graceful and experienced boxer. His long arms made him tend to the Out-boxer style, and his technique was naturally beautiful. The trooper, on the other hand, was a slugger. This made him nearly the opposite of Holt, but he was just as commendable. Holt fired off a bolo punch with the sound of the gunshot, landing directly below the trooper's nose, on his red mustache. The surprising angle of this punch allowed for easy first contact, and was a strong first move.

"Lucky dog, your stache padded that one." Holt teased.

The trooper swung with a heavy cross, thrusting it forward from his abdomen up to his shoulder. If it would have hit Holt just right, it could have brought the match to a swift close. But luckily, he anticipated this move, and threw a check-hook, dodging the trooper and making another hit of his own. His footwork was impeccable. He had just landed two rather rarely used punches right off the bat. He leaped backward to create some space in between them, but his adversary swarmed in with a few jabs and another cross. Holt pulled away from the first, parried the second, and was hit on the third.

The trooper's punch dealt damage equal to both of Holt's, so he quickly understood that he needed to make defense a priority until he was sure he could make contact with a strong enough punch for a knock-out.

Dooley was bobbing and weaving, he was slipping and sliding, he was gliding in an elegant manner, analyzing and gathering data with every punch the trooper tossed at him. When Holt believed he had learned some of the trooper's patterns, he tossed the occasional jab in to fire the officer up and force him to expend more energy. Soon enough, he had significantly tired out the man behind the mustache. Holt saw his chance and decided to move on the offensive. He threw a decoy cross to get the trooper's hands up, who blocked his punch and more importantly, his own vision. Then he launched a hook with all of his power, hitting the trooper square in the temple.

He staggered back a bit, but seemingly absorbed the heavy hit like a tank. Holt kept his composure and tried again. He jabbed, crossed, jabbed twice more, and then used his left forearm to yank the officer's fists down from his guard, and hit him hard with a right cross to the chin. Still, the mustache man remained in the fight, though he was a bit dazed. Holt was impressed. The trooper switched his stance to southpaw, and began throwing right jabs at him. Holt's eyes widened, astonished at this move and how well his opponent fought both ways.

"A real switch-hitter! This is my first time fighting someone so proficient," he said, with no audible response from the trooper.

Holt was in a full crouch stance at this point, doing his best to dodge the unorthodox punches whizzing by his face like rockets.

The other officer that slid into the pool had now made his way back up the stairs, which slightly distracted Holt from his current opponent. He slipped a jab, and fell out of step, unrhythmically bobbing another jab, he then took a heavy uppercut to the chin.

Holt's head whipped upwards and sent the rest of his body flat on his back. He felt the sprinklers gently tapping his face as emergency lights flashed on and off in between the droplets. The trooper took his handcuffs and grasped Holt's limp arm. He wrapped the first cuff around Dooley's wrist snugly, feeling like a knife to his bone. He was defeated. It was rare to see this sadness in his eyes. He truly thought he was the hero of this story. He thought he was destined to make it across the country and hold the hand of someone dear to him. Instead, the rugged grip of his newfound enemy pulled his hand up to place the other cuff on it.

It was then, in the nick of time, that the building came crashing down around them. A tornado from Dagwanoenyent traveled through the building, ripping it in half and opening up his line of sight to his Mini Cooper. Holt kicked the officer off of him and yelled for the boar to run to the car. They managed to escape the peril of falling, or rather, flying debris and got in the car safely.

The tornado came whirling through again, lifting the car and its crew off of the pavement and spinning them around and around, like a child's lifeless goldfish down a toilet bowl. The boar, in the driver's seat, put his hooves on the wheel as if he was steering. Holt pulled out his journal and jotted down his thoughts on the matter.

"A myercell kept me from the jail cell. The thunderstorm brought up the warm humid air, and sent the cold air down with the rain."

After a good while of spinning, the group was car-sick to say the least. Holt held on to Private Sherman and protected its branches.The twister loosened its grip on the car with every orbit becoming slightly larger than the last. They rotated around the center, skipping across the ground like a stone across the pond. The pig began to mimic an airline pilot, asking them to prepare for landing. Holt helped shift the car into neutral.

"Good thing the plains are so flat, everywhere is one giant airstrip."

They landed in a field a hundred some odd miles northwest of garden city, into Colorado. He knew that this was the doing of flying head, and he really was thankful. He had been given a second chance at life. He described to the boar about his clash with the mustached trooper, to which he replied that neither of them had a mustache. [74] Dooley laughed and swore that he did, as he had grazed it with his own knuckle.

"Golly, Holty, after all you have gone through to get to your destination...I just hope it is worth it." the pig said.

"She is," a peaceful tone in Holt's voice rang out. "She really is."

---

[74] Holt is described as very observant. Was the pig blatantly wrong, or was something else afoot?

CHAPTER 7

(Echolocation)

The quirky group had finally crossed into the Mountain Time Zone, and appropriately, the snow capped Rockies of the Centennial State were playing peek-a-boo through the Colorado Springs skyline. Holt found himself standing over the historical marker of Nicola Tesla's secret laboratory, in deep contemplation. The great inventor was infamous in the town, partially because of the time he had accidentally shut down all of the city's power with a massive lightning bolt that he himself had impressively created. He claimed his experiments were successful and that he could provide wireless electricity to the entire world. However, the townspeople quickly stopped supporting him after this incident, breaking down his lab to pay the cost of the generator he destroyed. Many people say he was a mad genius, and some even believe he had some supernatural help.

His chilling correspondence with the American Red Cross may be evidence to support the latter: "I have observed electrical actions, which have appeared inexplicable. Faint and uncertain though they were, they have given me a deep conviction and foreknowledge, that ere long all human beings on this globe, as one, will turn their eyes to the firmament above, with feelings of love and reverence, thrilled by the glad news: 'Brethren! We have a message from another world, unknown and remote. It reads: one… two… three…'"

Dooley wrote down in his journal this quote from his memory. The pig's radio stopped playing music and began producing deafening static. Muffled noises came through rhythmically, and possibly…intelligibly. Holt's head swiveled to its attention, and he lifted it from the pigs tusk's staring at it in awe. He placed it back on the pig, and jotted tallys in his journal, corresponding to the sound. To the average onlooker, he was insane.

"What are you doing, so frantically there, Holty?" said the pig.

"I'm decoding it," he said, furiously making marks on the paper. "I think it's telling me to 'dig' or something of the likes."

"There are no words coming out.. It's just radio noise," the pig said, clearly confused.

"I'm not going to take the time to explain it to you."

He walked into the grass and inspected it, and then began scooping up some of the dirt with his hands. He made a few holes in the ground, and on the third, his fingers brushed upon something cold in the dirt. It was copper. He did his best to unearth it, but its hefty size proved difficult. The pig begged him to stand back up and told him that people were staring. Holt looked back and saw a small crowd that had gathered, and decided to leave it alone for the time being.

"Fine. Discovery will have to wait for the opinions of the small minded!" he yelled.

One of the spectators was a mother with her daughter. She shielded the eyes of her child with her hand, as if Holt's actions were an unwanted influence. He was emotionally unaffected by the crowd's obvious disapproval, but he didn't want to wager his safety by gathering the attention of governmental authorities. Dooley decided to stay the night nearby, so as to re-visit the digsite in an untimely manner for tourists. They found a cave nearby, where Holt figured they would rest more easily than cramped in the car again.

Gently, a breeze made itself the cave's spokesperson, whistling in and out of the entrance. Holt spotted another petroglyph, yet again corresponding to the same one he had seen before and drawn in his journal. An eagle-like figure, with lightning from its beak, seemed to be in opposition with a horned snake-like creature, who watched from the water. A minimalist human stood between the two.

The pig began to snooze, as the radio returned to its deafening static, causing Holt's curiosity to act up again. He believed that when uncoding the concealed message, it was telling him to explore the cave further. Tiptoeing around Sherman and the boar, he ventured further through the cave without waking them. Dooley soon realized that he was actually in a mine, when he saw remnants of the miner's tools, as well as artificial holes that had been chipped away in the walls.

There were a few passageways to choose from, but Holt was well versed in exploring unknown areas and knew a few helpful tips. He recounted that most humans, when confronted with a directional choice, choose the left side subconsciously. Making a habit of this is often what causes one to lose themselves. He also remembered that a safe way to remember the passages you take, is to leave a marker.

Harboring handfuls of dried chokecherries and juniper berries in his rucksack, he decided to use them as his trail marker. He left them at every turn he took, as he went deeper into the cavernous mine. Eventually, he began to hear what resonated like a knock. He followed this sound to an oppressively confined chamber, where he beheld milky crystals that were as big as his body, and multi-colored mineral deposits that were assuredly valuable. There was an old minecart sitting in the middle of it all, with a pickaxe and bucket, ready to gather the surrounding treasure. He was dazed by the beauty, but not stupefied. He had enough self restraint to question the reality of his situation, rather than to immediately start harvesting the resources.

"Who was knocking on this minecart? Show yourself," Holt requested. After waiting a minute with no response, he tried a second time. "I'm not going to mine any of these deposits, without first speaking to who led me here." Listening to the sound of his echo speaking back to him off of the cavern wall, he again wondered about his own sanity.

Holt pulled out his elk skin map to see if anything out of the ordinary was afoot. He saw the map draw out a leprechaun-like figure, wielding a pickaxe and other miners' garb.

"If a leprechaun lives here, I would really like to speak with you," Holt said.

Out of the silent cave, he thought he heard the murmuring of a soft, yet grumpy voice.

"They always think we are leprechauns," one said.

"Hush, Cole, you dimwit!" yelled another.

"It's spelled like 'Coal', not 'Cole!" he retorted.

"I'm not even spelling it, I'm simply speaking it!"

"But you were thinking it, weren't you Malachite?!"

Finally, Holt decided to break up the confrontation he started, alerting the two that he could hear everything. Glancing backward towards his food trail, Coal and Malachite were squatted down progressively consuming it until no marker remained. They each were just under three feet tall, with disproportionately large features. Their slender nose alone was bigger than their own forearm, and ended in a round tip. Ears like maple leaves were pressed against the sides of their little bobbleheads. Both were wearing miniature mining uniforms and held their own tiny tools.

"Hey!" Holt said sternly, "I was using those to find my way out of here."

"You can see us?!" [75] asked Malachite.

"Well why wouldn't I be able to?" inquired Holt.

"We just assumed you were a regular human," said Coal.

"And that I am."

"If you are a regular human then so are we!" Coal said laughingly. Malachite elbowed him in the stomach as if to suppress his loud mouth.

"What do you mean, exactly?"

Malachite threw his grubby little hands over Coal's mouth, to stop the words from coming out, but he fought his way free, exclaiming that Holt was a "seer." [76]

"Hush, Coal, you know we can't speak of such things," Malachite loudly whispered. He looked at Dooley and realized that there was

---

[75] I believe this same question has been asked to Holt before.

[76] Seer is an increasingly important term to understand in the interest of this story.

nothing they could say to cover up what had been seen, figuring he might as well introduce themselves. "Sorry about your trail, miners used to feed us by leaving food in here, and I thought you were doing the same thing...we are tommyknockers,[77] you know."

"Were you the ones sending messages via radio transmission?" Holt asked.

"Yes we were! But that had nothing to do with you. Normally we can communicate that way to humans who understand Morse code," said Malachite.

"Whenever the mines were used, it was the only way to warn the dumb humans when a cavern was going to collapse," said Coal.

Holt realized that they must have been talking to someone else when he received their message to dig, meaning that whatever he was unearthing at the Tesla site earlier must have had purpose for the city's infrastructure or utilities. Holt didn't worry anymore about the subject.

"So, weren't you knocking earlier?" Dooley said nervously.

"Yes. This area is right on the brink of falling in," Malachite calmly stated.

"Are you kidding me?! Get me out of here right now!" Holt exclaimed, attempting to backtrack his path.

"What's wrong? Can't you just use your 'seer' powers?" Coal said, before taking another elbow to the ribs.

"I'm not a seer!" Holt yelled.

---

[77] Tommyknockers are legendary subterranean creatures, who have occasionally been known to help, or act mischievously to miners.

They followed close behind, watching earnestly to see how he would save himself. Holt, due to his impeccable observation skills, was able to remember each of the paths he had chosen in reverse order, leading him directly out. The cave around him had not yet collapsed, and he was feeling a mix between relief and suspicion.

He questioned the tommyknockers, who still claimed that it would cave in soon, but without much definitive proof, Holt felt duped. He would have liked to go back inward to the mineral deposit, but the swearing of the tommyknocker brothers made him believe the risk was too high for the reward. As he was chastising them, he stood in front of the petroglyphs, where he apparently bore resemblance to the man in the rock art.

"Coal, look. He looks exactly like the man in the drawing."

Holt realized they were referring to the stick figure behind them, and laughed. "This literally could represent any human in existence!" he exclaimed.

Dooley wondered about their claims that he was a "seer", but didn't dwell on it long. He was tired of their shenanigans, and ready to move on to the next waypoint along his journey. The group retreated to their car and left behind any thought of the tommyknockers, deciding to rest in Denver and indulge in the city life for a day.

———

Denver is nicknamed the "Mile-High City", as it is one mile above sea level. Coincidently or not, the amount of conspiracy theories involving the Denver Airport could be stacked a mile above sea level as well. There were other intriguing spots scattered about the city as well, but Dooley decided to take a day off from his supernatural adventures, and just relax. Although, he did spend a few minutes investigating a blue mustang sculpture entitled "Blucifer" [78] that was well-known for falling on its creator and killing him. Besides that, Holt enjoyed a plain iced latte at *Corvus Coffee*, went to the *Tattered Cover* book store, and listened to "Rocky Mountain High" by John Denver on the pig's magic radio. It was a quick day of uneventful rest, compared to the experiences of his expedition, and they felt re-fueled to move onward. I only include this, to let it be known that Holt Dooley had normal days too. Nonetheless, the following day they would find their way to the Denver outskirts, notably Lafayette, where an event of high interest took place.

"Why do I keep seeing people in costumes?" asked the pig.

"Humans are strange," the plant presumably answered.

"It comes from an old Celtic tradition called Samhain, wherein they would dress up to scare off ghosts. October 31st was the date they believed that the spiritual dimension[79] overlapped with the physical one we live in."

"So do we need to dress up to ward off the ghosts too?" asked the pig.

"No, most of the people celebrating don't actually know the origins of it, so it is safe to assume that they aren't actually trying to frighten any paranormal entities. However, if you all would like to dress up, I suppose we can do that."

---

[78] Horse statue made by Luis Jiménez, who died when a piece of the statue fell on him in his studio.

[79] Yet another use of the word "dimension"; could this Halloween story have some validity?

So, in preparation for Halloween, the three unlikely friends and the radio visited a local store, and fabricated some costumes. What I mean is, they actually used the materials in the store without purchasing them, and were swiftly kicked out. I'm not entirely sure of what Holt Dooley had in mind, but he had a few pipe cleaners taped to his shirt, and a few other things he picked up from the crafts section that nobody knows the names or purpose of. The boar picked up an apple in its mouth, as that was all he was capable of doing. Holt also managed to smuggle out a Christmas ornament to decorate the plant with.

"Extraordinary," said Holt. "Everyone looks great, and everything is looking up."

"Why don't we trick or treat?" the pig asked.

"Great idea." Holt paused for a minute, "And another good suggestion from Private Sherman! We should break out the map and see what kind of spooky thing happens tonight."

The group followed the map to a new neighborhood, which notably appeared fake. Some brand new, fully constructed neighborhoods exhibit a strange mood, as if they are a scene that only exists in a happy movie, yet somehow they can radiate creepiness instead of happiness. It was assuredly designed with New Urbanist [80] philosophies, as Holt made known. Dooley parked the car illegally on the street downhill, and they walked to the first doorstep.

---

[80] Urban design movement that promotes walkability as well as includes environmental relationships

"Looks pretty empty," Holt said, while knocking with the same melodic knock that most Americans seem to strangely know. [81]

Faintly from inside, the deep thud of footsteps approached them. The door swung open and revealed a man dressed like a vampire. The old timey kind, like Dracula, rather than the teenage heartthrob, *Edward Cullen*. Introducing himself as "Theodore Glava," he explained with a thick Transylvanian accent that he didn't have any candy, as he wasn't expecting "trick or treaters". He was the developer of the neighborhood, and his house was the only one being occupied so far. He invited Holt in for dinner, but asked that the 'pork' stay outside, as he kept a tidy house for showing interested parties. Holt leaned to the boar and the bonsai tree saddled on top, and told them he'd save some food for them.

"So, what are we having then?" Holt asked with a smirk. "If it's mashed potatoes, I'd like mine with extra garlic salt."

Glava stopped in his tracks and shivered for a second, "I don't have that here."

"Wow, that accent is good. Do you do any acting? Dooley said, as he opened the pantry, and then the fridge. "Well, you sure don't have a lot of food in here, Mr. Glava." The reality of the situation quickly became clear to Holt. The map had led him to an actual vampire.

"It is a spec house, you know," said the vampire.

Dooley pulled his piece of driftwood out and began to fiddle with it. "Did you know that the force behind tornadoes is so strong, that pieces of straw have reportedly pierced tree trunks? I doubt that is

---

[81] Likely a reference to the knocking pattern called "Shave and a Haircut," and "two bits" which makes up seven notes in a knocking pattern

true, but it is not entirely impossible... considering they have reached speeds of 205 miles an hour." He turned his back to the vampire and continued. "And humans, well, the fastest hit in badminton was recorded at around 264.7 miles an hour. That's quite a bit faster than the tornado."

He looked back over his shoulder and saw Glava standing suspiciously, almost like a jaguar ready to pounce. He began speaking again, unphased.

"I guess what I'm trying to get at, my friend, is that, while I may not be able to shove my little piece of driftwood through your heart with the force of a tornado, I like to think that I'm resourceful enough to compete with the badminton player."

Glava swiftly moved in behind him, close enough to feel his words.

"It's just a costume," he said maniacally.

Just as things were looking grim, a confident knock rattled on the cheap front door, as Holt jokingly asked if it was a "real" vampire.[82]

Most unexpectedly to you, I would imagine, is the character who kicked the door open. He looked as if he had been living out of a shed in the woods. He looked as if he stunk. One arm was held by a sling, and with one he held up a not-so-shiny badge, as he yelled that Holt's time on the run was over. Chase Griffith survived.

"Excuse me, do you have a warrant?" Glava shouted.

Holt's quick thinking allowed him to interrupt Griff's stammering with an advantageous lie, "He doesn't need one, he's a deputy

---

[82] Referring to the old rule that vampires must request permission to enter a homestead

111

marshall. In fact he's probably already commandeered your house for the marshal's service. Next he's likely going to split us up and ask you to go outside so he can deal with me one on one."

"Exactly. Creepy guy, scram! I'll deal with you in a minute."

It was only seconds after Glava left that he decided he would kill Griffith as well as Holt. Griffith was in the middle of gloating to Dooley the speech he had prepared for his capture (though he legally did not even have that authority), when Glava interjected.

"May I come in?"

"No!" shouted Holt emphatically, before turning to Griffith. "Look, I hate to ruin your moment of victory, but the reason I told him that you are a deputy marshall is so that he would believe you could take his house as your own. Now he believes he has to have your permission to come in, so that he can ultimately drink my blood."

"Listen here Holt, I don't know how to tell you this but you are mentally unstable. That guy out there is wearing a vampire costume. In the same way that you are wearing...well,whatever costume you are wearing."

"Please, may I come in?" the vampire asked again.

"No!" Holt yelled a second time.

"Holt, just don't try to resist or you're going to experience a world of pain. You're going to come with me back to South Carolina."

"Marshal, sir, I need to come in because I'm sick and I've left my medicine in there, may I come in?

"Laughable excuse," Holt murmured.

"Yeah, just give me a second!" Griffith said, allowing permission to the vampire.

Glava predatorily stormed in, but was just steps after Griffith...who was steps after Holt. Dooley burst through the window and ran to the next closest house, with the other two following close behind. Like a football player who would dive for a catch in the endzone, he broke through the neighboring house's window and watched as the vampire struck Griffith in the back. The investigator then swiftly pulled his taser and put enough volts into Glava to kill a man. Without skipping a beat, Griff hopped in the window after Holt. [83]

Holt screamed, "This house is now property of the United States Marshal Service!" in his best impression of Griffith.

Before the vampire even got back on his feet he asked them again, "May I come in?" He tried to convince them that he just wanted to fix the expensive window they had just broken.

Finally, with chills up his spine and wet down his trousers, Griffith caught on to the real scenario. No regular person could instantly recover from being tased like that. With eyes like saucers, he asked Holt what to do. At this time the vampire had the idea to rip apart the house until it no longer was a house, so that he would be able to get to them. He ravished through the framework and all rather quickly, with the force of a rhinoceros, I might add. For lack of time, the only plan they could develop was to run to the next house and fake commandeer it. Managing to barely escape a second time, Holt had stalled long enough to formulate a real plan. He told Griffith to distract the vampire while he found some wood to use as a stake. Meanwhile, the boar had waltzed back up into the

---

[83] Chase Griffith seems to have a lot more resolve to act with authority, regardless of the fact that he is just a P.I.

113

neighborhood blaring Christmas music on his radio, with the plant and its ornament.

"Hamlet! It is WAY too early for Christmas music, who do you think you are?" Holt yelled, before leaving the investigator.

Fortunately for Holt's sake, the vampire, rather than ravishing through the foundation of the house again, decided to reason. A cold deep voice asked from under the window sill, "What is your name, officer?"

"No, you can't come in!" Griffith screamed. "Cool kids only!" he decided to add, unaware of what tactics might work best on the vampire.

"Well, cool guy, I'll make this deal with you, I don't find it particularly amusing to rip apart these homes I've spent my hard earned cash on. If you allow me to come in, I'll spare you and only kill Colt" Glava said.

"It's not Colt, it's Holt," Griffith replied.

"You're testing my patience. Tell me, may I come in? Or do you want to die alongside Holt?"

Griffith waited until the vampire started to rip the building apart, and then gave him permission to come in. Angrily re-routing to the front door, he scanned the area for Holt. Not seeing him next to Griffith, Glava turned himself into a bat and resorted to echolocation. As the sound of his screech bounced off every object in the house, through walls and ceilings, it revealed that only one human was there, jumping halfway out of the window again. The vampire went after Griffith and cat and mouse ensued again in remnants of the second house, then back to the first.

Meanwhile, Holt had run down the hill and back to his car, which unfortunately was booted in it's illegal parking spot. His plan "B" was to run back to Glava's house to steal his car. While Holt was downstairs locating the key, Griffith burst through another window in the house, rather than traveling through the one they had previously broken. He darted up the stairs to hide. As the enraged vampire aggressively tore through his own house, there were gaps and holes everywhere like the ravishing of a tornado that Holt had warned about earlier. Holt hid behind an open door waiting for the opportune moment to escape. Up on the second floor, Griffith had the bright idea of jumping on a loose board to break it and use it as a stake. Just as the vampire was nearing Holt Dooley, Griffith broke the board and fell from the ceiling landing directly on the vampire. The board's sharper end pierced through Glava's back, staking his heart to the ground. Holt, not as surprised as he should have been, whistled for the pig to rally up and take off with him in the now deceased Theodore Glava's car.

When Griffith oriented himself, he saw Holt Dooley escaping him. The investigator realized that Holt's 'plan' was simply to run away and leave him to die. "Wait a minute! I wasn't actually going to arrest you!" he yelled to Holt, who continued running.

However, he was feeling somewhat accomplished from beating the vampire. He wanted to take the broken board as a memento to his heroic slaying of the beast, but the board had already grown into a small tree.[84] The branches were badly contorted and knotted like pretzels.

---

[84] This is truly how the folktale goes, regarding the vampire of Lafayette, Colorado -- the stake that killed him supposedly grew into a tree.

A week later, Holt and his crew had made it to the Colorado/Utah border. Waking to the smell of blackening timber, Holt realized a controlled burn was set to take place in the area.

"Why would they burn the trees here?" Sherman was believed to have asked.

"I know it must seem barbaric, or even villainous to you, Private, but the intention is actually quite the opposite. Often the reason they burn a small amount of trees is to prevent a different stand of others from being burned. I know it can seem counterintuitive, but some amount of burning is healthy for the forest, and many organisms even rely on it. Much of the nutrients hiding in older trees are brought back to the soils when the ashes break down."

The pig chimed in saying, "Sometimes you have to take the bad with the good. This area is better for my mushrooms now."

"Yes it is, and now the sun's light will collide with more particulate matter [85] in our line of sight, making for a better sunset."

Holt began to write in his journal, reflecting on his time in Colorado:

Just as a bat uses echolocation to find its target, I fear my own "echos" may be too perceivable to my authoritative predators. Balancing the tightrope of duty and consequence, I feel a bit unsteady.

---

[85] Particulate Matter (PM) is measured to determine air pollution. Smoke particles are an example of this.

CHAPTER 8

(Smelling Salts)

Now, you might have a few questions regarding Griffith, and how he caught up to Holt in Colorado. This story's complexities will be revealed in time, but in order for you to have the best understanding of these, we will retrace our steps to Griff's mishap.

The witch, Rosie, had just placed smelling salts under Griffith's nose, bringing him to consciousness. It should be said that she had geniously concocted this aromatic spirit of ammonia, by destructively distilling the same antler that was used to make Griff's figurine.[86] He sat up and looked around, clueless as to where he was or how he got there. She asked how he was feeling, as she placed a salve on a deep gash in his head. Griffith, inquiring if the witch was the voodoo lady, quickly sprung a follow up question, wanting to know if she had beignets. Ignoring his request, she put the elk figurine in his curled fingers. Griff's arm was clearly in pain, seeing how even the slightest touch made him wince from its sensitivity. Possibly due to her having such a compassionate heart, she fashioned a make-shift sling for

---

[86] "Hartshorn" is an antiquated smelling salt ingredient. This detail is included for a reason you will find out further.

117

Griffith...although I must admit, she occasionally had hidden motives.

"Why are you doing all this?" he asked her.

"Do you want to know something about Holt Dooley?" She responded. "He is quite special. I've been watching him for a good while now." She pointed to her reptile scale, which was recording Holt in Springfield.

"How did you know I'm looking for him?"

"I'm a witch. Isn't it obvious, Mr. Detective? Oh, and also, I'm the one who called you and employed you to find him."

She told him about his elk antler figurine, and how it embodies the spirit of the elk it's made from. She said that the reason it worked was because she allowed Holt to take a map made from the hide of the same elk. The map had a hex placed upon it, wherein the one who holds it is drawn to keep using it. It had shifted owners many times, putting them in harm's way, often resulting in the owner's death. Then another unsuspecting human would be drawn to it, and restart the sequence.

Holt had caught her eye long before she *lured* him to her woods. [87] And She had caught his as well, she explained. "Holt and his wife were visiting a park, at the same time and place that I was. He waved to me as they passed, and his wife looked at him with great disdain. And don't be mistaken, he was in fact just waving kindly to a passerby. There was nothing flirtatious about it," she said, wagging her finger as if to make sure the point was certain. "The reason it surprised me so much is because nobody sees me unless I want them to. Just as you right now, Chase Griffith, can see me

---

[87] This is the first glimpse you see of the extreme manipulation that Rosaline utilizes. She seems to orchestrate a lot of the world around her.

118

because I've made myself visible to you. I did not make myself visible to him though. And clearly not his wife. She was upset about something else. When Holt waved to what she perceived was nothing but the thin air, it instigated some sort of fight."

She further detailed that she kept watching Holt for nearly a year, just as one would a television show. Sitting in her living room around her reptile scale, eating popcorn. It was a great drama.

In short, a man with a genius level of intellect constantly struggled with communicating to everyone, including his wife. She ran out on him a few times and out of love, he pretended not to notice...until she went missing. Now you wouldn't guess it by his appearance and outdoor skill set, but Holt was quite the tech guru. In actuality, the reason he acquired a lot of the skillset he has today, is because of his desire to save her. Originally, he worked in computer programming and was an avid artificial intelligence hobbyist. When his wife went missing, he developed an algorithm to recognize patterns relating to her, so that he could find her and see if something was wrong. He illegally mined data all over the Western Hemisphere, and in doing so, invaded other citizen's rights and privacy. As one might expect, it wasn't long until he was found out by government officials who made a deal with him. He wouldn't go to prison, if he would help them gather information on potential threats to the United States government.

He obeyed their rules and restrictions for a bit, but after he learned how to navigate their systems, he continued searching for his wife. It wasn't until recently that he got a hold of a clue: a conversation of text messages sent from a phone in Oregon displayed her patterns of speech. Holt immediately packed what he could and left, removing most technology from his life so that he may not be tracked and stopped. It was then that Holt and Griff met, and it was then that Rosie learned Griff existed.

"You checked to see if it was his wife?" asked Griff.

"Of course not! Why would I spoil the ending?" she replied.

"So then why do you need my help? Can't you just magically zap a happy ending from your fingertips or something?"

"That is not for me to decide. His good ending would be someone else's bad ending. Regular people just exist in a different realm than me altogether. It's better that someone from his world helps, rather than me. But I *will* help you help." She winked.

"He's got the feds after him, and he's running to find his wife in Oregon, who may not actually be his wife. And you want me to make sure that he is represented with the proper information when he gets caught and goes to court? Or what?"

"Yes, that is what you will be compensated for," she said, showcasing to him a sack full of cash. "How you interact with him is ultimately up to you, but he did draw the short straw in a sense, and we are leveling the playing field. I imagine you will feel quite free since the world believes you are dead now, use that to your advantage." [88]

Griff asked if he could have some sort of magical powers, and she refused. However, Rosaline's last sentence awoke some sort of power deep within him. Additionally, she did offer to pay for his flight to Tulsa, Oklahoma, as that was his best guess as to where Holt would be traveling through next.

The private investigator landed in Tulsa, made a quick stop at Hurts Donuts, [89] and tried to determine where Holt could be. He

---

[88] Consistent language like this from the witch seems to showcase some sort of battle she believes she is waging with fate

[89] One of the highest rated doughnut shops in Tulsa

kept his eyes peeled, in the doughnut shop at least, and waited for his elk figurine to aid him in his search. The figurine was fashioned into a strap-mount around his chest, probably repurposed from sports videography. This seemed to be an eyecatcher, as people began to glare at Griff in the same way they would at Holt. It tugged him out the door into his rental car, where he sped northward into Kansas.

The elk figurine brought him all the way into Garden City, where he watched Dooley's car be taken up by the tornado. He followed the tornado as far as he could before it was out of sight. Seeing as the storm clouds were resting over Colorado, he drove through the night to Denver. From there he tracked Holt to Lafayette, where he fortuitously slayed a vampire.

Griff began to feel a sense of something greater than himself in working Holt's case, satisfying his otherwise insatiable inferiority complex. Though consciously he would believe the case to be an annoyance, he *needed* this interaction to subside feelings of inadequacy. Faking to be a detective, and having a coincidental weakness for doughnuts could only provide some relief, but Rosaline had given him a real purpose, even if he didn't understand it yet. This was his true compensation, which no monetary reward could satisfy.

That about does it. In the same way that smelling salts brought Griff back to consciousness, you should be more or less up to speed now.

CHAPTER 9

(The Wild West)

Saloons. Cowboys. Tumbleweeds. Utah is an icon of the Wild West. Its vastly geologically diverse terrain provides tourists with stunning backgrounds for their pictures, and once provided cover for gunfights. It is called "The Beehive State." I'm not sure why I included that last little factoid, but I do know that I will be sharing a lot of Holt's experiences throughout the state, as he spent more time here than anywhere else. So get in the spirit of things; grab some jello, fry sauce, or make some funeral potatoes[90] and enjoy the ride. I'll try to keep it concise.

Holt inched his way down a narrow slot canyon, the color of rust. "You may need to lose a few pounds." He shouted back to the pig, who was having more trouble squeezing through than he was.

"Why are there no trees here?" the plant may have asked. [91]

"Well, if you're wondering about this canyon specifically, there is certainly a lack of light and water. Those two factors are requisites

---

[90] Stereotypical foods for Utahans

[91] The narrator always exhibits some sort of skepticism to Holt's dialogue with the bonsai.

for plant life. However, up past these walls, there are plenty of plants that are well adapted to this arid environment."

The friends were, unintentionally, almost to the infamous outlaw hideout called Robber's Roost. Butch Cassidy and his "Wild Bunch Gang" had once lived there. The walls of the canyon acted as a hallway leading up to a magnificent sandstone arch, near the Dirty Devil River. Holt tied a rope around the pig, climbed the wall-face, and hoisted the pig upwards with a makeshift pulley system. It was a humorous sight, wherein the boar dangled helplessly, swallowing all of its pride. They crossed the arch over the canyon, into a closely-packed protected rock house. There sat four humans around a campfire, enjoying the scenery. Holt got goosebumps as he approached them, and politely asked if he could join them.

Shocked by his temerity, they were offended that he brought a pig to their sacred spot, and asked him how he found them anyway. He articulated that it was part of the trail map he obtained for free at the bureau of land management office, and they all spit into their respective spittoons, sounding off four melodic and metallic notes from their cans. Holt thought it odd that they bothered to use spittoons outside, but didn't inquire about it. One of them gently, with his fingertips, lifted the hat from his beer belly, and delicately fit it to his head. He brandished a revolver and asked them to leave.

"You better be getting a move-on," the cowboy scowled.

"Unless you are looking for trouble," another shrilly vocalized. "I'm itching for some action." This one wore a black-cloth horizontally banding her eyes, where holes were cut. She had a face like a rattlesnake, with an equally venomous smirk. Long hair draped behind her shoulders in a fashion loosely tied at the end. Next to her lay a couple of bags of gold. She had presumably stolen it from pawn shops or wherever else in this day and age you can actually find gold actively used as currency.

"Pretending to be outlaws?" Holt rudely asked.

This provoked a third member of the squad to chime in, saying, "Your odds of surviving a few more comments like that are mighty slim there, bucko. This here is Riff Cassidy, he's got royal blood in 'em." He gestured to the cowboy. "Not to mention he's got some mean riffs on the ole guitar over there. The pretty one is Robin. Quite a fitting name for one of the modern world's last successful bank robbers. She sure is a bandit by trade."

Holt somehow deduced a decent amount of information about the speaker, from the playing cards in his hands, and the red handlebar mustache.

"And you're the gambler of the group?" Holt interjected. "Is that why you all live in the wilderness, because you lose all the money that the bandit can bring in?"

"Touchy subject, amigo, but yes, I am a gambler. Just a bad run of luck. My name is Reid Fox. Do you know who we are?" the gambler questioned.

"Are you what's left of the Wild Bunch Gang?" Holt sarcastically retorted.

"Why yes, we are. Are you sure you want to be hanging around a den of thieves?"

"I suppose it depends. You haven't introduced that fellow yet." Holt pointed to the last member of the gang, who didn't seem to be very bright, mind you, and it wasn't because the fire's light was lacking.

The last member had a golden-plated horseshoe bent around the top of his skull fashioned like a headband. He was catching flies with his open mouth, and was clearly unaware that they were talking about him.

"He was in a traumatic accident involving the game of horseshoes." said the gambler.

"Legend has it, only the most noble of heart can pry that horseshoe from his head. Riff gave it a try, and when it didn't work, we just had him travel alongside us until we could do something noble enough to get it off and sell it. He's been part of the gang ever since."

"Doesn't pull his own weight though," said the cowboy, as all four simultaneously spit into the spittoons again.

"If I manage to get it off of him..." Dooley started.

"His name is Bartholomew. We call him Bart," the bandit hissed.

"Thank you. If I manage to pry that horseshoe off of Mr. Bartholomew here, you all have to let us camp here. And share the beans. Deal?"

They agreed to entertain Holt's suggestion, skeptical that he would find any success, and watched as he took a wide stance behind Bartholomew. Cracking his knuckles, and subsequently rubbing his hands together, he felt he had readied himself for the moment of glory. He made a small anecdote about how it was akin to basketball, wherein your ritual before a freethrow determines your success rate, and that's why he cracked his knuckles before rubbing his hands together. Three-fourths of the gang scorned him, and one agreed, adding the unrelated comment that he was a Utah Jazz fan. Holt, back in position, slowly and dramatically reached for the golden horseshoe with both hands.

"On with it already!" the cowboy shouted.

Bartholomew, unaware that Holt was about to tug his head off his shoulders, was peacefully roasting a single bean over the fire, with quite a skinny stick. A twig, if you will. Holt, grasping the horseshoe, exclaimed to everyone that it was cold. They didn't care. He began to pull, and the legendarily stubborn horseshoe slid clean off Bart's head like butter.

"I'm noble!" he gloated, as the boar looked at the horse next to him and bragged about being Holt's sidekick.

The bandit pulled her mask off, as if to get a clear view of what just happened, and the cowboy sat straight up. Reid applauded Holt with sincerity.

"Ah, I loosened it up for you," the cowboy discounted.

"What, a few years ago?" said the bandit.

Holt's moment of fame was quickly overshadowed by the next event that took place.

Bartholomew pulled his roasted bean out of the campfire and off of his stick with his carefully shaking thumb and index finger. He meticulously proceeded to place it directly on his head where the horseshoe had been. The others watched in amazement as he grabbed a piece of twine, and tied a circle from his chin, to the top of his head, making a bow on the belly of the bean.

"What on earth are you doing?" asked Reid, slightly concerned.

"Protection," he replied.

Holt, invested in the drama, questioned what he meant, and was told that Bart is always concerned with protecting himself from aliens. They all used their spittoons a third time.

"Bart, that bean ain't going to do a thing for you. It'll be Riff's trigger that stops any kind of goblin running up on our camp." The bandit waved her hands around for emphasis.

"Aliens aren't real and neither are goblins, Rob. You're going to make Holt runaway telling others the stories of how strange we are rather than how inspiring," said Reid.

"Oh, so you're going to tell me Goblin Valley is just named after something that just ain't a goblin?" she responded.

"Actually, the prolific formations known as 'hoodoos' there, imaginatively resemble goblins, which is what inspired the name," Dooley chimed in.

Between Capitol Reef and Canyonlands National Parks, the constellations are beautiful. In fact, Utah is home to some of the darkest places in the world, making an easy hobby out of stargazing. The Wild Bunch Gang and Holt's gang kept up the fireside chat, with all its poking-fun, and exaggerated stories. Eventually, when the cowboy slipped his hat over his eyes, one by one they all nodded off. Holt connected the dots of zodiacs with his eyes, until they finally sealed shut on aquarius.

Whilst they slept, a mischievous creature lurked nearby. It must have caught wind of the golden horseshoe, whether audibly, or by its sniffer, which sat rather widely on his face. It's nose protruded and came to a point at the end, like a cone. It had no eyebrows, and seemingly no definite lips, but it did have ears -- one short, one long, both tapered at the top. It's skin appeared as camouflage to the red sandstone around it, and seemed to have the same rough texture, like the top of a skateboard.

It nimbly made its way through the slot canyon, with ease. It was obvious that it lived and moved through this terrain daily. Taking one of its eight fingers, it dug its fingernail into the gritty sandstone and gathered up some of its sediments as it turned the corners of the canyon.

Silently, it crawled up the wall and traversed the arch, and was nearly upon them. Bartholomew had taken a few cans from the group and scattered them around the camp, to act as traps that would sound off and alert them to a sneaky enemy. The monster did not notice the cans at his bare feet, and kicked one that laid right near the pig. Against the odds, the elementary design of the trap worked out well.

The snoring of the gambler came to a halt, and Holt's eyes opened back up. He peered around the camp, looking for the source of the noise as he rubbed his blurry vision with the sides of his hand. He noticed a six-foot hoodoo, towering above the pig. Concerned that he was losing his mind, he whispered to the pig and inquired if the rock formation it was sleeping under was always there. The boar in its unjustified sarcasm commented that he must not have realized it when he decided to sleep right at the base of it. Sleepy Holt seemed somewhat satisfied with the pig's answer, and nodded off again.

After thirty minutes of eluding the group by standing still, the goblin began to move again. It hobbled over to the gambler, who happened to be one of the lightest sleepers in the group. It held out the fingernail it used before to scrape the sandstone, and placed a small amount of it in both of the gambler's eyes. One by one, it dusted the eyes of the gang, putting them in a trance-like state. [92] It was only when it reached Bartholomew, that it stopped, looked at his bean hat with a disgusted face, and decided to skip him. With the group sedated, it fiercely plucked a golden tooth from

---

[92] This resembles the folktale legend of *The Sandman*

the gambler, took the jingling sacks of gold from the bandit, and ripped the cowboy's spurs straight off his feet. It picked up the golden horseshoe from Holt's lifeless hand and abruptly placed it into one of the sacks, as if it burned its fingers.

The goblin, with the gang's belongings tied in sacks around a stick that it hoisted over his shoulder, navigated through the sandstone wilderness. A day's journey took it to a small abode that rested within a hole in a canyon wall, in the bottom of the valley. There were holes stacked in an organized manner, as if the canyon were a massive apartment complex. Another goblin face popped its head out of one of the holes and conversed with it.

"Quite the haul this time, Zovrudgukken!" it happily yelled to its friend.

"Save some for the rest of us, 'Sandman'," another said.

"No biggie, guys, just doing my thing."

The Goblin affectionately known as "Sandman" felt confident and accomplished, and was excited to share its findings with the other goblins in the hole that it finally entered.

"Honey, I'm home!" yelled the contented goblin, as he embraced a family unit of five.

"I was so worried about you! I'm glad you made it back safe," said a smaller stature goblin. "The kids have been fighting nonstop since you left."

"Kids, listen to your mother. Gelnallik, put the axe down," he exclaimed. "It's an antique."

Gelnallik's pigtails bounced as she waddled back to the living room. The father goblin, apparently also known as Zovrudgukken, asked if one of the younglings was keeping up in school and staying out of trouble, and endearingly called it the "best half-toothed snot slug around." He then took a seat on a hand formed sandstone bench and began to read from a stone tablet, with petroglyphs etched into every open space.

"Gotta love the Sunday funnies." He chuckled to himself.

The mother goblin asked if the father could help in the kitchen, to which he replied that he was too tired from his lengthy journey and his courageous battle with the humans. The mother goblin melted down the gold pieces in a cauldron and added in some other minerals for spice. She served it into a few cups and set the table for dinner. Picking up the golden horseshoe, she felt as if her fingers burned and threw it aside with a shout of agitation. She exclaimed that it felt like poison and had a bad odor.

Now the Wild Bunch Gang had spotted the tail end of the goblin, escaping in the night with their belongings, only due to Bartholomew's relentless shaking of their limp bodies. The bandit's stolen bags of jingling gold pieces, the cowboy's spurs, the horseshoe, and one of the gambler's teeth, were all missing.

Mixed emotions flooded the camp, with the bandit claiming the creature had the ears of a goblin, and the once calm and collected Reid Fox, now expressing a more rowdy and aggressive side, but denying that it could be anything other than a human. He was the maddest of the bunch, and darted after the goblin. Holt grabbed him by the arm to talk some sense into them, and the gambler spun around in a rage, and punched Holt in the jaw. Dooley contemplated fighting, but calmed himself and told the group he had a plan.

"Holt is a darn good boxer. You do NOT want to mess with him," the pig snorted.

"How do we know you're not in cahoots with that burglar, and this isn't some big ole heist you'd been planning?" the bandit asked.

"Well for one, don't you think I'd be off by now running next to him into the sunrise with your gold?" Holt replied.

Holt told them that if the creature was in fact a goblin, there might be even more gold stashed up at its home, and it was just going to lead them straight there. They were in general agreement, and took off on a reconnaissance mission, as well as a team of five can, plus a pig and horse. Private Sherman was left at the roost to soak up the sun.

They traveled for a full day, and since the goblin was too fast for the group to trail, they sent the bandit to scout it out and bring details back to their camp. The goblin peered over its shoulder once, but The bandit flattened to the ground, evading any suspicion. From the top of a cliff's plateau, She watched the goblin crawl into its "hidey-hole" as she called it.

The gang made it to Goblin Valley, where their thief's residence was. They belly crawled to the top of the plateau and staked out the valley. Both Bartholomew and Holt were frightened at the number of hoodoos, and Holt suggested they turn back. They then questioned his loyalty, but were interrupted by a creepy comment from Bart.

"There they stand. An army of beasts, waiting. Guarding the mountains of gold buried in their homes."

"He's right!" Holt said, "There was a hoodoo in the camp where Hamlet slept, and when we woke, it was gone and so was our gold. Those hoodoos are not just sandstone pillars. Those are goblins."

The gambler, bandit, and cowboy laughed at his assertion, and made their way down the cliff, through the valley, and to the home of the goblin in question. They meandered in single-file like a creek alongside the hoodoos, looking up at them in awe. Holt reluctantly followed. They stood upright next to the hidey-hole's walls, and as the gambler motioned with his hand, they simultaneously jumped through the large entrance into the goblin's dining room.

Both groups, the gang and the goblins gawked at each other in surprise. It was as if they had caught the goblins in an embarrassing act. A young goblin broke the silence, sprinting fiercely toward them with an axe. The cowboy swiftly pulled his revolver and shot the goblin dead.

"Gelnallik?!" The goblin yelped and moaned and ran to its daughter.

The gang rushed in guns-a-blazing and shot, stabbed, and pummeled the remains of the goblin family. Holt guiltily asked if they knew what they had just done, as he picked up the horseshoe, and shoved some other pieces of gold in his pockets.

"They were eating a family dinner and we just massacred them," Holt cried out.

"They are monsters who stole from us. We are just taking it back," replied the cowboy.

"Is nobody going to talk about how they were just about to eat the gold?" the pig asked.

As they gathered their belongings onto the horses back, they heard the crackling of rocks, and suspected that the abode might cave in. Reaching to the entrance of the hidey-hole, their pupils constricted, and caused a few brief seconds of adjustment to the light around them. As their vision became clear, it quickly became known that the graveling sounds were coming from the hoodoos that were breaking open in unison. As pieces of sandstone eroded from each formation, rather than falling to the ground, it reformed like how the waves of the ocean molds a beach. Out of nowhere, hands and feet, arms and legs, and goblin bodies took shape throughout the valley.

It might have been silent if only one were re-forming itself, but the sheer amount of them all doing this simultaneously, provided a sort of loud white noise in the background. It might have been comparable to the sound of a helicopter, if it were a thousand feet in the air. At such a convenient time, the boar's radio tuned in to a radio host saying, "I'm not sure if any of you listeners are about to have some battle of fantastical proportions, but this one goes out to you. The perfect battle song, 'War Pigs', a Black Sabbath cover by Cake."

Pinned into a slot canyon, with both sides pouring in streams of angry goblins, the group took their stand. If they were in a less defensible position they would have lost this battle swiftly, regardless of their proficiency in battle. But there they stood, like the three-hundred Spartans, defending themselves from thousands of Persians.

This was largely a battle of hand-to-hand combat, as the only ranged weapon in the group was the cowboy's revolver with about sixty rounds in his ammunition belt. Furthermore, he wasn't a mythical cowboy, so he didn't always hit his exact target. He stood in the middle of the group, alternating bullets at both sides of the canyon.

The bandit wielded a dagger with a curved blade, and two sticks of dynamite. She was doing her best to plan their escape, occasionally providing support behind The gambler and protecting Bartholomew.

The gambler had seen more than a few bar fights, and displayed his worth as a brawler on the side opposite to Holt, as they both did their best from letting the goblins devour the small space they maintained. Bartholomew held his bean out toward the horde of goblins and did his best to ward them off. Surprisingly he did a great job providing some distraction.

Next to Holt, the horse was spooked, spinning in circles while bucking and kicking. Holt dodged most of the horse's kicks except one, which clipped his ear, nearly taking off his head. It seemed the Goblins steered clear of the distressed stallion and funneled in toward Dooley. He worked out a system where the boar was piling bodies and creating tripping hazards as he proceeded to knock them across the head with the horseshoe.

"I thought you were supposed to be good at boxing?" the gambler yelled back to Holt.

"When your knuckles are broken in five minutes I'll still be fighting," he said. "Robin?"

"Working on it. I think our best chance is going to be to blow up," she paused, pulling one off of Bartholomew and stabbing it. "...Blow up the entrance, and hope there is enough debris to climb to higher ground.

"That's all you got?" the cowboy asked.

"Horse." Bartholomew whispered.

They went with the dynamite plan, where they fought their way close enough to the entrance, that they might be able to do more damage to the weaker points of the walls, without as much danger to themselves. Holt moved to the front to help them edge forward, and the horse did a stellar job of fending off the rear, while the cowboy dropped any goblin who made it past. The bandit tossed the first stick of dynamite out to the base of the canyon entrance, and they waited for the explosion. One of the goblins quickly picked it up and snuffed it out.

"You threw it too early!" shouted the gambler.

"That's great. As if we needed more trouble, now you gave a horde of monsters an explosion stick. A kind gift. Let's hope they don't return it," the pig stated.

"Consarn it, Hamlet! Are you even doing anything to help?" Holt yelled.

"I'm the DJ," the pig responded.

Using profanities, the gambler yelled at Robin, telling her to hold the next one longer and throw it right before it's ready. The bandit tossed the second one, which had a much shorter fuse. Another goblin picked it up, and well, you can imagine how it died, I'm not going to go into detail. A few rocks fractured and toppled down from the walls, but nothing significant. The goblins quickly overcame it and pushed them back to a more narrow section of the canyon again.

"We're doomed!" the pig shouted.

"I'm running low," the cowboy stated, "There sure are a lot of them."

"Isn't there something they're afraid of? Maybe light?" asked the gambler.

"How would that make sense? Goblin's love shiny things, and shiny things don't exist without light reflecting off of them. Besides, we are out here in broad daylight." Holt remarked.

"Horse!" said Bart.

"The horse is fine, Bart, it's actually doing better than all of us," replied Robin.

Holt Dooley, racking his brain for a solution, reminisced on an old Korean folktale about goblins he had read about. The story had many adaptations, but generally went like this:

A goblin lived with a human. The human grew weary of it and decided to make it leave her alone. The human thought of a way to trick it by swapping stories of what scared them both. The goblin told her that it was afraid of horse blood, and the human said she was afraid of riches. One day when the goblin was out, the human scattered the house and property with horse blood, and the goblin could not enter anymore. Out of spite, the goblin threw gold and silver into the human's property, only making her richer and happier.

Like a light bulb turning on, Holt told them he knew how to escape, but that the horse would die. The cowboy was not in favor, but conceded when pressured by the rest of the gang and ensuing goblins. He stated that if anyone was going to kill his horse, it would be him. The gang readied themselves, and the cowboy used his last bullet to kill his horse. A tear streamed from his eye, and down into the sun touched cracks of his leathery face.

Holt took the dagger from the bandit and slathered horse blood over himself. He took the place of the gambler who did the same, and so on, until they all were covered. At a staggering rate, the goblins retreated away from the group. They were able now to just walk straight out of the valley.

"Well, now that we're invisible, maybe we should ransack some more homes," the pig said.

"I think you mean invincible," said Holt.

"I think you're both imbeciles," the gambler stated.

With all their belongings weighing heavy on their shoulders, they set out back to their roost, and made it a priority to get a new pack animal. Goblins angrily hurled rocks at them, but no real threat ensued, except the other stick of dynamite out there, which fortunately never made a second appearance. If you ever make it out to hike around Goblin Valley, Utah, just know one of those hoodoos might be holding on to some explosives and maybe a grudge, so be on your guard.

The group gifted the golden horseshoe to Holt as a memento, and told him he was officially initiated as part of the Wild Bunch Gang. He told them that he wasn't going to be living in Utah long, and was just wasting time until the cold of the winter fades and he could go north again. Thanking them and saying their goodbyes, he picked up a well rested Private Sherman, saddled him on the boar, and headed off to Escalante.

BARY & BEAN

The petrified forest in Escalante is captivating for two reasons. One, it's a petrified forest; and two, the curse. The park blatantly prohibits visitors from taking any of the petrified wood as a souvenir, but due to the sheer beauty of these rocks, people often disobey. Like clockwork, the park receives packages in the mail of returning pieces of petrified wood, along with stories of how horrible luck fell upon the one who took it. The amount of times this happens is alarming, and has since been recognized by locals as a legendary curse.

Learning of the curse of course put this destination on the map for Holt, and he formulated a plan. He analyzed the accounts of the curse's victims, and decided the curse didn't necessarily fall upon the one who took the petrified wood, but lingers with the item as long as it is out of the park. He believed he could weaponize the curse. Holt, the plant, and the pig, walked some of the trails until he found a piece that he claimed was calling his name, and stole it.

Readying himself for any effect the curse might bring him, he hurried to St. George, where he planned to find a public computer and do some research. They barely survived a simultaneous blowout of all four tires on the car they had stolen in Colorado, and were forced to walk the rest of the way.

After some digging on one of his newfound enemies, he managed to procure an address, which he wrote in the middle of an envelope. He placed the rock inside of it, along with a note that read, "Detective Griffith, here is some incriminating evidence for Holt Dooley's arrest," and sent it back to South Carolina. He hoped someone would receive this, and the ensuing storm of bad luck would compel Griff to go back home for a bit. Griffith's mailbox received the petrified wood, and soon after also received quite the wallop from a local teenager with a baseball bat. It had since been struck by lighting, wherein the envelope burned up and the rock was misplaced on the road. A biker then accidentally ran over it with his wheel, which caused him to wreck. Not that the rock deserves a play-by-play, but luckily for him, it never actually ended up in Griff's care.

Anyway, Holt Dooley decided to hunker down in St. George and the surrounding area, to wait-out some of the cold until it was safe for the gang to travel north by foot. Zion National Park was a beautiful place to spend Christmas, where he kept a roaring campfire, and adorned a pinion pine tree with various items from his rucksack. With his journal in hand, and map in the other, Holt noticed they were unintentionally camping in an area that the map had already drawn out. He looked over his shoulder at the pig who was snoring, and Private Sherman was resting on the blushing red dirt between them.

"What do you think, Private? Are we about to be sabotaged by some ghost, ghoul or goblin? Do you think you could take watch while I get some sleep?"

Holt began to dream of the beautiful valley they were in. His eyes rolled back and forth in his head as he slept, and he occasionally hummed a sort of dialogue to himself. Suddenly, Holt's soul became unbound from his body, flying up above himself. [93]

"Consarn it, Private, I thought you said you would take the wake shift…" he said to the apparently sleeping bonsai tree, before seeing his own body. "Woah, is that me? I suppose I should prioritize a meeting with the barber soon." He tried to gain control of his hovering soul, but was not well versed in arial movement.

About a hundred yards off he saw a herd of hogs closing in on them with a large cloud of mist among them. There was a man in the rear, who was holding a melon in one hand, and a 18 inch kingpin in the other. Holt tried to fly down to where his body lay, swimming through the air, and somersaulting downward at slow speeds. The man with the melon stood above his body and stared for a minute, before Holt could reach himself. Finally tumbling down onto his own chest, he grasped his shirt and tried slapping his body's face back and forth to wake himself up.

The man with the hogs watched this debacle and laughed heartily, like Santa Clause would. Holt's spirit stood up and faced him.

"Why are you standing over my body like that?" Holt asked.

"Well to haunt you of course! I swore to evict anyone who tried to settle my land when I was alive. Now I do it dead." He winked.

---

[93] Astral projection

"Well, we are not settling here, just resting until we can move northward. So you have no need to haunt my helpless body." Holt looked over at one of the ghastly hogs who was confidently standing with one of its hooves perched on his body's head. He aggravatedly shewed it off and noticed a bunch of them gathered around his boar who was still snoring.

The man with a melon seemed to take great pleasure in his discomfort, and encouraged the hogs to trample their bodies as it had no real effect anyway. Holt grabbed the man by the back of his head, and with great force pulled it downward onto the melon he was holding, cracking it open. His demeanor changed from a jolly, mischievous man, to an angry one. He told Holt that if he didn't leave the next morning, a great tragedy would ensue.

Holt fired back, telling the man that if he by chance managed to kill him, he'd never leave Zion, but stay there as a ghost to spite him. The man was shocked at his audacity, and began to tell a story to intimidate Holt.

"All of this land was once mine and my small family's, only neighbored by the Watsons and the Walkers. I had a large lot of hogs, for which I was nicknamed 'Hog' Allen, and a plentiful farm of squash and melons."

He went on to explain that he rightfully beat a Watson boy with the cart's kingpin, since the boy accidentally dropped it, smashing the man's finger. As the other Watsons pulled him off of the boy, he vowed that they could not stay in his valley.

After a long day of working the farm harvesting the fruit of his labor, he took a bite of one of his better looking melons he had left inside of his cabin. He quickly became sick and screamed out for his wife to heal his aching head. When she ran into the room, he was lying dead on the floor.

142

He claimed that he was not actually dead, but sleeping due to a poison inflicted by the Watsons. His wife had since moved to Cedar City and decided to dig up his grave, to move his body to her new home. As they opened his casket, his hair and fingernails had grown, and his body lay in a contorted position frowning. His wife, horrified, asked to close the casket back up and leave him.

A year had passed since his death and a mist rolled down the valley's golden staircase and rested over his grave. The Watsons were out riding their horses, and when confronted by the mist, continued onward. One of the horses, miss-stepped, bucking off the young boy upon its back onto the ground. The thud resonated through the mist, and the young Watson strangely passed away without a drop of blood.

After yet another year had passed, off went another Watson dying with the mist, again without any bloodshed. It wasn't until the third year, after the fall of their third son, that they remembered Hog Allen's vow to evict them from the valley. They packed up and left, as the locals renamed the area "Hog Heaven," saying that Hog Allen still resided there in his purgatory.

He told Holt that just as he doesn't see the Watson boys wandering through the valley, he just as assuredly wouldn't see him. He warned Holt a second time to leave the next morning.

Holt's spirit landed like an ethereal angel [94] into his sleeping body and climbed back in as one does with a sleeping bag. It wasn't just the threat of Hog Allen that spurred the group to movement, but also that he woke to a light dusting of snow on his face. He

---

[94] One of the most famous hikes in Zion National Park is named *Angel's Landing*

gathered his belongings, and the group traveled back to St. George, where it was just a bit warmer.

The boar asked Holt a question that resonated with him, as the strings do to the insides of a guitar's wooden frame.

"Holt, this girl you want to see... we have travelled for such a long distance, fighting off things that most humans wouldn't believe, let alone understand. Why are you letting the cold hinder you from seeing her? Private Sherman and me.. we are ready. You don't have to worry about us."

Holt's fingers found his old piece of driftwood, and his head tilted back to ponder the sky.

"I don't know. I guess it's more than that. We are drawing nearer, you know, and I've only just begun to think of what *she* would want. I've only been married to her for a short time. And she's already seen many other people throughout our marriage." His fist rose to the corner of his eye, to clear the blurriness from his vision. "I think this whole time, I've thought I'm on the way to save her.. and as selfish as it is...I've hoped that she needed saving. But I may get there to find her living happily with another who has replaced me.. in fact I think that is the most probable option."

Holt reiterated how he had tracked her down through a computer algorithm he created, and they were following this unlikely notion to the coast. He didn't feel it was necessary. It wouldn't change the outcome. Yet, the boar's question got to him. It prodded him forth, whether snow, government authority, or anything extraordinary were to step into his course.

Holt Dooley had never felt a more welcome feeling, than when Diamond Fork Hot Springs[95] sheltered him from the winter winds. A waterfall rushed down a pungent smelling mineral deposit, where it landed in a natural pool of steaming larimar-turquoise water. Spilling over its brim, it filled many other pools and puddles of varying temperatures; some warm, some too hot for comfort.

As soon as Holt would move, the frigid atmosphere outside of him would give him chills. He submerged his body all the way to his chin, with his shirt laying folded upon the top of his head. The boar and Private Sherman were a few yards off, sitting by a fire.

Out of the blue, quite literally, the hair on his arms stood up. He heard the heavy hobbling of a bird through the snow, and glanced at it, as it made its way over toward him.

"I don't have any food for you, buddy. Move along," said Dooley.

At second glance, Holt believed he saw an orange glint in its eyes, and he spoke cautiously. "I've seen a lot of things Mr. Crow. Your boldness doesn't scare me."

"What's wrong, Holt?" the boar yelled.

"I can't say. And it's not because you are far away. I couldn't whisper it to you even," he shouted back.

Holt believed that the crow was strange, but not anything he couldn't handle. Although, he did hear of the supernatural stories of Sherman Ranch, and for their sake, decided not to risk mentioning his suspicions aloud. You see, there is a legend that a type of shape-shifting creature haunts and terrorizes Utah, and if

---

[95] 40.0845424,-111.3549516

you speak its name, it is much more likely to make an appearance. For this reason, I can only allude to its details, not its name. [96]

The creature has been called a polluted shaman, a fallen angel, and a humanoid beast. Its origin is murky, as there are many different Native American traditions regarding it, but a lot of stories claim that they can appear as a crow, a coyote, or a wolf. Whenever it appears in human form, it is said to still carry animal characteristics.

Holt tried not to maintain eye contact as the crow hopped a little more toward him. It is said that if one locks eyes with this creature, it is able to submerge into your soul, and steal your skin. He wasn't ready to be floating outside of his body again, but neither was he concerned, as reportedly, they mainly attack people of the First Nations. Holt is only 1/16th Native American, so he figured he had a 15/16 chance of encountering the creature without confrontation.

The boar and its shenanigans, meanwhile, had misplaced its radio, and was shuffling around in the ashes of the fire to make sure he didn't drop it. Its tusks were stained in white ash, and it grew scared that its beloved radio had melted. It wasn't long until it burnt itself, which spurred a run of great speed to the not so soothing hot springs.

Possibly due to the large volume of steam, or maybe just the surprise of the unorthodox gait of a boar running in its direction,

---

[96] After researching Navajo legend, I would recommend reading for yourself about this creature, as I will also not mention it by name.

the crow failed to move out of the way. It was abruptly stabbed by the tusks of the boar, leaving white ash on its wounds.[97]

"Well, I guess I'll never know." Holt sighed.

"Holty, I can't find my radio!" yelled the pig.

"You left it here and told me it would help me relax."

"And you didn't even turn it on?" the pig said.

Holt looked over and saw a beast running away from them, with the appearance of a human, and a few feathers of a crow. It swiftly disappeared, and Holt never mentioned it again.

———

For the sake of anyone listening, I am going to speed through the next bit, as it is intriguing, but not exactly necessary to understand as of now.

-Provo-

While in Provo, Holt had followed his elk skin map to BYU. He saw a large crowd gathering toward the basketball stadium and decided to sneak in. Watching as a cougar mascot named "Cosmo" danced, flipped, and cheered its way down the floor, he saw that it matched the drawing on his map. His curiosity drove him to follow the mascot after the game, and interact with it, ultimately revealing that nobody was inside of the costume. It made more sense now, why it was able to do tricks and flips that seemed humanly improbable. Holt then went to an ice cream shop

---

[97] Coincidentally, this is reportedly one of the only ways to kill this creature, by using a tip coated in white ash.

downtown and talked to a couple of young men who had nametags pinned to their chests, with the title "elder" printed on them. Dooley asked them for directions, to which they began to give him spiritual direction instead. After a riveting conversation, he waved goodbye to his new acquaintances and made his way north.

-Snowbird-

Many of the older stands of trees in a forest still have noticeable senses in our day and age. For instance, Aspen trees[98] have eyes painted as black as tar on their chalky bark. They are always watching, while others are listening, and some are feeling the occasional passerby with their woody phalanges. As Holt hiked up the Wasatch Range, a conifer tree, burdened with a heavy pile of snow, recognized Holt on his course. I know now, why it desperately wished to reach out and tell him to stop his journey, though I don't know how it knew. One of its many appendages dropped its snow as he walked under, in an attempted wave. A tiny waterfall of white powder left the tree's arm swaying up and down, as if it were greeting Holt. The dull noise of snow landing around him, sounded like one pushing air through their lips repeatedly.

"Ah, a direct hit," Holt said, wiping off some snow from a sled. He never noticed the attempted communication.

Dooley was tugging his backpack along with the sled's rope, unnecessarily I might add. You see, he had stopped at a store in Salt Lake City, and upon asking for a "toboggan" he received a sled, rather than the soft knit hat he was expecting. In the Eastern U.S. that is what "toboggan" means. Anyway, on a whim, he

---

[98] Referring to six species of trees in the *Populus* genus

decided to purchase the sled instead. Then, on a whim, they decided to go sledding.

Finally, reaching the top of Snowbird Resort's "Pipeline Couloir" the gang strapped into the sled and pushed off. They tumbled to the bottom uninjured.

-Salt Lake-

Holt's boot pressed down on the cracked and crumbly shores of The Great Salt Lake. It was, in fact, quite salty; and it was, notably, great in size. Antelope Island displayed magnificent colors of a typical lake's blues and greens, but it also contributed silvers from the salt, and red from "Halophilic Bacteria" that Holt wrote about in his journal. He pulled out a bottle from his rucksack, and scooped some salt crystals inside it. He began to journal again, and was supposedly interrupted by Private Sherman. Holt told the plant that the reason he journals so much is to keep a record of all his travels. He said that he wanted to share all the things he had seen with his wife when he found her. He additionally told the plant and the pig that even though he didn't get to experience these memories with her, he was at least happy to share the times with them. He was content with their friendship.

"Nonetheless, I think it's time I shared with you all that I have mostly plotted out the graphemes of the script on the map," Holt shared. "I can't exactly translate every word. Even so, there are cognates with the latin based languages, and occasionally I can gather some meaning."

"What does it say now?" asked the pig.

Holt, with map in hand, turned around and watched as the drawings upon its surface shifted dependent on direction, almost like a compass.

"If I turn this way it looks like it says 'whales', and if I turn this way, it looks like it might be a phrase related to 'ghoul of Salt Lake'".

"So are we going to ride on some whales or what?" asked the pig.

"Well, considering the ghoul seems to be drawing nearer to us on the map, it looks like we may encounter it first. Should we leave?"

"Of course not! We mostly end up coming out with an advantage after these encounters. Ride it out." the pig greedily smiled.

"I haven't read enough Arabian [99] folklore to know, but I don't think we'll be getting any good benefits from meeting it. Maybe further honing my ability to fight, I suppose."

They sat on the salty ground, and watched as a one-man paddle boat traced the outline of Antelope Island. The shabby boat looked as if it were constructed from the boards of an 1800s cabin. The captain did not wear a hat, nor did he have any hair. His grey decrepit skin was wound tight round his bones, and he looked as if he was confused.

Holt decided he would confront the ghoul. He lightly jogged over to it, and it stopped paddling. After they looked directly into each other's eyes, the ghoul spoke up.

"You there...you can see me?" [100]

"Yes of course I can." Holt replied.

---

[99] "Ghoul" is an Arabic term having to do with a spirit that oftentimes haunts graveyards

[100] I'm sure I don't have to elaborate on the commonality of this trending phrase.

"A tourist has never seen me before. You must be newly dead. If you tell me where you are buried I can help you back into your grave." it said, licking its lips.

"Do ghouls not eat the dead? I don't think that was very sly, my friend. Regardless, I am not dead."

"Well, I am no ghoul! My name is Jean Baptiste. I am a gravedigger for the city."

"Ah, I should have known. I've actually read your story."

"My story?" it responded.

"Yes...the one where you stole clothes and belongings from the cemeteries of Salt Lake, got banished to an island on the lake, and went missing thereafter."

"How...How do you know that? It has been so long."

"A little thing called the internet. Though I can't use it nowadays," Holt said.

They conversed about their stories and backgrounds, and the ghoul actually exchanged some useful information. It told Holt that he could hop in its boat, where it could bring him northwest across the lake, and when Dooley declined, it told him of a hot air balloon maker in Idaho, who might be able to get him where he needed to go faster. In exchange, Holt offered to remove from the internet the information on the evil deed that transformed Jean Baptiste into the ghoul, clearing his name, but not his condition. [101]

---

[101] After some digging, it does seem that not much exists on the internet about his 'heinous deed' as Holt called it.

With a new plan in sight, he plotted his route in his journal to a university computer lab, on the way to the hot air balloon maker. Essentially, it read Ogden, to Logan, to Bear Lake, to Driggs. So, he decided to trudge along through the winter snow, with a newfound hope in his journey. A hope that he might more quickly, and just as assuredly make it to his damsel, who may or may not be in distress.

-Logan-

Logan, Utah is a city with a lot to boast about. For one, incredible scenery is abundant, filling the hearts of its citizens with desires of outdoor recreation. Every day after class, whether rain, snow, or sunshine, multiple Aggies of Utah State could be found adventuring the Logan Canyon and the surrounding area. There is even a song about it entitled "College with a View", which was conveniently playing on the pig's radio when they stepped into town.

Holt waltzed on into a computer lab and through means only the most technologically savvy would understand, began to eliminate all of the internet's worst information regarding the ghoul, Jean Baptiste. If you look up his story today, parts are still left out. Now since he had a screen in front of him, he decided to make it a little easier on himself directionally, and plotted his exact course to Driggs, Idaho by foot, writing directions in his journal. Meanwhile, while eavesdropping on a conversation between fraternity boys, he overheard something about a "pig dinner" and how they had a "whole pig" this time. Worried about the possibility of it having to do with his boar who was wandering campus, he darted out of the computer lab looking for him -- for he had grown fond of his travel companion. Unfortunately, and a rare occurrence for Holt Dooley, he forgot to cover the tracks he had so carelessly left on the computer.

Relieved, he found the boar on the second floor of the Fine Arts Visual building, adjacent to Todd Johnson, a professor at the school. Holt apologized, and racked the professor's brain on a variety of topics, from urban planning philosophy, to Native American history. Ultimately he gifted Holt a fishing rod, and told him of some great fishing holes on his way to Southern Idaho.

Holt was hungry, and decided fish wasn't an appetizing choice for his breakfast at that moment, causing him to ask around the campus where he could find the best restaurant in town. The gang and him took a walk around a little park named "First Dam", where he left the pig and Sherman, as he went on to have breakfast at the renowned "Herm's Inn". Herm's is a local favorite. Iconically, customers tend to doodle on their napkins as they wait for food, and consequently, the restaurant chooses some to hang up as part of their decor. Holt sketched a somewhat abstract, minimalist drawing of himself, followed by the pig, as they looked to a menagerie of odd characters that he had encountered on the journey to find his wife. [102] He proceeded to eat the "Carnitas Skillet" and was fueled up to tackle the next chapter of his travels.

---

[102] This description fits what appears to be the back cover of Holt's journal.

CHAPTER 10

(Physical Forces)

Bear Lake, sitting on the border of Idaho and Utah, has been said to rival the dazzling crystal waters of the Caribbean. Holt noted that the stunning blue coloration of the lake is due to "suspended calcium carbonate" resembling "patinated copper". Before he reached the shore, Holt had purchased some of the best fishing line he could get his hands on, with the little amount of cash he gathered from all of the group's sly endeavors. It was named "Spider Silk" and had a motto that read "stronger than the webs of your favorite superhero". He also spared some cash for a raspberry shake[103] for the pig and the tree, but later regretted his decision as the pig slurped so loudly. They set up camp on a beach opposite to the town, and Holt enacted his habit of leaving the pig by the fire, while he would wander elsewhere. It was an essential means of clearing his head.

Casting his first line into the partially frozen water, the string, as thick as a spaghetti noodle, waltzed through the sky. It resembled the St. Louis Arch making a parabola, from his wrist to the hook.

---

[103] Bear Lake is known for its raspberries, particularly in shakes. Many local restaurants competitively boast the best raspberry shake.

The line was pulled back from the drag in the reel, and demonstrated a good amount of air resistance, as the slightly rotating projectile created swiftly changing pictures of cursive. Holt anticipated and analyzed many physical forces at play during his recreation, and was excited to further read into the action of actually catching a fish.

Dooley got a bite. Feel free to skip forward if you are uninterested in the following physical forces described. The angular motion of his hand twisting and lifting the rod in response to the bite, placed the hook in its mouth, where the tensile strength of his line was tested. Its weight pulled the line taut, which bent the pole displaying more tension. Torque acted upon the fish, when a change in its downward direction took place. I knew you wouldn't skip it.

Overly-eager, he reeled the hook out of the water without the fish. Readying himself for his second attempt, Dooley thought he spotted an opaque, shadow-like spot in the water and casted towards it, landing the line a little bit past his target. It was stationary, until he snagged his hook back in, lodging the hook in the fish. This "snagging" is an illegal practice in many areas, but Holt didn't care for that law too much. The opaque spot grew larger as it appeared to rise in the water column to the surface, and revealed a much mightier foe than he had guessed. When it became more visible, Holt realized that what he thought was the whole fish, was merely the tip of a fin. It raised its slimy forefront, placing his eyes barely above the water as a crocodile does when hunting, concealing the rest of its mass. It had a strange shape, with its head bearing a similar shape to a giraffe, but mimicking the texture of a hippopotamus. Holt could blurrily make out some of the rest of its body, which was lengthy like a large snake, but also having a hierarchy of fins. It had beige skin with speckled navy running the course of its body. It was a leviathan of sorts.

Gripping the new rod tightly, he refused to let go when the Bear Lake Monster tugged him off of the icy shore and into the paralyzing water. As he was being dragged under, all he could think was how impressed he was that the thick fishing line had not broken. He began to brainstorm how to save his rod and cut the line, but the water pushing against him was too much to handle. It hadn't been but a few seconds, until his joints began freezing up. The monster spun around and came towards Holt with its jaws open, showcasing its teeth, which were small, and sharp like a surgeon's scalpel. The line then exhibited enough slack for Holt to stretch out an arm's length of it, which he held outward as a matador does to a bull. The leviathan was swimming furiously towards him, and Holt generated enough movement to elegantly evade the monster's bite, and simultaneously place the line in its mouth.

Not only did the line not break when facing the impact of a perpendicular collision from the aquatic beast, it forced Holt's body overtop of the monster onto its back. He was bare-back riding the The Bear Lake Monster, with the fishing line in his hands as its bridle, and his legs locked around the meeting of its neck and backside. He attempted to steer the monster with the line controlling its head, and motivated it to move towards the shore. Refusing to be tamed, the ancient beast fiercely raced to the shore at speeds rivaling the 21st century car. When it neared the lake's surface, it used its colossal fins to immediately stop its body, launching Holt through the air like a rock from a catapult. Somersaulting all the way to the boar and the campfire, his finger's were still enclosed around the fishing line.

"And that was the great force of inertia," he said to himself.

"I see you learned to flop like a fish when you were under there," the pig said. "That was a nice landing."

157

He pulled the fishing pole in from the line in his hands, and proceeded to curl up near the fire so as not to die from the cold.

———————

The crunchy snow sounded like a snare drum under their footsteps. As they walked into the city limits of Driggs, Idaho, Holt looked in his journal for directions to the hot air balloon maker. He saw an old wooden sign with the name "Montgolfier"[104] written on it, and continued down the curvy dirt path to a house of cobblestone. The grand Teton Mountains were looking over the home as if they were its protectors. All the houses in the region demonstrated a close relationship with nature, hiding in the rolling meadows, with trees scattered about, as if they were sprinkled on the landscape from above.

Holt walked around the back of the house, and witnessed both an old man and young boy standing in tandem next to a meandering spring. Steam was rising from its water, while the young man was holding some sort of fabric over it and periodically letting go. The fabric would briefly lift off of the ground and come crashing back down. The boy looked up at the old man and told him that there was still too much condensation. The old man turned to bring the material back inside, and saw Holt standing there watching their experiment.

"Can I help you?" His British accent preceded his appearance.

"Sorry to sneak up on you there…are you Mr. Montgolfier?"

———————

[104] Joseph-Michel Montgolfier and his brother, Jacques-Étienne Montgolfier, invented the Hot Air Balloon, and were responsible for the very first piloted ascent from land by humans (1783).

"No," said the old man. "I am merely an employee. That is Mr. Montgolfier." He pointed to the boy, and continued back to the house.

"I'm busy right now. Schedule a time with my secretary," the boy said with his back turned, still deep in thought about the steam. Mr. Montgolfier spoke in a child-like voice, yet in an orotund, matter-of-fact manner.

"Have you considered using diamond as a material for your project?" asked Holt.

"Why no, I guess I haven't.. How are you so sure of what I'm doing?" asked Mr. Montgolfier.

"Well, from your legacy and from what I just witnessed, it seems obvious you are experimenting with steam as a source of lift for hot air balloons."

"You're quite right."

The boy turned around and revealed his baby face to Holt Dooley, and extended his hand upwards to him. Now, Mr. Montgolfier would be tall enough to get onto a bar stool, but in doing so his legs would dangle awfully high from it. He was only about a decade old, and if he were still in school, he would have been the shortest in his class. He dropped out of school and got his GED, as he felt it was a waste of time.

Holt shared with the boy his desperate situation, and asked if he could "get a lift" to Oregon. Mr. Montgolfier, pompously told him that he was feeling generous, and that they would leave after he finished his new solar-balloon prototype in a couple days. It would be the first big test flight. Holt happily decided to camp outside of his house in preparation for the journey.

The night time came in peace, and the soothing rippling of the stream made for easy sleeping, but Holt wasn't relaxed. A bizarre thought plagued his mind. He was uncomfortable with the old man. Perhaps it was that he got no introduction, or perhaps it was the British accent. However, his paranoia spurred him to action. He tacitly unzipped the insulating bag enveloping him, and carefully lifted one leg out, then the next, not waking the pig. He stepped on the sides of his feet, and attempted to keep down the sound of the brittle snow. Peering into a slim window, Dooley saw the old man standing in the kitchen, under the cover of darkness. There was a light illuminating the side of his face from a cell phone, and Holt snuck around to a closer window, where he might hear some of the old man's muted whispers and learn his motives.

"The one you were asking about...he is here," the old man said, "Sorry, I only just now was able to call. Do I still get the reward? He is just sleeping outside of Mr. Montgolfier's estate."

Holt's displeasure was shown in his grimace, and his fast trot over to a large workshop where the prototype was located. He pulled up the garage door to find Mr. Montgolfier in an oversized mechanic's suit, and a welding mask. He was working on the solar aircraft at nearly 2:00 AM, and humming tunes through his mask.

"What are you doing up so late?" Montgolfier asked.

Holt explained that the secretary was a "Benedict Arnold" [105] and that it was fitting considering his British accent. He told the boy that federal officers would be there in minutes and he needed to

---

[105] One of the most famous traitors in history, with his name becoming a synonym for betrayal during the Revolutionary war, when he attempted to give over his American troops to the British. After his plan was uncovered, he fled to the British and became a general, fighting against the same soldiers he once commanded.

fly out as soon as possible. The boy reluctantly agreed to Holt's proposal and began stuffing a gobag. When all his quirky items were in, he wrote a quick note that read "You're fired," presumably for the old man. Holt didn't completely understand the generosity of the child, how he was willing to jump into an adventure so easily, but he did gather that he was tired of his current life, and especially his bothersome secretary.

The prototype hot air balloon was a large black mass that worked based on solar radiation. As it lay deflated in the shop, it resembled a black hole.

"Are we using the solar balloon because it is winter time?" Holt asked the boy.

"Yes, it might be too cold to rely on propane for this trip," said Mr. Montgolfier.

"So, we are doubling efficiency by the black material absorbing all of the sunlight that the snow is reflecting. Smart." replied Holt.

"And snow reflects up to 90 percent of UV radiation."

Holt gathered his belongings and told the boar and Sherman to ready themselves, while Mr. Montgolfier inflated the balloon. After twiddling his driftwood piece in deep thought, he replaced it with his golden-plated horseshoe, and preemptively put his bag in the hot air balloon basket. He figured the government officers would be after him any minute, and the balloon wasn't ready. He devised a plan, utilizing the reflective snow, to buy him some time.

Borrowing materials from Mr. Montgolfier, Dooley managed to swiftly make a promising trap to distract the officers. He had a mix of potassium perchlorate, magnesium, and aluminum, which he compiled into a makeshift flashbang. His idea was to lead the officers up a small forested hill, away from the balloon, and flashbang them, while he sledded down to safety. It would only save them a couple of minutes at a maximum, but that was all they needed until the balloon would be ready to launch.

Holt ran up the hill and loosely pulled back some young tree branches and locked them into place behind the thicket. He was fashioning an easy pathway for himself, and a more difficult path for the officers when he would release the branches as he ran. He wrapped a string around a lighter he set in place, which would hopefully light the short fuse he made for the flashbang. He readied his toboggan at the top of the hill along with the string he could pull before his descent. Everything was in place.

As he came back down, he heard the screeching tires of the federal officers' car right on que. Humorously, he took his place at the bottom of the hill, in the same way a track runner does before the gunshot, goosebumps and all. As they slammed their doors and came sprinting after him, he bolted up the hill, leaving them in the dust. He was hoping for a *Tom & Jerry* esque chase scene, but it didn't quite go as expected. Dooley was in fact, in incredible physical shape from traveling on foot so much. He made it through his path and to the sled, where he pulled the string to ignite the makeshift flashbang. However, upon diving down the snow laden hill, he saw that the officers had not followed him through the wooded thicket, but had barely made it to the top of the hill. They turned to chase him downward, as the flashbang blasted through the woods and caused them to pause in their tracks. They both flattened to the ground instinctively, in case Holt had recruited a shooter on his team, and watched as he climbed into a hot air balloon. He was relieved to not have to use his horseshoe again.

"Blast off!" said the boar, as they took off to the clouds.

The officer with the mustache pulled his sidearm and put a few small holes in the balloon's canvas before they were out of sight. He pulled out his phone and, spurting out a few numbers as coordinates, requested air support to follow the hot air balloon. After a frustrated argument with each other, the officers ran back to their car and sped off.

Now, a hot air balloon can withstand a few gunshots, but they certainly weren't equipped enough to take on a chopper. Unwittingly, Mr. Montgolfier proclaimed victory over the officers and cozied up to the pig and Private Sherman, as Dooley learned to "steer" the balloon. Hot air balloons don't regularly have a mechanism for changing lateral direction, so they typically rely on riding wind currents to get to their destination. On the other hand, they are equipped with a means of propulsion upwards, which is the basis of their travel, by changing altitude depending on the desired wind direction. Mr. Montgolfier's prototype was different though, their basket had a revolving extendable umbrella of sorts, which would catch the oncoming air and produce drag wherever they needed to utilize it.

Usually, the inner confines of one's feelings and personal experiences seem to be locked in a vault in their head, until they trust someone enough to give them the combination. *Unusually,* Mr. Montgolfier was ready to talk about his life. It was as if this adventure was the new beginning he needed, to quite literally, rise above his past. He explained to Holt that his parents had died in a hot air balloon crash, and left their riches to him, their only heir. To make matters worse, the treacherous old man was an employee of the Montgolfier company, who continued leeching his dead parents' money, by claiming he was watching over young Montgolfier and his new wealth. You see, he was not yet old enough to legally be responsible for it. Yet, he did take the responsibility upon himself to develop safer means of air travel, to honor his father and mother.

Concurrently, in Utah, Chase Griffith had tracked Holt's trail to Logan, partially by means of the elk figurine, and partially by his unwavering luck. The witch was eagerly watching through her reptile's scale, both the lucky fumbling of Griff, and the meticulous movements of Dooley. She had a growing concern that the "show" as she called it, was going to end too soon, and worried it would be cancelled before the desired climax. She was on the edge of her seat as Holt strolled into Driggs Idaho, not realizing the mistake he made by planning a route on the computer and leading the feds there a week before him.

It seemed her convictions had shifted. She used to be disciplined enough to keep away from being too directly involved, but now, with Holt having an undesirable outcome, her sympathy outweighed her restraint. And troublesomely, there are rules against this kind of act. This intervening into the *regular* human world[106] without proper clearance was a criminal act in her own circles. Knowing this, she still saddled her broom and flew to Logan, to get Griff, and ultimately to help Holt escape the federal officers if needed.

Navigating the winter air and precipitation, she flew into the city of Logan. She asked around for anywhere in town that might sell doughnuts, as she had discovered this to be the fastest way to find Griff -- maybe even quicker than just checking his location, she wagered. However, it took three attempts. After checking *Johnny*

---

[106] Again, some interesting language providing possible insight to us and our current situation.

O's Spudnuts, and then *Shaffer House Bakery,* she finally found him in *The Junction* on Utah State's campus. At first sight, rather than a regular social greeting, Griff led with telling her that he can get as many doughnuts there as he wanted for the small fee of 10 dollars. He believed it to be heaven, and she couldn't care less.

They left in a jiff, with Griffith significantly weighing down the back end of the broom, but not enough to stop them from flying. The broom appeared as if it was buoyant in water, and their movements on top of it displaced the atmosphere with their hanging limbs. He held around her waist like the second rider on a motorcycle would.

As they hovered over Mr. Montgolfier's estate, they spotted the wooded thicket adjacent to it, and decided that would be the best spot to conceal their landing. Nearing the ground, they watched a car abruptly pull up, and Holt ready himself. They hid in the brushes, just out of sight, watching to see if they needed to help Holt.

"How good are you at fighting?" Rosaline whispered.

"I tag criminals for a living. Of course I'm good at fighting. Holt wouldn't stand a chance against me," he said confidently.

"Not Holt, dummy! Those guys," she said, pointing to the officers as they slammed their car doors.

"You're suggesting I attack some secret agent looking guys?! I'd be wanted just as much as Holt. Not a chance in.."

"If you don't help, I'll report you for impersonating an officer," Rosie said, with a wink.

"Impersonating?!"

"Shh! They are coming this way," she whispered.

Holt rushed up the hill and ran right past them without noticing, and onto his sled, which was within just thirty feet of them. Holt pulled the string, setting off a flashbang close to where they were squatting. The witch and Griff were dazed and holding their heads as if the explosion truly endangered them. Possibly the most damage that it did was to their ear drums. As soon as they gathered their hazy vision, they could see Holt, hopping into the hot air balloon basket and making his escape. As the officer with a mustache pulled his sidearm, the witch threw a rock that barely budged the officer, making him think his partner hit him. He screamed at his partner and they both were confused and annoyed at each other. They ran back to their car while the witch looked at Griff for an affirmation of their victory.

"What on earth were you thinking, throwing a rock? Could you not have just used a wand to make him bad at shooting?"

"Holt is so smart isn't he? He must have formulated that plan on a minute's notice!" The witch's face lit up.

"Are you kidding me? He is *not* smart. He literally could have just hid in the brush or something. That 'plan' was useless," said Griff. "And it's not like they're done with him, they are probably calling in reinforcements as we speak."

The two plotted their next move, and Griff wasn't sure he wanted to even work for her anymore. He reluctantly told her his thoughts, and that they should probably just go back home. Rosaline was unhappy, of course, and after realizing that blackmailing him wouldn't help much, she used a "hail mary" play. She told Griffith that she would grant him super powers, and that she would magically make sure he wouldn't get in trouble. She was a witch, after all.

"Here's the deal, you are going to be a man of your word, finish this job, and I will make a personal guarantee that nothing is going to happen to you. When you do, you'll be rich."

"You promise?" he asked, hopeful.

"Cross my fingers,[107] hope to die," she replied.

Apparently, this was enough confirmation for Griff, because they got back on her broom and followed Holt from a good distance. It wasn't long until they heard the sound of a helicopter, coming in to intercept Holt. Presumably, the reason they brought a large helicopter wasn't to injure Holt, but to pressure the air balloon back down to the ground, where they would arrest Dooley and fly him away. Being quite a bit ahead, Holt's crew was still out of earshot.

"They called in a bird?!" Griff shouted.

"Remember what we talked about? I'm going to make you invincible. You're going to get in the cockpit and stop them," she exclaimed.

"And nothing bad can happen to me, right?"

"Right."

She could not in fact grant Griffith invincibility at this time, as she didn't have a spell for that memorized, and maybe didn't even have a spell at all. Anyway, her bluff proved effective to Griff, as he was radiating false courage. The helicopter unknowingly approached them from the rear, and the broomstick aeronaughts held their ground...or rather, airspace. The pilots of the helicopter were astonished, decelerating as they saw what appeared to be just

---

[107] Doesn't the phrase go "cross my heart"?

a man sitting on thin air, flying forward. They could not see the witch or her broom.

She guided it underneath the helicopter, where Griff climbed up the landing skids, to the door. Dauntlessly, he put his sanguine face in the window and banged on it with his fist. Frightened, the main pilot's hand tweaked the steering, almost causing Griff to fall to his death, unless saved by the witch at standby. They stabilized the aircraft, and the investigator, still believing he was invincible, was not worried, but motioned to the pilots to let him in.

The co-pilot, to his own misfortune, must have believed he was helping someone in trouble and decided to help Griff inside. Promptly escalating to violence, Griffith had no other plan than an attempted punch directed at the co-pilot. After having easily dodged the punch, the helicopter started to experience some turbulence, causing him to stumble backwards and dislodge his energy drink beverage onto the control panel.

"Just as planned," stated Griffith unironically.

The pilot, assuming the intruder had the upper hand, resorted to drastic aerial maneuvers, in order to knock the intruder around, so as to incapacitate him. In doing so, the co-pilot slammed his head on presumably the ceiling or the ground, knocking him out. The pilot looked back at Griff, who was laying next to his comrade, with his eyes shut as well. Turning on the autopilot feature, he went back to cuff Griffith in place.

"Surprise Attack!" Griff yelled, as he swept the pilot's ankles out from under him, in the same way a lumberjack would to a large timber. The pilot dropped the handcuffs in the process, and Griff snagged them up just as fast as they fell. With brute force, he locked the pilot's hand to the frame of the helicopter, where he could not reach the controls.

After Griff's victory he prepared himself to jump out the door. The pilot pleaded with him to let him at least steer the helicopter to safety, to which he replied that he wouldn't fall for a trick like that, since he was aware of the autopilot feature. Griff hucked his body out of the aircraft, leaving its fate in the unconscious co-pilot's hands. The witch darted after him, and managed to get Griffith to hold on to the broom with his hands. In the pull-up position, he told her that he may just let go since his muscles were feeling tired, and she revealed that he was not invincible. After he had a panic episode of pulling himself up, she lied and told him that he had just ran out of invincible juice, and they needed to go back and re-group at the ground. Griff really was not the brightest self-proclaimed detective.

"It's funny, I don't remember drinking any juice..unless..you must have slipped it in at The Junction! That's what I call retrospective observance. A detective skill," he said.

She told him that she could not in fact protect his reputation and himself from the consequences of his actions until after he had completed the job of spying on Holt for her. He was not excited about being Holt's "baby-sitter" as he called it, but he agreed to see it through. He told her that her obsession with Holt was unhealthy, unless of course she was going to eat him, as he assumed eating people was nutritious for witches. Blushing, she laughed and told Griff that witches don't eat adults. She also concluded that Griff had managed to acquire a concussion.

Meanwhile, Holt believed he saw two people flying on a broom in the distance, but they flew out of sight before he could make out any details. He almost decided to wake up the rest of the hot air balloon crew, but being night time, he figured he might have just been seeing things again.

Mr.
Montgolfier

CHAPTER 11

(Snow Became a Waterfall)

Holt Dooley was exhausted. There are some things that one gets used to when ditching the conveniences of everyday American life, and there are some things that are more difficult to normalize. He categorized being hunted by the federal government in the latter. He was actually so tired that he traded his fierce determination of saving his wife, for a bit of sleep. This doesn't sound like such a grievous mistake, but when you are piloting a mildly tattered hot air balloon prototype with no prior experience and you fall asleep, then you lose your way.

Mr. Montgolfier woke up Holt, yelled at him for his complacency, and asked him where he thought they were. The pig confidently said Oregon, whereas Holt disagreed entirely.

"Actually, I believe these are the Cabinet mountains below us. We are in Montana."

Hearing an assortment of complaints from the boy, snorts from the pig, and nothing from Private Sherman, Dooley did his best to calm them down as they got their bearings. Holt spotted a snow golem below walking next to what Holt called a lava hound. He noted that it was a peculiar sighting, as the two species don't typically live in harmony. [108] The radio, with its impeccable timing, started playing the song "Christmas Island" by Lake.

The bullet holes in the balloon had grown overnight, with the wind currents ripping the material. Deeming it unsafe to continue, they began their descent to a clearing in the mountains of Libby, Montana. A meadow exists near Leigh Lake, a glacier-made waterbody that rivals views of the United States' national parks. It was here that the balloon landed in the snow, like one leaping into bed after a hard day's work.

As the black canvas of the solar balloon laid lazily on the ground, Mr. Montgolfier was already planning its repairs and his way back home. Holt, feeling somewhat guilty of leaving an unaccompanied youngster to fend for himself all the way back to Southern Idaho, invited him to continue the journey to Oregon along with the rest of his gang. Mongolfier said he would consider the offer, and have his answer before they left their new campsite.

Just as a grand finale comes at the end of the show, a blizzard arrived to celebrate the end of winter. The wind howled and rattled the balloon canvas, which they were using as a tarp over their shelter. Snow would commonly creep in, just to melt with the heat of their bodies. They were staying warm by sleeping on a layer of dirt placed over the hot coals of a fire they made upon landing.

Mr. Montgolfier had trouble sleeping due to Holt, endlessly explaining the workings of the world to his plant. Rather than being resentful, the wise child decided to join the conversation to tire Holt out more quickly.

---

[108] Seemingly an allusion to the television show *Adventure Time*

"What do you make of this blizzard?" he asked Holt.

"Well, the moon did have a rather large ring around it tonight, so it was expected."

"What do you mean?"

"When there is a halo around the moon, it will rain or snow soon," Holt replied.[109]

Assuredly, Mr. Montgolfier was both intellectual and knowledgeable, but he was unfamiliar with a large portion of the insight that Holt harbored. It fascinated him, and kept him asking Holt questions, over and over. Everyone Dooley met seemed to do this. He was like a walking encyclopedia, but with more of the charm of an adventure fiction book. He talked about the grizzly bears and other fauna of the area, then talked about the flora, and how the Pasqueflower is the first one to bloom and welcome in the springtime. Finally, his words came to a halt, and the group fell asleep.

Mr. Montgolfier dreamed about his parents, and realizing that he had no one to go home to, decided to stay with Holt. He woke up to the pig and the plant sleeping still as statues, and Holt nowhere to be found. He crawled out of the shelter to the blinding sunlight, ultimately revealing a humorous sight. A hundred yards off, Holt had torn the canvas of the hot air balloon and fashioned it onto some branches, making a massive fan. He was swinging it back and forth, keeping something in the air.

"What are you doing, you stupid oaf?! How am I supposed to fly back home now?" screamed the angry little boy.

---

[109] Weather lore, found throughout many sources, including the *Farmer's Almanac*

"Can't talk, concentrating," said Dooley.

"You better talk!" said Mr. Montgolfier, sprinting full force toward him.

"Hang on, this is important. I'm going to waft this snowflake all the way down to town and figure out a way to capture it."

Mr. Montgolfier looked up at the colossal snowflake, which measured over 16 inches long. Pleasantly surprised, he told Holt that if he'd known it was a pursuit to further the world's scientific knowledge, then he would never have been upset. He also insisted that Holt just try to capture the snowflake on the canvas, rather than waft it all the way to a town and risk its destruction. Holt was feeling tired, and considered that the odds were actually higher he would unintentionally damage it. He decided to let the snowflake fall onto his fan, which only mildly damaged it.

They woke up the pig in a hurry, and rushed for miles down trails, to the nearest town of Libby, Montana. They followed a creek, flowing from the glacier lake, and Holt decided he was fine with drinking from it, whereas Mr. Montgolfier did not, warning of microbes. Dooley stated he was fully aware of the risk, and had come to terms with it over his journey. He picked and ate rose hips as he saw them, passing some back to the boy, who passed them back to the pig, who ate them happily.

Montgolfier's eyebrow raised [110] at Holt yet again, for answering Private Sherman's supposed question about the rose hips. Holt explained that it wasn't odd for him to eat these, as they weren't very closely related to Sherman's own species of plant. He went on to describe scientific nomenclature, and how in the list of

---

[110] It seems that Mr. Montgolfier doesn't hear Private Sherman speaking.

kingdom, phylum, class, order, family, genus, and species, Private Sherman differed from roses all the way up at the phylum which is often alternatively called "division" when referring to plants.

"The rose family is of the Magnoliophyta division, whereas the redwood is of the Pinophyta," Dooley clarified.

"Where did you learn all of this information?" asked the pig.

"Hamlet, why are you even wondering, it's not like you're going to get your dirty hooves on a keyboard to research anything," Holt joked. "But as for you, Mr. Montgolfier, there is a great resource called 'PlantSnap' that you can access to help you start identifying plants."

He glanced behind him to see the boy typing it into his phone. Disheartened, he yelled his typical profanity, and plucked the phone from him and launched it as far as he could into the woods. He couldn't believe after telling the boy of his backstory, that he would be dumb enough to bring along a trackable piece of technology. He compared it to a deer being hunted, and running toward the hunter, rather than away. Mr. Montgolfier, being only around a decade old, still understood the ramifications of his actions and started crying.

Holt Dooley was experienced with many things, but not dealing with children. He grew tremendously uncomfortable, and immediately rummaged through the snow to find the phone. He gave it back to the kid and squatted down in an attempt to soothe him.

"I'm not mad. I was just surprised, that's all..." he started, "I'll get this sorted out and get the feds back off of my trail if they aren't already waiting for us in the town."

Mr. Montgolfier started crying harder, and Holt didn't know how to console him, so he told the boy he could ride to town on the boar. The pig was unhappy with the deal, but reluctantly allowed Holt to remove the plant from his back and exchange it with the kid. Holt continued his descent into Libby, with Private Sherman in his hands. Finding a library right away, he strutted over to the librarian and laid his canvas, displaying the snowflake, down on the counter. He told her that the world record size was 15 inches, and he believed that he found the successor to its title. She didn't bat an eye, but rather told him not to talk so loudly. Disgusted with her ignorance, he strolled around the library for a way to safeguard it. He took some super glue and preserved its icy crystals in place.[111] He pulled an old map display directly off of the wall, and snuggly fit the snowflake and canvas inside the frame. In a font that looked like an engraving, he typed and printed an inscription stating that it was "The World's Largest Snowflake" at approximately 16 inches, and that it was donated by Chase Griffith. To this day I am not entirely sure why he included the last part.

He then began to work on the computer, to change the location of the phone and divert the feds. On the screen a pop up image appeared of a witch riding a broom. Holt looked for the "x" to click out of the window, but the 8-bit witch dropped a letter from her pouch, and flew off-screen anyway. The letter tossed and turned like samara seed[112] in flight and then fell off-screen as well. Directly afterwards, the librarian asked if there was someone by the name of Holt Dooley there, and delivered a paper from the printer to him. Being the only other person there, he sarcastically told her it must be someone else, and took the note anyway. Holt eyeballed it in suspicion, and then opened it to reveal a message that read "It

---

[111] This preservation method actually works, I checked.

[112] Fruit of the maple tree

would benefit you not to change the phone's location from your present town."

"Baba Unaka," he said to himself.

He was unsure whether to trust her, or to believe that she was upset from him stealing the elk hide map, so to play it safe, he formulated a new plan. Rather than changing the phone's location *from* Libby, he decided to change it *to* Libby, in a way that would allow the feds to know he did in fact change it. This, he thought, would both fulfill the requirement of the witch's memo, as well as his own instinct. He hoped it would stir the pot enough to keep them off of his trail. However, he was now concerned that the witch was watching him, and analyzed her as a threat. His journey had provided him with many memories and acquaintances, so organizing his thoughts wasn't necessarily an easy task. Yet, he pulled out the decorated mental file of Rosie and placed it on top of his desk -- I'm not sure if that metaphor conveyed the message I was trying to send. What I mean is that even though Holt had encountered a lot of wacky stuff at this point, Rosie was so memorable to him that it was easy to recall her and assess her as a threat. Is that better? Anyway:

He came outside to the pig bucking like a horse trying to knock off Mr. Montgolfier.

"Calm down Hamlet, what's wrong?" asked Dooley.

"He kept pushing the radio buttons after I asked him not to," the pig replied.

Mr. Montgolfier attempted it again, re-agitating the pig who circled around and accidentally crashed into the plant, who was sitting on the ground. It's hoove cracked the little bonsai's pot, sending Holt into a fury. He slapped the pig on the back with his

177

hand, and forcibly pulled the kid off. Gathering up some of the pot's pieces, he went back into the library and used the superglue to fix it.

"This should hold him for now, let's get back on the road," he sighed.

"Private Sherman, always was his favorite, he didn't even check to see if I sprained my foot." The pig whispered to the kid.

"He is trying not to get too attached to you in case he runs out of food," Mr. Montgolfier said, without even hearing the pig's complaining.

Night fell around 4:00 PM, where Holt Dooley and the gang decided to rest by the Goat River, in Troy, Montana. Holt briefly bathed in the frigid water, the first time he had done this since the Bear Lake Monster tugged him in unwillingly. This time he sat voluntarily, and let the heat retreat from his skin to the innermost parts of his body by his own accord. As his body was partially suspended, his fingers started to lose their dexterity. He felt the mostly round shaped gravel beneath him, and the slipperiness that existed due to the "aquatic plant biomass," he later wrote. Before he felt like leaving, his fingers stumbled upon a sharper object in the water. As he brought it close to his eyes for inspection, he hoped it was a Native American artifact, and charged to the light of the campfire to confirm. Mr. Montgolfier praised Holt's ability to make fire in cold conditions, and Holt brushed it off. Furthermore, Dooley did apologize for his anger toward him and the pig, and told the kid he was happy to travel alongside them. He also asked the pig if his hoof was okay.

They asked why he was looking at the rock he brought back from the water, and he confidently swore it to be the head of a Native American stone axe. He said that he wasn't sure of what tribe the territory belonged to, but he was sure of its authenticity. Mr. Montgolfier was shocked by the odds that he had just found the world's largest snowflake, and then a real artifact, and slightly questioned how accurate he could be. Holt told him that everyone has the ability to observe, but few people utilize it on a deeper scale than necessary. He claimed this was the reason he encountered extraordinary events in his travels while others remain oblivious.[113] Furthermore, Holt shared the functionality of the projectile-point authenticity system, and in such detail, displayed how the sharp ends of his artifact were knapped into shape. At his exhausting end point, his information was so comprehensive that novice critics would be positively assured. The group was already asleep before he was done excitedly spilling his thoughts.

The next morning, Dooley curled his bag upwards, slightly putting a strain on his arm muscles. His bag had grown heavy from all the items he had gathered in his excursions. Rather than seeing the extra weight as burdensome, he saw it as an opportunity to train his strength and endurance.

"You know what this adventure reminds me of?" Holt asked his friends.

"*Friends* the sitcom?" the pig replied.

"Um...no."

"The story of how *Captain Ahab* rounded up a dangerously fierce crew to hunt down *Moby Dick*?" asked Mr. Montgolfier.

---

[113] From an onlooker's perspective, this doesn't appear to be the entire reason Holt can "observe" as he called it

"That's a little closer, with the exception that I'm not looking to kill any whales... or anything for that matter." Holt scratched his head.

After Private Sherman ostensibly mentioned *Lord of the Rings*, Holt was tired of their guesses and told them that the question was actually rhetorical. He didn't expect them to correctly guess the piece of history he was about to unveil to them, as he wouldn't have even brought the subject up if he didn't think he was going to be the one to teach it to them.

"There was a movie that came out a long while ago entitled *"The Revenant."* It was based on a real man, Hugh Glass, and his troubles in the early 1800s. The film shot a scene wherein his character floated the Kootenai River and down the falls. That is what reminded me, because it was filmed just off the highway that we traveled past."

"Why didn't we go see the falls?" asked Mr. Montgolfier.

"I was distracted by your weeping," said Holt, rolling his eyes. "Anyway, Hugh Glass experienced a lot of things that nobody believed, still to this day. It's funny, I found myself doubting some of his tall tales, like surviving a grizzly bear mauling, and dragging his broken leg across a hundred miles, evading the Native Americans and others who wanted to kill him, and so on. But I believe we have experienced even more than him."

"Not Mr. Montgolfier, he's only been here for one scene and it wasn't even that exciting," argued the pig.

"Please stop with the interruptions. I mean to say, surely my wife won't believe a word I say when I explain all these events...but I find some comfort in sharing them with you all. If I had nobody to share these memories with, I might wonder if I would go mad."

The bonsai brought an idea to Holt, reminding him of his heavy pack, and all the items that could act as evidence of his adventures. He hoped that they would hold weight in proving his stories, rather than just weight on his muscles.

It wasn't long until the group progressed from Montana, into the northern border of Idaho, near Canada. The first town they came across ended up being Holt's favorite place on the entirety of his journey. It was the epitome of charming. It was picturesque. It had managed to obtain some major benefits of a city, but with a mere population of twenty-five hundred people. One of the northernmost cities in the lower forty-eight states, it was named after the old ferry that used to run across the Kootenai River. Not to beat a dead horse, but one of the last reasons Holt loved it so greatly was that it was the gateway to three unique mountain ranges, which allowed it to harbor some of the last remaining populations of a few endangered american species, namely the woodland caribou.

"Mark my words my friends, I will move here, and live out the rest of my content life with my love. Accompany me if you will, but I will not live anywhere else."

He felt somewhat apologetic for the week he spent camping out there, but he had fallen in love once again. Of course to love a landscape is different than to love a human, but he was smitten. He decided to restrain from divulging the name of this town to anyone else, in hopes that his love wouldn't be found by others. It is true that there does exist some contagious sense of ownership to this town. I should know, I do currently live here after all.[114] And for that same selfish reason, I keep its name secret from you, and sacred to me.

Holt Dooley splurged from his poor pockets on the town's luxuries every day he was there. He went to his newly favorite book shop, where a black cat roamed through the bookshelves freely, and purchased a work about an explorer, David Thompson. He bought some of the world's best sandwiches from an Amish bakery, and then devoured burritos from a restaurant that he wrote in his journal made his "soul shine". He slowly enjoyed his drinks in the most creative and eclectic atmosphere imaginable in a downtown coffee shop, where locals go to interact with old friends, or to lonelily watch others do so. He felt that anything under the sun could happen there. He filled up the pages of his journal on the second floor, where he exchanged information with strangers to learn where to sightsee iconic hikes of the area.

After seeing one of these immaculate sites, he decided it was too overwhelmingly beautiful, not to share the experiences with his wife, reminding him to take his leave. Specifically he wanted to undergo with her the novelty of seeing a grand scene for the first time, as this is a reflective occurrence of exceptional proportions. He had used up a first-time hike on a wondrous waterfall, but was still a virgin to the many other falls and overlooks in the area. Those scenes he desired to share as a romanticist, since he did view the landscape like a painting of this genre. And of course, who only might share in romanticism than his love interest.

---

[114] I think you will agree that this is a massive clue to the identity of the narrator.

CHAPTER 12

(The Levelheaded Shift)

From the great and nameless town of his dreams, he made his way south to yet another city of astounding natural elegance: Sandpoint, Idaho. Schweitzer Resort and Lake Pend Oreille are the recreational gems that contribute to the humble state's nickname. Similarly, a wine bar called "The Longshot" is a bastion of creativity that inspires the locals to be the best version of themselves, while Evans Brothers is an award winning coffee roasting shop that with warmth from a mug, enchants like a siren, the seafarers and the bundled up skiers alike. Lastly, I believe it would be an injustice if I didn't point out the Pack River General Store, in its culinary expertise, hidden in the backwoods. An epitaph to days past is framed on an old piece of cardboard, stating "Coins, guitar picks, and bullets" need to be removed from pockets before using the washer. Holt spoke very highly of these in his journal.

Dooley steadied himself after feeling the earth move in a small tremor.[115] Brushing it off, he took his time reading historical displays in a local museum, and was enthralled by one about the NAVY. One of the most prominent submarine testing locations in the U.S. was on the same lake he strolled alongside earlier. He felt as if he could happily waste time in the intelligent, bustling outdoor oriented community of Sandpoint, but was experiencing guilt for the leisure he wasted in the last town. He reminded himself that he was on a voyage to save his wife and continued on out of the museum, even whilst seeing a depiction of a submarine on the elkskin map, as well as another lake monster.

"I've already dealt with one of those anyway." He thought. "But a submarine... I sure would like to see that."

An idea sprung into his mind, and he was far too curious to ignore it. He bravely went back into the museum, and had the pig stage an attack on Mr. Montgolfier, where he could distract the elderly employees enough to not realize what he had stolen. Sure enough, he walked out of the museum with a real NAVY uniform in his bag, and retreated with his group to the woods that surrounded Sandpoint.

The uniform was a tad bit short on him, and he was a bit shaggy looking to be an officer of the military, but he figured his persuasive language was enough to convince anyone of doubts. He took off a few miles east to Hope, Idaho, where the submarine testing station was headquartered. He had read that the particular base was known for impeccable security, as the design of U.S. naval warcraft was a valuable secret commodity.

---

[115] When the earth begins to shift, tremors can sometimes be felt, which in the past have been used to try to predict larger earthquakes. That, I believe, is the symbolic meaning behind this detail.

With the utmost confidence, Holt Dooley arrived at the gates, which were adorned with barbed wire, like tensile across the entire perimeter. He was met by a clean cut guard, who's face gave way to skepticism. He called in on his walkie-talkie before even conversing with Holt, making his superiors aware of a "hobo with an obsolete NAVY uniform" engaging the premises. One officer, after reviewing an image of Holt in the security camera, vouched for him and told the guard to escort him into the building. The officer explained that he had purchased an old-timey singing telegram as a gag for the head engineer's birthday.

Holt was surprised at the ease by which he infiltrated their base, with an old uniform no less, and without even talking to anyone. The officer that vouched for him relieved the guard and brought Holt to the door that led to the head engineer's room, and debriefed him. He told Dooley that they were working on a new submarine design, but it was okay to interrupt. He encouraged him to burst through the door singing and doing his routine, but to direct it at the one in the biggest chair. Giving him a push on the back, Holt went through the doorway and the officer slammed the door shut behind him.

The group of engineers stared at Holt intently, and the head of them ridiculed Holt for his interruption, and then his appearance. Soon enough, the head engineer realized that Dooley was not actually an officer but some sort of gag for his birthday.

"Whatever you've got to do, get it over with," he said sternly.

Holt had pieced together his assumed role as that of an entertainer and began to sing the John Mayer classic, *"Walt Grace's Submarine Test, January 1967."* Trying his best at the second verse, a spider had repelled down from the ceiling and landed on his forehead. Terrified, Holt's singing became a ghoulish yell, as he rattled his head like a crazy man, swiping it with his backhand.

Not seeing the spider, the head engineer mistook this for some sort of odd denouement, where Holt's back handed swipe to his forehead, was an irreverent salute.

"I was never one for slapstick comedy, but you, solely with your looks may be laughable to someone. You may leave now, thank you."

Holt, mustered up his pride, and commented on the submarine blueprint he had seen on the engineers' table. His constructive criticism did not fare well with the head, who had just asked him to leave, and interrupted each of his explanations.

"Give me a quick chance to explain. Maybe I'll surprise you." Holt said.

"What could a buffoon like you provide to an engineering team like us. I'm sure you don't have the proper credentials, let alone a highschool, or even kindergarten diploma," the designer scorned, giving Holt the noticeable tell of nervousness on his skin.[116]

"I don't believe a piece of paper makes you more intelligent, more creative, or more capable than me... all of which are primary factors in a good engineer. Am I correct?"

"Alright then. Let's see you come up with something. What is your big shiny idea?" he said, putting Holt's creativity on the spot.

"Well... to start, maybe you could develop a more energy efficient submarine if it was designed based on using its own buoyancy as a primary means of propulsion. In the same way a plane uses gravity to glide through the air, a submarine could use its buoyancy to glide through the water."

---

[116] Goosebumps again?

"What do you think the ballast tanks[117] are for, numbskull?"

Holt began furiously drawing a design in his journal. In less than a minute, and amidst the insults of the engineering crew, Holt designed what he called a "corkscrew winged submarine". The journal page wasn't a complete constructive blueprint, but was rather in depth for the brief amount of time he spent. He tore the page out and gave it to the head engineer, who glanced at it, crumbled it and tossed it to the porcelain floor. Discouraged, Dooley left the station and rejoined his group. He was slightly humiliated and didn't share about the experience with Mr. Montgolfier, whom he feared, looked up to him. After they left, one of the lesser ranked engineers with a red mustache picked up Holt's paper, studied it, and kept it for himself. In the near future, this engineer would become known in his circles for "discovering" one of the greatest innovations in sub-nautical history.

"It lived up to its high security reputation," Holt said. "A spider landed on my head before I even had a chance to see a submarine."

"How'd they know you hate spiders?" asked the pig.

"Lucky guess, I suppose."

Further southbound, they reached another city, named Coeur D'Alene. Holt realized he had an affinity for this city as well, though it was larger than the last two. He began to realize that the different cities of Northern Idaho had a bewitching effect on him, almost like the lotus flowers had on *Odysseus*'s crew in *The Odyssey*. Holt termed it the "Syringa Effect" after the state flower. Dooley found himself journaling in the CDA Coffee company, about the city's wondrous innerworkings, until his elkhide map

---

[117] found between the submarine's inner and outer hulls, controls the submarines buoyancy

revealed something that broke his brief hiatus. It directed him toward the visitor center, and told him to converse with someone that looked like an old frontiersman.

Feeling the earth's second noticeable tremor in a short amount of time, Holt paused for a moment, but decided not to address it. He entered the modern architecture desiring to blend in as a visitor, and inquired about a bus route, train ride, or some faster means of transportation than walking. He didn't see a frontiersman, but the French-Canadian woman working at the desk did tip him off to some useful information. He learned the meaning behind some of the placenames in the area.[118] The reason there were so many French words, had relation to the Gallic trappers who settled the area long ago, who would trade furs and other materials with the Native Americans.

Dooley saw "Hell's Canyon Jet Boat Rides" on a brochure, and decided that the fastest way to travel inconspicuously might be by boat, down river. He took it, and on its miniature map, quickly plotted a course to the snake river, which he assumed was the fastest way to cover more ground southward.

"Maybe you would find a canoe more comfortable than a motorboat?" the lady asked. "My father has an antique canoe he's been trying to sell, and maybe you could make a good deal with him." She pulled a picture up on her computer of a *Craigslist* ad, with a wrinkly man named Honoré holding the even older looking canoe.

---

[118]Lake Pend Oreille, was named after the shell ornaments the Native Americans wore on their ears. Coeur D'Alene means "heart of an awl" and is how the French referred to the Native Americans in that area.

Holt recognized the man as the one from the elkskin map, and decided to take her up on the offer. She wrote down an address on the back of his brochure, and he left shortly after.

He knocked on a heavy oak door that displayed a nameplate with the inscription "Beaugrand". The man from the ad opened the door.

"Are you Honoré?" asked Holt.

"Yes, what is it?" His old voice trembled within a french accent.

"I wanted to inquire about the canoe."

Beaugrand turned around and went deeper into his home, and up to the second floor. Holt could hear it from outside: the hollow sound of the boat, clunking down each stair one by one, and then dragged carelessly through the house to the doorway, scraping his wooden floors.

"I must warn you," the man started, "this boat will absolutely fly."

"Figuratively, right? When you say 'absolutely', you are not intending literal connotations, correct?" Holt asked.

Old Beaugrand didn't give much assurance to Holt's clarification, but nodded in confirmation anyway.

"Well...alright...so how much again? I don't have a lot, but I can trade you this Native American artifact." Holt rustled through his bag and pulled it out.

"That is merely a rock," Beaugrand replied. "Fine, I'll take it." He snatched it from Holt and kicked the canoe out the door, rudely slamming it behind him.

"What a steal! He practically gave that away!" said the pig.

"I don't think so, Hamlet. Artifacts like the one we traded can go for high prices to the right buyer."

"But he did seem as if he wanted to get rid of it, Holt." said Mr. Montgolfier, hopping inside of the canoe and expecting to be dragged by Dooley.

"Well, maybe you all are right...which would confirm my suspicions. An author that passed away in the early 1900s wrote about a canoe, and he shared the same name as that old man."

"What is so suspicious about a canoe being fast?" the little redwood tree might have asked.

"Glad you asked, Private. When he said 'fly' he did mean it literally."

"What would prompt someone to get rid of a magical flying canoe?" asked Montgolfier.

"It's not magical. The *La Chasse-galerie...*" He wiped off the dust on the canoe's siding, uncovering its name. "As legend goes, a hunter made a deal with the devil to acquire this canoe."

Mr. Montgolfier was again impressed by Holt's knowledge of folktales that seemed obscure to him. He asked Dooley and the party why they weren't excited about flying around in a canoe, and Holt told him that he would not participate in the devil's deal. Upstairs, listening through the screen in his open-window Beaugrand replied to Holt's statement in a hushed murmur. "You will sooner or later, Holt Dooley."

The group had been traveling through a small patch of woods bordering Idaho and Washington for a while, and Holt was growing tired of towing the canoe through the woods. It was holding not only his belongings, but also Mr. Montgolfier who lazily rode along. This particular forest wasn't extraordinary by any measure, but was the last geographical mark from the biome of treed wilderness, to that of a sandy brushland wilderness. Additionally notable, they had just reached the top of Micah Peak, which had a small clearing, where a couple of old cell phone tower relics stood. These towers were becoming more antiquated with low orbit satellite technologies, and it seemed these hadn't been used in almost a decade. From bottom to top, the main tower was made into a graffiti sculpture,[119] with horned beasts from some other realm and also familiar animals colorfully sprayed over its bolts. The most prominent creature that he could make out though, was an eagle. Finding this of high interest, he compared it to petroglyphs he had seen along his travels. Side by side, adjacent to the towers, they took in the view of Liberty Lake in front of them, and Lake Coeur D'alene behind them.

"Why'd you choose to go directly over the mountain, rather than circumnavigate it?" Montgolfier asked.

"Yeah you do seem awfully worn out, Holt," said the pig.

Holt, spoke lightly, in between his hard inhaling and exhaling, "It's not uphill both ways, you know."

He further elaborated that the snow was getting sparse, and would only be harder to tug the canoe on dry ground. The higher elevation route was actually easier for him, and he could plot his future route by determining where the last remnants of snow still

---

[119] An important description, as it greatly resembles a totem pole. This has significance later in the story, you will find out.

persisted. He told them that soon enough they would enter a more arid region, which meant less resources. They decided to camp on the peak for the night and enjoy their last bit of time under the cover of canopy. They were going to be wide out in the open soon.

The next morning, a thick cumulonimbus cloud as grey as slate overcame them, and their campfire sizzled with the sprinkling that ensued. Holt didn't suspect the storm was ominous, and began to tell the bonsai redwood about differing types of clouds, explaining some basic meteorology. Interrupted by the clapping of lightning, Holt realized that they better pack up and retreat away from the cell phone towers. But the storm rolled in too quickly, like a bowling ball on the hardwood floor, and the towers were the pins. He had never felt a storm as powerful as this, shaking the ground below him like an earthquake. Dooley witnessed lightning reach out and touch the top of a tower, much like God touching Adam in *Michelangelo*'s famous painting. [120]

I must add to the story that I was shocked to witness this next part. Flashes of brightness whipped around like a flail, with a ball of lightning at its end. The bass-boosted beating of the thunder forced Mr. Montgolfier to plug his ears with his little fingers. Holt was clutching his driftwood piece with a grip, which if translated into a handshake, would send shivers down the recipient's spine.

As if Holt was watching a three-dimensional movie, an electric eagle burst through the graffiti and sent bolts of lightning his way.

---

[120] *The Creation of Adam*

The radio began to play its quite appropriate last song as a goodbye -- "The Lightning Strike" by Snow Patrol.[121]

"*Zapdos* is real?!" Mr. Montgolfier screamed.

"I'm afraid not.. I think this is a Thunderbird!" Holt yelled back.

"Holt, it's going to be okay," assured the pig. "Whatever happens, it will be alright."

Holt ignored the stammering of the pig, and directed his words to the flashing light. In an attempt to use his silver tongue to diffuse the situation, Holt failed to remember, silver is the greatest conductor of all the metals. When Its expansive wings flapped, it was clear the storm was in direct correlation with it. A stray bolt from the Thinderbird's beak clinged to Dooley like a magnet. He lit up like a neighborhood house on Christmas. As one does in the mere seconds before death, he felt time slow with its power surging through his veins. Rather than reminiscing, he stopped his flashback and began to think of the future and how he would escape. But he had not even fallen to the ground during this, nor were his clothes damaged. He did not feel pain anywhere except a burning sensation within his clenched fist, where his driftwood was. He opened it to see an ornate carving, banding the wood. It was so finely whittled, that he had to hold it inches from his eyes to even perceive that it reflected the Thunderbird's own image. He gazed into the eyes of the great bird of lore, and lost something. I cannot entirely say what. Yet Holt's mind and the Thunderbird's

---

[121] The narrator mentions the song to be appropriate. I thought I would include this stanza in its relevance:
What if this storm ends?
And I don't see you
As you are now
Ever again

195

were locked in sync for a brief moment in time, and he wasn't the same.

The clouds began to fade away, and the bird dissipated, returning to the realm it came from. Holt could no longer hear the radio.

"Are you guys alright?!" Holt yelled.

"You're the one who just got struck by lightning!" said Montgolfier.

"Yeah, I don't entirely understand what happened, but I think it was trying to tell me something. Check this out," he said, holding up the driftwood to the group. "What do you make of that, Hamlet? Bizarre right?"

The boar looked up at him, and oinked as any regular pig would. Holt squatted down to meet it at eye level, and concerningly laid his hand on its head.

"Hamlet? What's wrong?"

The blank glare in its eyes proved worrisome to Holt. He told Montgolfier to ready the canoe and that they were going to find a veterinarian in Spokane. Pulling the bonsai off of the pig, and fastening it down into the canoe, he got the impression that it was being relatively silent as well.

"Sherman, please tell me you're just being bashful again…" He glanced over its tiny branches and inquired again, "Private? Say something! Please, I order you to say something!" His hoarse words alerted Montgolfier of Holt's suffering status.

He glanced at Mr. Montgolfier as if the boy would be able to fix the situation, and asked what happened. Claiming not to know, the boy said that the only one who got hit by the lighting was Holt himself. Dooley's hands covered his face as he knelt to the ground hoping that if he shut out all light to his closed eyes, no distraction could keep him from thinking through the situation.

"Maybe being shocked by the tower took away your ability to communicate with them. You know I never could hear them myself," said the boy.

"What do you mean you couldn't hear them? I heard you reply to the pig's insults many times. Private Sherman is a different story, nobody can hear him, but what do you mean?" Holt seemed like he was about to break down and weep.

"I don't know Holt, you must have dreamed that or something, if I replied to the pig, I never meant to."

Holt was so taken back by his comment, that he didn't know what else to say. He figured that if Mr. Montgolfier was right, and he did lose his ability to communicate with them, then at least they were healthy and alright. At least the only damage done, was to himself. He studied his piece of driftwood, as the pig came up to stand by his side. He was feeling downcast, but comforted by the boar's caring presence. Gathering everyone back into the canoe, he didn't want Mr. Montgolfier to think poorly of him, so he tugged it with all of his sulking and strength, not speaking a word, all the way to Spokane. During this somber moment, Holt remembered the fortune told to him by the rock and fungi being, Armillaria. *"Up on a pedestal for all to see, your last waking months will bring you a shock you will not believe. Your time on this earth will come to a peaceful halt, but your love will live on."*

Though still somewhat unclear to him, he recognized that maybe a portion of it had actually come true. With the constant shifting of the earth and its plates there are earthquakes...and with the bombardment of new stimuli on the mind, we change in knowledge and experience, adapting ideals. Holt underwent this shift of level headedness.

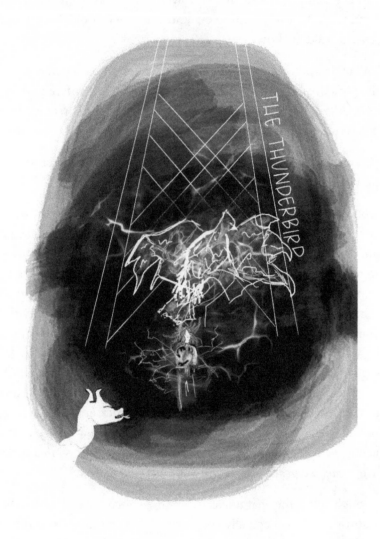

CHAPTER 13

(The Visitor)

Skulduggery, a heinous wrongdoing in the social realm of humankind, is not so nefarious outside of it. And while the witch might be praised for her dishonesties by her colleagues, she was beginning to taste the bitterness of self-reproach. You see, Rosaline had not been authentic with neither Griffith, nor Holt. Not necessarily in a way of inaccuracy as some might picture, but simply by not telling the *whole* truth. Oftentimes one finds that this type of deceit can be even more harmful than a direct lie. Additionally, she had acted outside of her authority by helping Dooley escape, which was another wrongdoing, but ironically one she didn't feel as much guilt over.

Rosie had sent Griffith out yet again to keep close tabs on Holt. She refused to accompany him, saying that she had important business to attend to. He was on a wild goose chase though, as Holt's ability to use his elk skin map was taken away by the Thunderbird. This meant Griff didn't have a tangible means of finding Holt again. He continued, nonetheless in the direction that he was ordered, hoping that his old friend "luck" would come to his aid.

In the meantime, the witch was expecting a visitor. One she had not yet known, but anticipated, due to her recent slip-up. Right on cue, the man with the red mustache appeared at her abode, for the second time in his life. The first time, you might remember, was when Holt first saw him lurking in her forest. Sly as a fox, yet bold as a lion, he confronted Rosaline outright.

"Are you the seer they call Baba Unaka?" he asked, encroaching on her home's entryway.

"I am she."

"I don't like to show up unannounced…" he stated.

"Well, 'unannounced' doesn't necessarily mean unwelcomed," she formally responded.

"With your pleasantries, I hope you can separate myself from the unfortunate news I am required to deliver to you. I assume you might be expecting it."

The witch decided denial was her safest option, and did her best to elude the guest's accusations. Unfortunately for her, he had witnessed many of the events firsthand. She didn't know how he had done this, despite the one great "tell" of his species, or she would have been able to make a crucial move in this chess game she had unintentionally started. It was then that she began to grow suspicious of his various appearances. Regrettably, hindsight is always in 20/20 vision.

You see, it slipped the witch's mind that he was a seer, just as she was, but with a different title. He was a *Hideling*. Hideling's have many oddities and secrets that can ultimately lead to their downfall, but their ability to conceal these things is what makes them so successful. For those who don't know, a Hideling has the ability to see through the eyes of any living thing, whether it be a tree, a human, or maybe even a toad. Now there are two ways to detect a Hideling, and neither are to be used as a truly confident means of evidence, but sadly the only evidence that can be used. The first way is only seen by its current prey. When they are stalking, the only one who can see them is the target themselves, not even a whole party who might be accompanying them. And by "see them," I mean see the slight resemblance of their true persona. In whatever living thing they inhabit in order to stalk their target, they leave a remnant of their true physical characteristics. In the case of this one, it is his red mustache. Yet, so far in the plot the only person to actually see this red mustache has been Holt.

I primarily know this through reading his journal entries, and even through observing him when he encountered the creature, but let's retrace his steps for a minute. When he was first in the witch's forest, he inspected a tree with a red polypore that he described felt like it was watching him. In the Kentucky farmer's market he had a brush up with a red-mustached vendor, and the federal agent who had been after him displayed the same trait. The gambler in Utah, and the NAVY engineer also showcased red facial hair. In every instance, Holt physiologically experienced what can be described as the second "tell" of being stalked by a Hideling -- and if I would have paid closer attention I could have caught this detail and put ourselves in a better position than we are now.

Nevertheless, the other way to detect his species is that it will give its target goosebumps when they are being watched. This is their second "tell". If others in the target's cohort are knowledgeable of this, they might be able to spot the goosebumps on their associate, and help them reveal the Hideling. Yet, revealing it won't do much good, unless they can find its real body, and exclaim that they know it is a Hideling, using its name. When this happens, it will be forever cut off from its abilities, as goes the law.

It was then that she confirmed much of the conspiracy surrounding Holt Dooley. Of course much of this information was at first just her speculation, but had been validated throughout their talk. Alas, the misdemeanor reprimand dealt to the witch for her "mortal-affair intervention", would keep her detained, under the threat of death, from intervening again. If she herself would have participated, rather than just coerce Griffith into action, she might already be dead.

It may be a surprise to you, that such a governing authority exists outside of the commonly visible human spectrum, but it does.

Rosie called up Griffith, telling him Holt's exact location. Wondering why the witch didn't just give him this information sooner, she told him that she would elaborate in time. Rosaline had kept Griff working for her through a variety of means. By appealing to his pride, reminding him of his future payment, and a little bit of flirting, she was able to keep him mentally hostage without him fully realizing it. The new plan she established was for him to confront Holt, and tell him he is in danger. Griff was to try to impede Dooley from getting to his wife, as the witch feared Holt was being unwittingly led down a woeful path. Rosie believed he was not ready to hold the responsibilities he would be given.

CHAPTER 14

(The Euchre Gamble)

The irregular cityscape of Spokane, Washington is unrivaled by any American city for varying reasons. However, it doesn't own the colossal mountainous grandeur of Seattle and Mt. Rainier, nor does it have the sprawling light show that New York City offers to astronauts. What is remarkable about Spokane is more mysterious. Like buried treasure, quirky shops shine through the ground floor of the highrises. The parks that weave in and out of downtown showcase a few large waterfalls, where one can take a scenic gondola ride over the river. Artists and sculptors make their mark throughout the concrete and asphalt as if to say "_____ was here." I don't know how else to describe its setting, other than this: It is the most seemingly fictional city I have experienced. I don't know why, but something about it feels cartoonish.

Holt Dooley sensed this city's mysteries, although he had recently been seemingly "cut off" from the extraordinary world he was accustomed to. Dragging the canoe through the city's hardscape, its friction was as audible as the honking of car horns and disrupted the passing conversations. On any regular day, the sight of this would warn onlookers to a possibly disturbed mind, but this day was different. It was a city-wide annual CrossFit event, where heavy items were being pulled and pushed around as a competition of health and fitness. Because of this, the canoe managed to be a significant means of camouflage to his social irregularities.

Many competitors looked at Holt's canoe enviously, as a believably sensational work-out for one's strength and balance. In the days that followed, word spread to other cities' events, and a fad emerged involving canoe training, becoming an actual event in Holt's ever influential wake.

The gang stocked up on food and other necessities, in preparation for their next trek through the wilderness. Holt found his newly favorite sushi restaurant, named "Sushi.com"[122] where he ate enough tuna to go into a pseudo-anaphylactic shock sometimes referred to as tuna poisoning. Regardless, he continued on through the nausea to more exploring. Just a block across from the sushi restaurant was a store entitled "Atticus" which was a highly rated coffee shop, and close to that was a store named "Boo Radley" after another character from the same book. [123]

Sleeping under an overpass in Spokane, Holt coped with his inability to communicate with his crew, by talking to the homeless. A few of them lived under there year round, making conversation around trash fires. While it wasn't freezing that night, Holt had goosebumps that the fire didn't alleviate. Maybe it was from the nausea, or from inhaling the fumes of burning plastic, but Holt spotted someone who reminded him of the gambler down in Utah, Reid Fox. He approached him, and asked if he by chance knew the name, but was rejected outright.

---

[122] Ironically, the restaurant doesn't actually own that online domain. I checked.
[123] *To Kill a Mockingbird*

However, he did find that the man was in fact a gambler, who desired to play a game of cards with Holt.

"Have you ever played Euchre?" the man asked.

"Actually, yes...but I don't have a partner," said Holt.

"How 'bout the kid?"

"Mr. Montgolfier! Get over here, I'm going to teach you a card game."

Dooley explained the rules to Montgolfier, who was an incredibly quick learner. There is certainly an aspect of luck involved, but oftentimes can be overshadowed by sly skill and strategy, as with many card games. I won't elaborate on all of the rules, since there are quite a few and it is not a traditionally easy game to explain, but in a minute, I will give an overview.

The homeless man called over his partner, who strutted into the light, revealing his freshly shaven face, and comically holding his fake detective badge. It was Griffith. Upon seeing Griff, there seemed to be a microexpression of surprise with the homeless man, who suddenly seemed to lose the red tint in his facial hair. [124] On one hand, Holt didn't notice the slight change of color, but on the other, he actually anticipated a run-in with Griffith soon, and did not show the slightest bit of shock.

"Wow, Holt, you might be a tough opponent with that poker-face, I was hoping for more fright in those eyes," said Griff.

"Do you even know how to play?" Holt asked.

---

[124] If my timeline is correct, it is possible that the Hideling was shocked by the witch's immediate disobedience, and left his post to deal with the matter.

"Don't need to. The good guy always wins," he retorted.

Griffith requested that if Holt lost, he would have to come back to South Carolina and turn himself in, leaving behind the canoe for the homeless man. Holt countered, asking that Griffith would stop following him, and hinder any other authoritative forces from doing so as well. Both were doubtful of the other's promise, but figured it was worth a shot anyway. Before Holt ever saw the homeless man, Griff had pressured him to convince Holt to gamble with promises of payment, which turned out to be the canoe. The investigator was fortunate enough to have the Hideling unknowingly contribute to his plan, which drew Holt to talk with the homeless man anyway.

The game was to end at 10 points, which were counted by the winning of rounds. Rounds were won by whoever gathered the most "tricks" as they're called. Tricks are won by utilizing trump cards and regular cards to your advantage. Trump cards are different each round, depending on what is called.[125] Essentially, it is similar to a war, in that many battles must be won to be victorious. Confusing, I know, but so is the very world we all live in.

Unless one understands Euchre, the following interaction could be rather hard to follow, so don't feel bad about being lost.

---

[125] Here is a concise overview of the scoring as told by the manual in the *Bicycle* card deck:

Partnership making trump wins 3 or 4 tricks – 1 point
Partnership making trump wins 5 tricks – 2 points
Lone hand wins 3 or 4 tricks – 1 point
Lone hand wins 5 tricks – 4 points
Partnership or lone hand is euchred, opponents score 2 points

The game ensued, with Holt and Montgolfier consistently receiving poor cards, but managing to keep their wits. The homeless man was the most experienced of them all, and Griff the least, but the luckiest. Holt and Montgolfier used their superior intellect to reel in a few tricks, while Griffith had no attempt to even learn the rules, but threw whatever card he felt was the highest. Somehow he complied with the game's rules, but his incompetant, yet prosperous choices annoyed Holt, and even Griff's own partner at times.

Holt and Montgolfier were sitting at a score of seven, for which they really had to put in some gruelling brain-work. Team Griff held eight points which came easily, from the greater number of "trump" cards. The next round could end it, if Griff and his partner could secure all five tricks without being contested, or if Holt's team would be dealt a winning loner hand.

Montgolfier was dealt a jack of clubs, the second highest card in the spades suit, which was called trump by Griff's team. Griff had the chance to over-trump the jack of clubs with the only higher card in that round, the jack of spades, but didn't due to his own misunderstanding of trump cards. So, Holt's team managed to keep them from scoring two points, making the score now nine to seven. Holt weaseled his way into another point in the next round, making it nine to eight.

Griff attempted to distract Holt, claiming that the pig looked distraught, turning his attention towards it. Griff slipped the joker card out of his pocket and exchanged it for the low number nine card in his hand. Griff's team called diamonds as trump this time, as Holt apprehensively watched the cards unfold. For the first trick of the match, Montgolfier tossed a jack of diamonds, making Dooley grin.

"Atta boy," Holt said.

Griff placed the joker card on it, over trumping it, and jubilantly gloated.

"Where did that come from? I didn't know we were playing the joker variation of Euchre," said Holt.

"How has it not shown up the whole game?" asked Montgolfier.

Even the homeless man looked at Griff cynically. Rather than accuse him of cheating, Holt pressed on, hoping to steal the feigned happiness right out from under Griff. And he did manage to win the next two tricks, which placed them in the final stretch of the game. Griff was out of trump cards, and threw a king of hearts. The homeless man hoped that nobody saved the ace of hearts as their last card, and that he would be left with a canoe. They followed clockwise, and Holt's face did display disappointment this time. He had no trump cards, nor had he been dealt the ace of hearts. To his amusement, Montgolfier did have the ace of hearts, and nonchalantly saved the day.

"Euchre!!" Holt yelled euphorically. "I suppose I am the 'good guy' you previously gloated about?"

Griffith's brooding face showcased his displeasure. He really believed he'd win without even knowing the rules, and he almost did. He believed his cause was valiant and that it is hard to fail with pure motive. Sometimes it can be difficult to see your own motives as selfish. Though he did want to bring in a criminal, it was only for his own betterment and glory. Nonetheless, in his next request, he put his pride aside, hoping to adhere to the witch's plan.

"Holt, I'm going to ask you one more time to come back with me," he said. "Please, don't go to *Brookings.*"

Dooley paused for a moment before answering. How did Griff know he was going to Brookings? Did he have some connection to his wife who supposedly lived there? Holt considered many possibilities, but for him, this re-affirmed that the algorithm he used to find his wife was accurate, and he was truly going to meet her on the Oregon Coast. Even so, Griffith's pleading was alarming. Holt wondered if Griff's dense head was so ignorant that he couldn't see past his own desire's to bring him in, or if there was something that he himself just didn't know. Just like playing Euchre, Dooley weighed the possible outcomes of countless rounds to find a way to win. As expected, he believed his most advantageous move was to continue on his path.

"Even though your plea is entertaining, it disturbs me that you would go to such lengths to bring me away. For this reason, I know that some aspect of my expedition is more than meets the eye. And being the prideful man that I take you as, it doesn't seem fitting that you would sacrifice your dignity by begging me to leave with you. Regardless of whatever discomforting information you have yet to relay to me, I'm afraid I must go on."

Griff didn't intend to stay true to his bet in not following Holt, as that was his job, and his purpose. He would though do his best to keep others from interfering with Dooley, as it was in the best interest of him and the witch.

CHAPTER 15

(Fireside Folklore)

Through a series of creeks, lakes, and rivers Holt Dooley and his crew had made it through the majority of the mostly desolate southeastern Washington landscape. Tugging the canoe through the drier parts was surely a challenge, but he handled it well, and it was ultimately a faster way to the coast. Having to circumnavigate dams and other infrastructure was a pain, but not as irksome as his inability to talk to the pig and Private Sherman.

Mr. Montgolfier's words were really his only healthy company, as his occasional attempts to speak with the pig only ended in disappointment, with apparent unintelligible grunts and oinks. Holt saw Montgolfier almost as a little brother, and they enjoyed bouncing information back and forth between each other, like a mindful game of four-square. But again, they didn't pass the ball to the plant or the boar very often.

"What is she like?" asked the boy.

"Who?" replied Holt.

"Your wife!"

"Euna?[126] She's beautiful. Strong like ginger, yet elegant like jasmine. [127]

Holt's overall plan had been adapted in the light of the Thunderbird's advent. He did still plan on speedily traveling to the southern Oregon coast to see his wife, and eventually taking the plant to the redwoods national forest, but he was also concerned with what to do about the pig and Montgolfier. He thought about reaching out to Rosaline who might be able to fix the communication problem, but he doubted the possibility of even being able to find her again. He considered asking Montgolfier to live with him and his wife as a family, but didn't know how she would react. He also wasn't sure that she was in trouble at all… it was certainly a possibility that she was living happily, just blocking Holt out of her life.

It was the last day before they would ride the Columbia River, saddling the Washington-Oregon border, all the way to the ocean. Holt was sore everywhere from the weight of the canoe, and occasionally the weight of Mr. Montgolfier. When they triumphantly marched to the expansive river banks, they made their fire, and Holt sprawled out on the ground like a starfish. After gazing into the sky for a good while, He sat up to write in his journal.

"Today, gravity is a wrestler. Weighing in at approximately 180 lbs, it has been my own opponent, and one with unrelenting endurance. Once I reached the Columbia, it pinned me, for much more than ten seconds, forcing my neck, extremities, and

---

[126] "Euna" is a popular Cherokee name for girls, roughly translating to "waterfall".

[127] Lyric from the song "Mountain Flower" by LC Huffman

morale to the dirt. I don't know how much further my body can manage physically, and I'm not sure how much more I can compete mentally."

Dooley looked at his carving on the driftwood piece, and fell dead asleep. No matter how lengthy Holt's slumbers had become, Montgolfier refused to wake him, as Holt told him that in dreams, he felt the gratifying remnants of his old "condition". He dreamt uninterrupted for the next fourteen hours.

In his dream, he saw the petroglyphs that he previously recorded in his journal come to life: The Horned Snake was watching his lifeless, frozen body from the water of the Columbia River, and it was conversing about him with the red-mustached man that Holt was increasingly becoming familiar with. They cryptically referred to Dooley as the "Harbinger of Change". The massive wingspan of the Thunderbird brought forth rain, which blurred the sightline between the snake and Holt. It appeared both of the beasts were in great animosity, with Holt's body being the point of contention. Many of the folklore beings Holt had encountered aligned themselves accordingly under the influence of the Horned Snake and Thunderbird, while some stood by indifferently. Rosaline stood with Griffith to her side awaiting some grand, terrible denouement. Holt woke with a gasp, as if he hadn't been breathing.

"Consarn it, Holt! You startled me!"

"Do you kiss your mother with that mouth?!" Holt said, mistakenly. "I didn't mean...nevermind."

Upon hearing Dooley's dream, Montgolfier found it engaging, but encouraged him not to dwell on it. Holt looked again at his driftwood piece, mesmerized by its intricacies. He developed a thought that the Thunderbird may have done this to signify its

213

role as his totem. Still, he didn't know the purpose behind severing his paranormal communication.

They gathered up camp and fit the four of themselves into the canoe, floating atop the Columbia's current. On the right side of the waterway was the state of Wasington, and on the left was Oregon. It proceeds this way making up the border, until the river dumps into the ocean. The thrill of riding in the canoe fell short of Mr. Montgolfier's expectations, as the spacious river provided few obstacles.

"We should take this baby to the air, like it was meant to be. How did you say it could fly again?" he asked Holt.

"I don't quite remember. If I did, I might just agree with you at this point. The story had something to do with making a deal with the devil."

Holt was thankful for the replenished strength in his muscles, but resting doesn't always cure a haggard mind. He was actively counting down the time to his destination, which as some have experienced, illusively makes time move slower. Montgolfier wasn't as restless as Holt, but that made sense considering he only joined his efforts back in Idaho. There wasn't a decisive way of determining whether the pig or plant felt that way, but Holt just assumed they were feeling the same. At any rate, they sought out nightfall to put another day's distance behind them.

Breaching the city limits of Hood River, Oregon, Holt paddled the canoe to shore and dragged it up the bank. They considered just sleeping on the river, but Montgolfier was anxious about any possibility of drowning. Holt made camp for them at sunset, and went into the town to gather supplies. There was a pizza shop named *Solstice,* who's menu appealed to his smitten taste buds. Walking into the establishment, he held the brazen appearance of a wayfaring hobo, but to his advantage, this "granola" style seemed to be a popular look in Oregon. He ordered four large pizzas for each member of the crew, wherein they could all finish Private Sherman's leftovers. He also ordered a few of their "famous" s'mores. The naive waiter delivered all the food to his one man table, where he walked clean out without paying. His ears tuned in to the waiter behind him who yelled "Consarn it!" queuing Holt to increase his speed and evasive action. It wasn't the first time he had recently heard someone use his own expletive excluding Montgolfier. He believed the broadcasting of him on the news a while back may have spurred the movement of the phrase across the U.S.[128] From this moment on, I never heard him use it again, possibly due to frustration of its overuse.

Dooley and the crew ate on the riverbank until their stomachs were packed tight with pizza, but they decided to save the s'mores for later. Holt filled their sleepy heads with facts about Mt. Hood, a colossal local mountain. If it were earlier in their journey, Holt most certainly would have taken the detour to explore it. But, having full bellies, heads, and hearts they lazily imprinted on the shoreline.

The next night, after floating the Columbia, they made camp at Beacon Rock State Park. This wasn't but a few miles from Hood River, on the Washington side, but their tiresome efforts to travel around the dam warranted an early rest. Mr. Montgolfier had grievously stepped in a generous pile of unidentifiable skat, causing much negativity among the group. The smell was pungently horrid, and Holt refused to help the kid wash it off of his boot, saying it was "a good learning experience." Dooley

---

[128] I have heard many people use this phrase, as if it arose to fame rather quickly. Maybe this truly is the explanation. Even Holt's words seem to have considerable influence.

wondered what animal could have displaced such hefty droppings, but the stench was the primary concern. He could only imagine what the boar was thinking, with its superior sniffer.

Holt was feeling the slight annoyance one sometimes experiences with a younger sibling, and determined he would initiate Mr. Montgolfier into the great folk-American rite of passage, *Snipe Hunting*. In this gag of a ritual, the wide-eyed contestant is told to hold out a bag and wait, while the prankster purportedly flushes out a fictional jackrabbit-bird called a "Snipe", into the bag's reach. Expectedly, instead of following through with the plan, Holt was relaxing at the fire, leaving Montgolfier alone in the dark.

The occasional high-pitched "whoop!" was heard in the distance, as Dooley alluded that this was the sound the boy should use to attract them. After considerable time had passed, much more than a "whoop" was heard from the child, rather it sounded like a fearful yell of Holt's name. He jumped up and sprinted to the boy, who was cowering under a dead tree trunk.

"Mr. Montgolfier! Everything is alright! It was a prank." He placed his hand on the boy's shoulder. "There is no such thing as a snipe. Well, actually that is a lie, there is, but you weren't hunting any. And their description is different from how I depicted it to you."

"No Holt, I saw it!" said the boy. "It must've been seven feet tall."

"What did it look like?" Holt's tone changed from nervously joking, to stern.

"Like a bipedal bear...or a gorilla!"

Holt asked in which direction it was walking, and went over to see if he could uncover tracks.

"See?! That is the largest footprint I've ever seen," Montgolfier stated.

"I...don't see anything. Where do you mean?"

Holt escorted the boy back to their campsite, and tried to assuage his trembling. He felt bad for trying to trick Montgolfier, and decided to break out the s'mores to cheer him up. Dooley told him just to focus on his taste buds, and that they would be safe and sound in Brookings soon enough. Holt, before tasting the treat, journaled about it as Montgolfier ate.

"The sweet mixture of marshmallow, chocolate, and graham cracker has been a staple to American camping cuisine since 1927. In fact, an ample percentage of marshmallow sales is attributed to this one dessert."

Mr. Montgolfier experienced only a few minutes of enjoyment, before skittishly turning his head looking for the beast that haunted him.

"Did you hear that?" he asked Holt.

"If you are referring to the excessively auricular chomping of Hamlet's jowls, not only do I hear it, but I can't ignore it," he said, glaring at the boar.

"No, it sounded like a grunt or something."

"That, again, is the sloppy technique of our mannerless hog." Holt nudged the pig with his foot.

Montgolfier dropped the remainder of his s'more in the scorched dirt, and lifted his pointer finger to the surrounding woods. His gaping expression worried Holt, though he wasn't entirely sure he trusted the kid's imagination. However, his credibility rose when the pig, worriedly changed position, lying prone, sneaking back

217

toward their canoe. Dooley decided it was more advantageous to play along, and listened to Montgolfier, who claimed the beast was stalking them behind the pines. He couldn't see it, but he picked up Montgolfier's s'more, and tossed it through the trees towards its feet. The beast picked it up, sniffed it, and then gulped it down. It more confidently showed itself to Mr. Montgolfier, who described it as an enormous, hair covered woman with fierce teeth, and arms that could lift a car. He claimed it was then assertively motioning for Montgolfier to follow, and making a "whoop" sound like he had previously done.

"I think she can smell me," Montgolfier said fearfully.

"Who wouldn't be able to?" Holt retorted.

It was then that Holt began connecting the dots, though he still couldn't sense the beast. He believed this to be a female Sasquatch[129], which had smelled its own skat on Mr. Montgolfier, and mistaken him for her own child. He had heard that Bigfoot relies on its sense of smell. Before the beast were to try to take Montgolfier along with her, Holt stood in between them with another s'more. To the kid's horror, he claimed it upset the beast and she resembled a mother moose, ready to charge. Holt gave direction to Montgolfier to get Private Sherman and wait in the canoe, while he would lead the beast through the woods and come back to them to escape.

"It's just like how we escaped on the hot air balloon, alright?" Holt explained, "I'll be back hastily."

Holt sprinted through the trees, maneuvering like a gazelle, with quick lateral movements, so as not to get caught. In the same way, after watching a scary movie, many people can convince

---

[129] "Sesquac" as named by the Salish Native Americans

themselves of some horror waiting for them even in their own abode, Holt started to believe. When putting himself in this predator and prey like interaction, he began to actually experience his first bit of fright toward the bigfoot. Not being able to see or hear it chasing him proved a challenge he felt unworthy of, and decided to climb the next forked tree he saw, putting himself at higher ground. With the help of his adrenaline, almost instantaneously he was holding the top branches, and trying to detect any glimpse of sasquatch. Thereupon, he did notice a heavy wind pushing the canopy in the direction back to the canoe. Believing this may be an influence of the beast, he climbed back down and hurried back to the campsite.

Holt couldn't believe his eyes. Although, his disbelief wasn't due to anything he saw, but rather what he didn't see. The canoe wasn't there at the campsite. He fought back thoughts that he could be lost, by physically pointing to the remains of the fire. Dooley *was* at the campsite, but his friends *weren't* where they planned to be. He fell on his knees and slammed the dirt with the fists in dismay. The canoe was gone, along with the pig, the plant, and Mr. Montgolfier. He didn't see any tracks from dragging the canoe, and figured in his head that the boy would have been unable to do so anyway, considering his small stature. The only explanation was that the little aeronaut had figured out how to make the canoe fly, and was piloting it somewhere to safety.

"Well, if anyone can fly that thing, the kid can," he reassured himself.

Luckily, they had left his bag behind, which held a few of Holt's valuables. He attempted to use the elkskin map again, to see if it would aid in locating the paranormal canoe, but remembered that he could not read it anymore. He couldn't see the script that he once decoded, nor the lines that would draw out direction. Holt now held a regular elk hide, which was not too practical for him at this point.

He ran to the Columbia's shore, and looked for the flying canoe, but saw nothing. Having no means of tracking them, it was decided that the most probable way to see them again was to wait where he left them. He sat up all night, plotting the stars by pointing his driftwood piece to the sky, and writing them in his journal.

"I used to consider myself introverted. So why now do I struggle so much when my attention is drawn to social solitude. Loneliness has become a fear to me, darker than any forest, and stranger than any beast. I find it more unquenchable than the relentless beckoning of a growling stomach, when it hasn't reached its daily quota." [130]

Holt uneventfully waited there for another whole day, without any sign of them. He decided the next morning he would try searching the city of Portland.

The City of Roses is known for its idiosyncrasies, and for its pride in them. To such a degree that the city's motto is actually "keep Portland weird." Various protests had broken out over the years, covering some of the smallest subjcts of everyday life. Last year Portlanders infamously boycotted a popular U.S. brand of soap, in order to support their multiple local soap makers. While the cause of supporting small businesses is honorable, blocking off streets and transit for the protest only inhibited other small local businesses' from receiving their important daily income.

When Holt came through the city looking for answers, he naturally was drawn to a large crowd, where he could easily ask

---

[130] At this point, one might wonder at his sanity, figuring he had crafted all of these interactions in his mind.

multiple people if they'd seen a boy and a pig, or maybe a flying canoe. The crowd stood directly downtown, listening to a politician on a portable stage. Holt intermingled into the herd's ameba-like confines, standing shoulder to shoulder in the middle.

"We all know that the future is in a cashless society," the politician said. "It is time we stopped printing money, and started saving trees."

Many excited cheers were hurled around, as people threw in their support.

Holt nudged the person next to him and spoke up snidely, "Interesting idea if our money was actually made of trees. It's not. It's made of cotton and linen....and what about the homeless community, how will they make their living if nobody carries around cash anymore?"

"Hmm.. good point man, that policy doesn't sound too inclusive," said the crowdsperson.

"Right on, right on," said Dooley, attempting to use some lingo he had heard from another in the crowd. "Have you seen a ten year old boy walking around with a pig anywhere?"

"Nope. What's his name?"

"It doesn't matter what his name is, how would that help you identify him?" asked Holt.

"Maybe I know him. Portland is just one big family. You know!"

Dooley squinted his eyes and nodded his head, shoving through to a different portion of the crowd.

"Has anyone seen a flying canoe?" Holt loudly whispered.

The woman in front of him, assumed he was concerned with the recent lull in tourism income, and spoke up for him. "Some of us were wondering how you plan on fixing the tourism industry for our city. Specifically regarding canoeing and other water based recreation."

The politician attempted to answer the specific question off the cuff, as his team had not considered watersports to be a large part of his platform. "Why yes that does seem to be something we need to fix... and... that... is why we are proposing an annual jet ski tournament on the river!"

The crowd seemed alright with this answer until Holt made a comment about the new wave activity causing erosion on the river banks. Multiple shaking heads were seen showing their newfound disapproval.

He moved to another section and asked around, which somehow spurred the crowd into another dramatic display of disapproval to the politician. Dooley had unintentionally shifted the entire crowd's supportive mindset, into rejection of the candidate. Holt didn't pay much attention to the politician or what position was being contested, but I am sure this candidate proved unsuccessful after this event.

Still not finding the answers he was hoping for, Holt decided to try asking a different set of people. He believed that the demographic at Powell's Bookstore might be more knowledgeable or observant, and tip him off to the right direction. Only his second interaction with a random customer proved successful, wherein a woman claimed to have overheard a young man and a pig, saying he was going to Astoria. This wasn't much to go on, but was the only lead he had. He exited the building, and took off straight away.

Reaching Astoria was a long awaited milestone to Holt. The Columbia river met the Pacific Ocean, viewed from architecture that was aged to perfection. He might have more fully enjoyed his time there if it weren't for his frantic wild goose chase...or wild boar for that matter. He scavenged the city for information, and simultaneously ate stolen to-go food from *Surf 2 Soul*. His grown out beard was a comical contrast to the "Coffee Girl" sweatshirt he was wearing, which he nabbed from a local favorite coffee shop.

Speaking to a nice honeymooning couple on their stroll downtown, he gleaned that there was some sort of pig festival to take place south of there in Tillamook. He never made sense of the lead he got in Portland, so the one to Tillamook quickly became the best choice. He didn't actually think he would find his old crew there, but couldn't rule out the possibility. He believed they might be waiting for him in the town of Brookings, as they knew where Holt's wife, and his final destination was. He started his final expedition, down the entire Oregon coastline, from Astoria, to Tillamook, to Brookings, and all the cities lying within.

CHAPTER 16

(Unearthing the Past)

Whether you've found the heretofore happenings of Holt Dooley's life amusing or not, I can't blame you. You didn't know him, nor do you know what's going to happen to him. If you did, it might fill the interconifnes of your heart taking up all its space, as it does mine.[131] The remainder of his voyage down the Oregon coastline was much less eventful then one might guess, until he reached his final objective. Up until then, he traveled by means of his own two feet, with no companions, no paranormal encounters, and not even any trouble from governmental authorities. It was peaceful, yet somber. He appeared as any other vagrant, with his thumb up, looking to catch a ride.

The coastal towns of Oregon all have their own distinct appeal and foibles -- from the whimsical carnival-esque downtown of Seaside, to the trapping of tourists at Cannon Beach's iconic Haystack rock. Smaller towns like Manzanita, Depoe Bay, Dune City, and even Yachats all have their fill of visitors, but their nature is still

---

[131] This seems to be another hint to the narrator's identity.

palpable, with whale watching, rockhounding, and sand dune sports front and center.

Holt didn't make time to experience the day to day normalcy of any of the towns, as his focus was now solely on finding his wife, and friends. He hitchhiked to Tillamook, where he heard there was a pig festival, just to make sure that his old crew wasn't there. A charming agriculture town, known for the dairy giant that shares its namesake, was home to twenty or so pork meat enthusiasts for the weekend. They had taken over a small portion of town, handing out free samples of bacon and marketing their pork loins, chops, and ribs to one another. After talking to many of the vendors, Holt confirmed that his friends must instead be in Brookings. Though he was hungry, he refused all the samples, feeling sickly over pork for the first time in his life. His disgust only deepened upon seeing a familiar face yet again, despite the bet that they had previously made.

"Where's your posse at, Holt? Did you finally cook up that pig and sell it to these weirdos?" Griff asked, probing his teeth with a toothpick.

"What is your angle?" asked Holt. "If there is something you have to tell me, go ahead. If you are attempting to incarcerate me go ahead and attempt."

"That's confidential stuff buddy, just part of being a detective. But.. I have been told once again to keep you from Brookings. It's for your own good."

"If you can't give me more information than that, then I'm going to be on my way." Holt said, turning his back to Griff.

"Wait! What if I told you where your friends are?"

Holt stopped in his tracks. "Then what?"

"You don't try to find your wife. You go back to your friends and live out your life happily, running through the forest looking for candy or whatever it is you do."

Holt socked Griffith in the gut, and sweeped his leg, pushing him to the ground. Getting him in full-mount, he punched Griff in the face multiple times.

"Tell me where they are!" Holt screamed.

Griff was completely dazed and unable to answer. Not that he would have after that. Holt held Griffith's limp head by his shirt collar, and added insult to injury, "I know you are not really a detective. You would be a horrible one. Why do you keep this up?"

The pork enthusiasts watched, and some cheered, but Holt noticed his social mistake and hurried off.

———

In a beeline down Highway 101, Holt Dooley made his way to Brookings. The last town of the Oregon Coast hangs in its own hillside evergreens like a Christmas ornament harboring memories. One notable memory is held in the samurai sword downtown, respectfully gifted by a penitent, one-time enemy[132] of the city. It's a good story, look it up. The panoramic sitelines displayed appealing scenery of various forms, from the Chetco River, the white capped Pacific waves, and beautiful city parks named for the flowers that inhabit them.

Azalea park set the stage for where Holt had tracked his wife's text messages. One step in the park, and the adrenaline pumping through his veins was just as prominent as his blood. He declined

---

[132] Nobuo Fujita

his mind's bombardment of beautiful aesthetics, and replaced the stimulation with more closely detailed observations to determine his spouse's location.

His eyes locked on to a red car, with a note in the sunvisor. Upon further inspection, he seemed to recognize the handwriting. It was very scribbled, and almost as illegible as the *elkskin map* he had previously tried to decode, but nonetheless uniquely his wife's. The fact that her handwriting was so close to the location that he tracked with his algorithm, was too much to be a coincidence. He believed she must be in the house behind it.

Dooley's limbs grew stiff with his nervousness, and he felt a chill with the Oregon winds. He brushed it off, drew up his confidence and took one step toward the door. With the second step, his legs moved with half of the confidence, and with the third, he came to a halt. He wondered what he would say, if he should hug her right away, and he even wondered how to smile. He practiced a few smiles and said "hello'" to himself in a couple of ways, and off he went again to the door. The house was classically characteristic of 2000s suburban architecture, but not stylistically unique.

Holt Dooley's appearance had developed greatly since he started his American odyssey. Unfortunately, his image showcased something altogether different than what his soul represented -- almost like a *bonsai tree* seeing its shadow, and fooling itself to be bigger. The clearly comfortable body that one assumes when safely dwelling within the confines of life in the socioeconomic middle-class had been whittled down. He was much skinnier than his wife would have remembered, but definitely in better physical shape. Well, except for his fingers. He compensated from his original workday routine of typing on a keyboard every minute, by twiddling a small piece of *driftwood*. The groomed hair he had in the past was replaced with longer, knotted up locks, the same luster as a *witch's broom*. His affectionate, wandering green eyes were still just as observant as a *detective's* would be, yet with a hint of uncertainty. His *crimson tinted facial hair* was much more prominent than when he used to shave his stubble, standing next to her and staring in the bathroom mirror.

As he knocked on the door, his heart pounded in sync with the sound of footsteps on the hardwood inside. The door opened just a crack, with a pair of eyes cautiously hiding behind it. The exhaling sound of the letter "H" stumbled out of her lips in shock. It was the gasp, just before winning points in her scrabble game by using the corresponding "o", "l", and "t".

"H..h…Holt?"

Her shock was just as effective as the Thunderbirds electric bolt. She couldn't believe her eyes, but she had to. Her other senses helped affirm his presence from his piney scent, and reaching to touch his *cold snout*, which she lightly pressed like a button. His teeth were as sadly chipped as a *boar's tusks*, and his smile was as goofy as it ever was.

"What are you doing here?" she asked, glancing over her shoulder as if someone else was in the house. "How did you?"

"I came to rescue you!" he interrupted.

"Oh Holty… I just…" she started, "I don't know what to say." Her apparent maternal instinct kicked in, embracing him, and pulling his head to the warmth of her heart.

"You don't have to say anything! I'm here now. I can take care of you. Everything is going to be alright again." Holt's eyes were joyful and watery. "Here, I got this for you," he said with *child-like excitement*. "You would not believe the story behind this thing."

He pulled the Golden Horseshoe out of his bag and began to tell her of his happenings in Utah. She began to cry, a response he wasn't expecting, as it didn't feel to him like a "good" cry. He attempted to show her another artifact of his travels, the elk skin map. He told her of his friends and enemies -- the boar, the bonsai tree, Griffith and so on.

"Holt the doctor said it isn't good to let you indulge in your delusions." she said. "You need help. Look at me Holt! You need help."

"Euna look, I can hotwire any of these cars and get you out of here right now." He gently grabbed her forearm and tugged it. "Let's go!"

"Nothing is wrong! I am not in trouble. I'm happy. Did you not recognize my flashy red car right there? Same one I've always driven..."

Dooley paused for a second in deep thought, unsure how to answer.

"I drove here out of my own volition, Holt! I left you because of this kind of stuff, you're choosing not to remember."

"I don't understand."

"I left you. And I'm so, so, sorry. I really am. But I couldn't live like that anymore. The constant paranoia, and taking care of you like a child.."

Holt's mind was racing, and the fidgeting of his driftwood let Euna know he was taking the situation poorly.

"Holty? I didn't mean that negatively. It's just not my dream to take care of someone else for the rest of my life, you know?" She shook her head at the situation and at her lousy choice of words.

To make matters worse, Holt saw movement through the window behind her. The figure of a man had just strolled from one room to the next, unbeknownst of the drama outside.

"Who...is that?" Holt asked.

Her cheeks turned from pink to red, as she frantically looked over her shoulder and back at the house.

He thought he had a grip on the earth, but he was finding that all of the soil just fell through his fingers. Taking in a long, and difficult look at her, Holt pressed the sight into his memory like a dried flower in a book. Her hair was *straight as arrows*, with the *luster of knapped obsidian*. Her skin was as soft and clear as her quiet speech. She had strong cheekbones that he remembered kissing to feel her smile start. Poetically, I might add, she was wearing the same black dress as when she left him. He had been running towards her for so long, but this was the first time he ever felt like running away from her. So he did. He didn't stop until he hit the redwoods.

Euna yelled at him to come back, as his swift feet carried him away with the same fortitude as *Forrest Gump*. She looked down at the golden horseshoe in her hand, and the piece of driftwood Holt dropped on the pavement in front of her. Upon inspecting it, she saw that it was different from when she originally gave it to him to alleviate his delusions. She gasped. Seeing the intricately detailed carving on it, she quickly brought it back into the house.

THE
RED-
WOODS

CHAPTER 17

(The Prophecy)

As you already know, redwood trees are the biggest trees on the planet. Private Sherman, was akin to these beautiful organisms, but is just a snack-size version due to his small pot. Holt Dooley wrote about his old friend in his journal to relieve the pain of what he had just witnessed, in an attempted distraction.

"He always felt so constricted by his pot. Complaining and wishing he could be described as gargantuan, scraping the sky like his relatives. If I could only conjure him up again, I would tell him what I think now. Who's to say bigger is better or less is more? All things carry with them their own merit and burden. But while these barked behemoths sit in glory, they do idle the same old spot. Private Sherman, on the other hand, may have been smaller, but got to witness the glory of many wonders. Surely it is not better to be seen as beautiful, than to see beauty for yourself."

Holt Dooley pressed both of his palms against the tree bark and stared at the dismally grey skies. His cloudy eyes filled up with water, and rained just the same. He failed in his attempt to divert his tears from thoughts of his wife, Euna, and even from Private

Sherman, who he promised to bring to the very place he stood in now.

Euna said she believed all of his experiences to be figments of his wild imagination, and had good evidence for it. Consequently, a dreadful thought barged its way into his mind, and wouldn't leave. He wondered if he truly had made up these stories in his brain, being dually beautiful and sickly.

"Well, a promise is a promise," he thought to himself, and decided to try to bring Private Sherman into existence again. He concentrated on the tree's looks, from pot to branch, and then the smell of its soil. He went through their memories together, and drew up some picture that he hoped to translate from his closed eyes, to his opened.

"Holt?" yelled a far off voice.

His slouched posture straightened up, and his eyes widened. Remembering that Private Sherman didn't outright talk, he thought his wife must have somehow found him already.

"I'm sorry about everything, and to cause you so much trouble!" he yelled, in anticipation of seeing her.

He searched for her face through the thick trees. He wanted to be understood, but also wanted to be forgiven, since he had seemingly given Euna such a hard marriage, that she had to move across the country and find a different partner. But Euna was not to be found, something else was. Through the redwood forest he caught a glimpse of graceful maneuvering. He thought his mind was generating another of the many tricks it had been playing on him, but he was too upset to care. His head tilted as the figure became more recognizable. She was a woman he knew, in fact, but not one he expected. Her long red hair curled at its ends, and her smile was soft.

"Baba Unaka?"

"Call me Rosie! We've got a lot to talk about."

"Maybe start with you being a figment of my imagination."

The witch laughed. "I'm flattered, but whether you've been thinking of me or not, I am very much alive and kicking outside of that captivating noggin of yours."

"I wish that were the truth. Unfortunately for us both, I am in poor mental health."

The witch looked at him in disappointment, and disappeared into thin air. She swirled into visible distortion, almost as if being mixed in a cauldron with the atmosphere that surrounded her.

Holt let out a sigh. He *did* want it to be real. Even with his knowledge of these delusions he couldn't control the appearance of them, it seemed. After contemplating this, and right on que, the witch re-appeared.

"How about that? Could your mind have done that?" she asked with a grin.

"Apparently. I just don't know how to make it more permanent."

She burst out laughing for the second time. "Holt, stop it, you're making my side-ache. I didn't teleport because of your brain, I did that because of this black hole tablet. See, I just crush this in my hands and poof! I appear somewhere else."

Holt looked at her like a child who just learned that Santa isn't real. "Alright, I'll believe you...If you can teleport *me* out of here."

"And waste another one of these?" she exclaimed, "Do you know how rare they are? And to waste not one, but TWO of them for the purpose of your foolish doubting...alright let's do it. Take my hand."

He grabbed her steady hand and felt a surge of energy run through his body. It could have been the fact that his body was warping in the process of teleportation, or possibly the thrill that comes with a newfound spark. Anyone who has felt this thrill, has likely also felt the comfort that comes with progressing within a relationship. He was in need of this solace, and Rosaline had been waiting to give it freely. After all, it wasn't only Holt that was experiencing feelings.

In the blink of an eye, they landed where they originally met- in her humble abode nestled in the deep woods of North Carolina. Rosie, being as experienced as she was, landed like a cat on her feet, while Holt clumsily somersaulted into one of her shelves of organized clutter. It was just as he remembered it -- or subconsciously designed it, he thought.

"Do you remember our conversation here some time ago?" she asked him.

"Ah, let me see, the first and only time we talked. Yep, easy to remember since we don't have a lot of data to scroll through anyway. We bartered and you gave me direction. Then you kicked me out...It was quite physical you know?" he smiled.

"Still think this is all fake? All in your head? How could you bring this place back to existence so clearly, and yet not even remember our conversation. I didn't give you direction. I practically told you where my enchanted elk skin map was and your filthy hands stole it. Just as I planned," she said with a wink.

Holt paused in consideration for a moment, taken back by her rather strong point. Still hesitant, he dodged her question, and continued to inquire further about the map.

"Just as you planned? I suppose retrospectively, that makes more sense. It's a shame of grand proportions that the enchanted map seems to have lost its magic now...sorry about that."

"Oh, it works just fine. The issue is with you, Holt. Can't you just make a new one with your mind?" she laughed again.

"There is no need for such a condescending tone. Anyone in my position would find themselves confused as well. For all I know, you are a mere figment of my imagination, while in all actuality, I am speaking to a tree or a rock.[133] Maybe I never even left South Carolina in the first place."

"Didn't you tell your little pig friend that it is quite alright to speak to a tree? I seem to remember that."

"SEE!" Holt exclaimed. "How would you know that if you weren't me? Even in my imaginative state I don't recall you being there."

"Caught me red handed, I guess. I've been watching you. Sometimes reading your thoughts even," She said pointing to her seer scale. "Did you forget I am a witch? And one of the best, I might add."

Just as the final straw could "break a camel's back" so to speak, Rosie's comments began to weigh on Holt. Ascertaining that she was making progress, she decided to keep illuminating the situation for his sake, but also for her own.

---

[133] He *did* in fact experience this phenomenon earlier in his journey, when interacting with Armillaria -- or so the story went.

"Tell me, Holt, could you feel *this* all alone in the redwoods?" She leaned up, balancing on her toes like a ballerina, giving him a quick peck on the mouth.

Dooley reminisced about his commitment to his wife, and reminded her that he was married. She reminded him that if she was just in his mind, he had technically done nothing wrong. However, this feeling was all too real to him. How ironic that it took an emotional tug to finally move such a typically logical person. She watched his eyes unfocus, as he swam through his feelings and his confusion.

"Take a seat," she said. After gathering that she had somewhat convinced him of her existence, she proceeded to tell him something considerably more difficult. "I'm not sure how to actually tell you this, and I'm definitely not allowed, but here it goes. You are quite the topic of controversy, Holt Dooley."

Holt's stomach growled, and she supplied him with a hearty stew that had been cooking as if she knew she'd be having company. "Allowed? Who's going to tattle, and to whom?" he snickered.

"I'll get to that." She snapped her finger, turning his spoon into a fork. "What I'm trying to say is that you *see* things that most people don't. That makes you a see-er...well kind of, you are a bit different. Anyhow, there are other *seers*, like myself, who can sense the same irregularities. You, being a man of science, might comprehend these things better than me, or anyone else for that matter." She felt it was a smart decision to explain something unknown alongside the hope to know it. Holt may be more receptive if he thought of these supernatural occurrences as deducible through scientific observation and explanation -- and they are. However, not all scientific laws translate so strictly from one realm to another...in fact, that is actually a great means of categorizing them.

238

"Uhuh," Holt hummed, as he put the fork down and drank from his bowl.

"Are you paying attention? I'm about to hit you with the big reveal so listen up!" She snapped her finger again, and a snare drum fell off of a shelf and began to play itself.

"OTHER DIMENSIONS!" screamed a familiar voice through the entrance. "That's right, Sidekick, I'm back to whip you into shape. Put you in line so to speak. Think fast!" he said, hurling his shoe at Holt. It missed him by a longshot, knocking a bowl of squishies into Dooley's stew. Dressed in all designer apparel, Chase Griffith had finally been compensated, though he still continued working for Rosaline.

"How does *he* fit into the mix?" Holt asked, pointing to Griff.

"Like oil and water. It wasn't very long ago he found all this out either," she replied.

"But, he's right. Your experiences are extra-*dimensional*, if that is the word you want to use. Seers can come in many forms,[134] but they all interact with realms outside of which their own species dwells. For instance, Griffith, yourself, and I, all in some way or another can interact with beings outside of the human realm, which lies somewhere categorically in the third dimension. That is a large source of a witch's power! Griffith on the other hand can sometimes tap into alternate realities to gain the most desirable outcome in situations. Seers like him are called "fates". He would be vastly overpowered if it were more controllable."

---

[134] Perhaps the magic behind the elk skin map and the elk figurine is telling of the seer-like nature of the elk when it was alive.

239

"So if you're a witch, and he's a fate, do I have some fantastical title that grants me powers too?" Holt asked.

"Well, yes, and no. You're one of a kind."

"A freak!" Griff chimed in.

"Ignore him, he's mad that you got the better of him," Rosie said.

"He did not. It's not like I was allowed to fight back! Golden boy here is fragile," Griff retorted, rolling his eyes like a child.

"Back to your question, yes you have powers in a sense, but since you are the only one like yourself, you have no title. Golden boy will do," she said, winking. "Holt, you are an important piece of a prophetic puzzle. Many of the seers know this prophecy, and some of the higher ups, we call them *Overseers*, are in opposition regarding it. Essentially Holt, that means you have enemies."

"Conceivably so, but I'm not sure this rivalry would be mutual. Even if all of this is real, I don't have any compelling desire to evade or pursue that relationship."

Griff laughed loud enough to know it was fake, saying, "Why don't you just say that you don't care? It's so funny how smart you think you are!"

The witch ordered her broom to sweep Griffith out of the doorway. Initially he hesitated to comply, but after feeling the coarse bristles whip him a few times, he made his way out.

"I know, I know, 'What's in it for me,' right? Possibly just your life, but maybe your wife's life, and your future therin? I'm not sure, it could be anything. Whether they full-on murder you or not I have no idea, but I know something bad is coming," she said, trying to maintain stern eye contact with him. "Let me give you some background. One of the more powerful...or at least prominent Overseers in our region has always had bad relations with a few of the others. You've met before actually. Do you remember when you talked to that giant ball of lightning in the air? That was a *Thunderbird*. And the last of her kind believe it or not."

"As in...her species is about to go extinct?" Holt asked.

"I don't know about the timeframe on that, as I'm pretty sure they live for millenia, but yes, the implication is that once she dies, it's over."

"That's rough."

"Yup. So, she clashes heads pretty badly with this giant watersnake.."

"The Horned Serpent?" Holt interjected.

"Yes! How did you know that?" she asked.

"That fungi-rock creature, Armillaria, told me that Native American history is especially pertinent to my future, so I did some brushing up on a lot of the mythology from different tribes and cultures."

"Of course, I recall. Back to the drama. Those two Overseers have a very different opinion on something, and you are right in the middle of them. The prophecy says that one human, wedged in between the desires of the Overseers will be the tipping force of either an *epoch of calamity*, or an *epoch of peace*. We're talking generation upon generation."

"Hmm. And why do you think I'm *that* human?"

241

"Oh it's not just me. They've all been watching your every move and fighting over what to do about it."

"Are they are watching us right now, talking about this?"

"Nope. I'm craftier than I look. I'm sure they are scrambling on their thrones trying to figure out what is going on!" She chuckled. "We are safe for a bit though. You're probably pretty tired aren't you? You should relax here for the night and I can tell you more tomorrow."

"Actually I think I should go back home and just process everything. Regarding my wife and all."

"Back home? You'll be arrested as a federal fugitive. I'm not letting you off that easily," she joked.

Rosaline told him to make himself at home, as it would be his as well for the time being. Ergonomically, her house didn't have much to offer, but she did toss Holt a dusty quilt. He realized that if everything he had been hearing was true, then she was under significant pressure. Harboring him was surely illegal by her laws, putting a big target on her back. He couldn't risk her wellbeing by leaving, and he wouldn't even know how to leave if this really was one of his delusions. It was clear that Rosie allowed her fondness for Holt to get the best of her. One rarely jeopardizes their own well being for the advantage of someone they don't intend to have a connection with, in at least some way, shape, or form.

CHAPTER 18

(Back to the Chalkboard)

"That sure looks like the work of the Thunderbird alright, engraving a totem of herself into Holt's thinking twig. So conceited," said the Hideling, holding onto Holt's piece of driftwood.

"I feel so bad for him. Getting caught up in all of this...and then to make him believe he is losing his mind...it all seems so evil to me," replied Euna.

"Must I remind you of the coming calamity? Would you rather your husband be responsible for that?" he sternly said.

"There has got to be another way of doing this," she pleaded.

"You're right. There are a million ways of doing this I'm sure, but *The Great Horned Serpent* and his council have sifted through the outcomes, and chosen wisely. Trust in his wisdom."

Euna was not born a seer, nor did she entirely hold any title, but being a pawn of an Overseer has some perks, and disadvantages, of course. Holt had already made her aware of the existence of supernatural beings, though he didn't have the terms and means to elaborate on them. Whether she believed him or not didn't matter, as she was the only choice to be utilized in the manipulation of Holt.

The Hideling and Euna were in the process of packing up her belongings into cardboard boxes. The occasional tap of falling tears onto the boxes was a sound she grew accustomed to, with her worries ever present. Sure, moving her life around for a cause she barely understood was nerve wracking, but being left out of the loop about Holt and his safety was the main contributor.

Moving to a new location was a strategic play to keep the Thunderbird and its faction guessing. The conflicting Overseers were not in all-out war, nor are either sides equipped enough to do so even presently; hence their reliance on somewhat civil tactics to achieve advantage. The Hideling, who was loyal to the Horned Serpent, was tasked with keeping Holt and Euna somewhat separate, as it was believed that keeping Holt unhappy and unstable would keep him from being innovative. This was key to their master plan, as they believe the prophecy implied. You see, this battle between the Overseers was not as simple as evil versus good, but due to different interpretations of the prophecy. Those loyal to the serpent believed that modern human technology would reveal the workings of other realms and dimensional knowledge, ultimately bringing about the epoch of calamity. The Thunderbird's following, however, believed that technological innovation would bring peace across all realms. Both believed that Holt's unquenchable mind and innovative spirit would be the catalyst for the prophecy. After all, he has displayed a considerable amount of influence.

They purposefully allowed Holt to see Euna, so as to put him in a state of depression. The plan had worked out as they hoped, however she was feeling a moral dilemma in its success. She never wanted to hurt Dooley, and in fact felt a rekindled affection for him, knowing how far he had gone just to see her. It didn't help her emotions when the Hideling had mentioned some obsession that a witch had for her husband. He claimed he was sure that Baba Unaka was keeping tabs on him for the Thunderbird, just as he was doing for the Horned Serpent. Meanwhile, Euna's concern was mainly rooted in jealousy.

They loaded up her car and began to head east. She had asked to stay on the coast somewhere, but the Hideling believed things were only going to get more dangerous as the opposition eventually would become more desperate. This time, he *actually* wanted to hide, and he was good at that, seeing as I still don't even know his name. They were going to a different realm.

The easiest way to get a lower tier third-dimensional being to travel to another realm was by utilizing *totem poles*. Not all totem poles work like this, as there are many ornamental ones, created specifically to lure tourists. In traveling this way, they wouldn't necessarily move distance in the way that we think of it, but figuratively it would put a lot of ground between them, Holt, and anything else who might be lurking in the realm that humans know taxonomically.

———

Climbing up the ridgeline that leads to Crater Lake, one's soul is filled. And when one is afraid of heights, that soul gets so heavy that it falls. Euna was in for a treat. It's not often humans get to do what she was about to do. The Hideling knew of a hidden totem pole on an island[135] in the lake, that could only be utilized in a

---

[135] Possibly the volcanic cinder-cone island named "Wizard Island" in the middle of the lake

special way. As they reached the precipice, the view was unmatched. Steep drop-offs are set panoramically around the lake, where the background is endless forest, and rugged mountain tops. A sunset here is a treat, fresh like citrus. Like cutting an orange in half and viewing its subsets, light is reflected onto the walls in similar polygons from the water's waves. He put the car in park and checked to make sure her seat belt was fastened.

"Hold tight or you'll hit your head on the roof," said the Hideling.

"Wait, what?!" she nervously asked.

He reversed into a precise position and smiled at her. She tried to open the door, but he button-mashed the lock button over and over, as the engine roared like a lion with its full power. They flew off the top of the ridge, and her seatbelt held her mostly to her seat. One hand firmly on the passenger window, and one on his shoulder, she couldn't hear her own screams over her fear.

At the same time, a child sat on an overlook bench playing with one of his toy cars. Funnily enough, when he imagined his toy jumping from the ridge to the island below, he witnessed the scene in actuality. His jaw dropped, wordless. He shook his head when the car vanished before crash landing on the island, knowing he would never have evidence for what he saw. He didn't attempt telling his arguing parents, as he predicted that they would assume his outlandish imagination was just acting up again.

Euna had stopped screaming, and much like the child, sat wordless, in amazement at the world she had just entered. The totem pole had lit up like the Thunderbird when they were falling, and "struck" them for lack of a better word, transporting them to another dimension. The car that they once sat in, still looked like a car, and the landscape around still resembled the one she was just in, but with a bustling city built up all around them. The

246

inhabitants were anything but human, and the Hideling looked different, though the distinction was unperceivable to Euna.

"What just happened? This place... this is beautiful!" Her countenance changed and she looked at the Hideling more seriously, "Am I dead?"

"Might as well be! The totem pole brought us to a convergence of realms. This is the city of Giiwas." [136]

"I thought you said the other dimensions would be incomprehensible to me. This looks the same as earth, just with little aliens everywhere and architecture from the future!"

"Oh trust me, you see this realm in a very different way than I do. I wouldn't be able to describe what I see to you, since you have no language that correlates with these physical laws, or shapes even. By the way, those aren't aliens, they are just as much residents of earth as you are. Some species are much much older than humans, so you are actually more of the foreigner here."

"Nice ride, Cube-heads!" [137] shouted a lifeform slithering through the air past them.

"Hey now, do I look like a Cube to you? Pretty daft to not see the difference between her and I!" He shrugged his shoulders at Euna who was scowling at him.

She couldn't be too upset though, as she was overwhelmed with curiosity and intrigue at the sight of the city. All the trees she once overlooked, now overlooked her. Though still rooted in their same position, they were lively with their expressions, animated with

---

[136] Klamath Indian name for Crater Lake.

[137] Maybe this is an insult from organisms of higher life-forms to lower tier 3D beings? Similar to our insult "square"

247

their communication. The architecture was built with materials she almost recognized, but the structures seemed to move quite a bit more. With atmospheric conditions that the structures absorbed, they resembled some characteristics of a spider's web.

"What's the population of Giiwa?" asked Euna.

"Billions...since we are counting various species, unlike humans who only count themselves. We don't measure by population, we measure by social to structural capacity. So this city is a stage 4 with the SSC at 85 percent. That is roughly equivalent to the human city of Salt Lake City."

"Isn't it more likely that I'll be spotted here, especially since as a cube, I stick out?"

The Hideling winced at her usage of the word, showing her his disgust before speaking. "What did I tell you before? Trust those wiser than yourself. I know what I'm doing."

They wandered in and out of the city corridors, navigating the strange social world around lifeforms that were just as busy as humans. As they approached a high-rise that shone like car lights to an astigmatism, Euna could hardly keep from looking through her fingers, which she incongruently used to block its brightness. It appeared to be made of gold, or at least a material with similar color and luster. The entrance had a neon sign in the shape of some two-headed snake, with its forked tongue sticking out as it flashed on and off.

"There are so many things here that resemble human inventions."

"Many of them are human inventions. It's the one thing your species is good for -- *creating*."

As they entered, she was surprised at how open the interior was, with offices and the like placed organically about. Although there were variations of floating platform-esque areas, no "floors" as she thought of them existed until about the 20th story, and from there it was for privacy. Furthermore, Euna was shocked by the giant employee who seemed to be regulating vertical travel in the structure. With the name tag "Cerberus",[138] it sat slouched to keep his head from touching that 20th story ceiling. It leaned all the way to the front doors where they stood, and asked where they needed to go. The Hideling mentioned that he was a friend of the Great Horned Serpent, and the giant's already massive eye grew a bit larger in surprise.

"Right this way, sir," he said, holding out his hand for them to step into. "I thought I recognized that red-mustache," It continued, making the Hideling visibly uncomfortable. The last thing a Hideling wants is to be remembered.

"Why don't they just have some sort of elevator?" Euna asked.

"Then Cerberus here would be out of a job," the Hideling replied.

They soared to the ceiling, where the giant squashed them to its surface as one would when smashing a bug with its shoe. Fortunately for them, the substance that made up the floor was gelatinous, and they phased directly through it. The Hideling confidently walked up to a secretary and identified himself, who waved them to a room down a hallway and to the back. This appeared much more like the corporate scene that Euna was used to. They entered late into a meeting where he pulled out her seat for her, and sat beside her. The beings who were already around

---

[138] "Cerberus" in greek mythology, is the name of the multi-headed guard dog that regulated the entrance of Hades.

the table didn't seem as friendly as she hoped, but she held her head up high anyway.

"The Great Horned Serpent requires action. Now is the time to move. Holt is nowhere to be found, and presumably the Thunderbird is working her magic on him. There is no other option," one said.

"I apologize, what is the option we are discussing?" asked The Hideling.

"A freeze out," said another.

"Woah, woah, woah! That would escalate the situation far too quickly. There is no way the Overseers would vote for that, and even if they did, the bad blood with the Thunderbird is going to come to a boil."

"We already have a majority vote. It's been confirmed throughout all of our liaisons. Wasn't it obvious with the last vote to have the Thunderbird remove Holt's seer status? Ironic that the old bird had to be the one to carry that one out."

"This hasn't been done in centuries! Are we even sure it would work effectively with the technologies they have set in place nowadays? And how do we know it would actually work on Holt anyway? Is he not part-seer?" asked The Hideling.

"Calm yourself!" one commanded.

"The Great Horned Serpent himself has exclaimed there is no better time than now to push that boundary. We'll be putting a hold on Holt, while obtaining enough data to determine how far they have come," another one elaborated.

"He is not actually a seer! That is what is so dangerous about him -- the fact that he can see, and instruct others to do so as well!" a third member chimed in.

"What is a freeze out?" Euna asked the Hideling.

"Stopping time. They want to stop time for every species that lives primarily in the human realm."

Another in the assembly spoke up about a message he had received from an anonymous source, offering intel on Holt's location in exchange for the driftwood piece that Euna had acquired. Euna blushed as they turned to her to validate the existence of the piece, and her hands shook as she handed it to the Hideling. After no more than a minute of debate and inspecting it, the group planned to enchant the driftwood, to be used as a tracking device after the transaction would take place. Hopeful that either the intel, or the driftwood would be a revealing tool to Holt's location, they made an agreement to meet with the anonymous client. At the same totem pole that the Hideling used to transport Euna into their realm, he would exchange the driftwood for information. If I only knew this at the time, so much would be different now.

CHAPTER 19

(Out of Check)

You can only doubt your senses for so long. Over a week's time, Holt had been so immersed in this new reality, that he put any concern of being delusional out of his head. Rosaline caught him up on the conspiracy revolving around him, both sides believing he would bring either colossal calamity or multidimensional peace. Rather than pressuring him to choose a side, It was clear that she couldn't care less about who was right. She was more concerned with keeping him safe.

Holt now understood that the boar was one of many patrons of the Thunderbird who had been helping him to reach Euna. The exhausting notion that his adventuring kinships had artificial origins clouded his foresight. He even learned that "Hamlet" was likely not the boar's actual name.[139] The image he had developed of the boar, a loveable fumbling dimwit, was somewhat inaccurate, and that bothered Holt. Was the boar actually aiding him and

---

[139] This could be why the narrator never calls the pig "Hamlet", only Holt does for the most part.

leading him all of this time?[140] Dooley focused on what it said to him before encountering the Thunderbird: "Whatever happens, it will be alright". The generic and nonchalant nature of the pig's last words was evidence that he knew more than met the eye. Holt became unmotivated, only half listening to the witch and Griff in any given conversation.

"This is not the Holt Dooley I've grown to know. The old you was as sly as a fox. Where is your craftiness?" asked the witch.

"A sly fox with no motive is just a fox."

"It sounds like the Holt I know though. Just going to curl up and die because his ex-wife doesn't love him. Wallow in his sadness a bit for attention."

"Griff, keep it up and you're out of here. And Holt... I don't know what to tell you. I just know sulking isn't going to help you feel any better."

"Can you show her to me?" asked Holt.

"It would be difficult, unless you have something of hers I can use."

Holt felt in his pockets for the familiar piece of driftwood he frequented. This is when he realized it was missing. She had given it to him on their honeymoon, and he had since used it to alleviate his mind anytime he needed to think through his "delusions". He hoped it was left at her doorstep, and that she kept it as a token to remember him by.

---

[140] It would seem that the patrons of the Thunderbird desire Holt to have as much interdimensional interaction as possible, while others obviously disagree.

The witch had fibbed to him though. Of course she was talented enough to spy on Euna if she wanted, but she didn't think it would be an advantageous idea. She intended to stall him from receiving any current information on Euna, or his old crew. Even so, later that evening when he wasn't around, she did end up checking up on the status of these other characters, as one checks on the weather when concerned for a storm. Therein, to her great displeasure, she learned about the "freeze out". Since Holt's seer status had temporarily been removed by the Thunderbird, she believed he would be frozen in time, with the rest of the normal people of their realm. Rather than alert Holt to this information, she planned on getting him somewhere safe, where he would settle for the time being and reduce his chances of being seen. She believed that she didn't have enough time to prevent Holt from being frozen, but that she could help him if she could keep him hidden someplace where no faction would think to look when time would stop. In anticipation of some desperate action of the authorities, Rosaline had been hard at work developing a means to hide Holt, herself, and a few others.

You see, a while back, after the Hideling came to her and threatened her, the witch had constructed a sort of barrier, spanning dimensions to keep herself, and anyone around her from being seen. She utilized not only her own abilities as a seer, but also Griffith's, though it was unbeknownst to him. If your memory recalls, Griff is incredibly lucky. And I explained previously, this is due to him being a seer, called a "fate". While finding a fate who can purposefully harness their power consistently is implausible, the witch was able to harvest some of his power. Rosie's "barrier" was concocted by living in the most favorable outcome to her desire, over all alternate realities. Being mainly limited by close proximity to herself and her psyche, she was of the belief that she needed to not allow Holt leave her presence, until he was in an inconspicuous location. This barrier was an incredible feat, considering some of the clairvoyant abilities of others, which were now somewhat incapacitated as long as Holt was near her. Despite her efforts, Rosie was still paranoid that the Hideling knew where she lived, and that the Overseers would be witty enough to eventually overcome her smoke and mirrors.

Rosaline held small animal figurines on the flat surface of a board game, replacing each of them frequently to understand new scenarios of the future. Holt could tell she was strategizing, but didn't pressure her to tell him much about the figurines and what they represented, as he only half-cared anyway.

"Why are you even interested in helping me?" he asked.

"If I don't, I'm worried you'll usher in an era of calamity. I just want to help you get back on your feet," she replied. "In the end, you are going to make everything alright."

"If you two are getting sweet on each other, I'm outta here!" yelled Griff, attempting to seem disinterested. Holt analyzed Griff's out of place comment and determined the witch might be holding Griff mentally hostage by some underlying feelings for her. Rosaline shook her head and hoped Griff hadn't somehow witnessed their recent kiss.

"What do I do now?" Dooley asked.

"What do you feel like doing?" she replied.

"I don't know if I feel anything."

The witch gathered that Holt was experiencing symptoms of depression, and felt she should spur him to make some decisions that would fall in accordance with the plan she had been concocting. She didn't feel as if she was necessarily manipulating him, but just helping guide him through a difficult time.

"Is there any place on your travels that you felt you would like to revisit?" she asked.

"There is a town I haven't stopped dreaming about since I left it. Where skies are as vibrant as a mountain bluebird's feathers, and my peace gently floats alike."

"Surely you don't mean that town in Colorado where I slayed the vampire," said Griffith.

He did not. Holt was referring to the great nameless town, which if you recall, he swore to his old crew that he'd move back to. Contrary to his old nature, he harbored unrealistic thoughts of going there and meeting back up with them. Though sometimes a healthy coping mechanism, dwelling on unrealistic thoughts can also make one vulnerable. And on occasion, friends take advantage of vulnerability for the greater good. This is what the witch had been planning for Holt in his dismal state, and for the betterment of life in their realm as a whole.[141]

"I can at least do one favor for you," she said.

"Let's hear it."

"I might, possibly, could maybe be able to grant you one wish."

Holt's eyes lit up as if he had just tasted hope again. "When you say 'wish', are you referring to a *Monkey's Paw*[142] kind of wish or a genie in the bottle kind?"

---

[141] The language used here seems to be justifying the witch's actions, a point not to be looked over.

[142] Short story by W.W. Jacobs, wherein wishes come at horrible prices

"Let's say the genie rules apply here...what would you want? Think long and hard because I wouldn't be able to do this twice," she replied.

Griff used some expletives, questioning where his own wish had been this whole time, and the witch sent him on his way. His presence was not only annoying them, but also making her tactics of manipulation less assured, with a third variable of conversational outcomes.

"I know exactly what I want. I have two options. One would be that I wish for Euna to fully comprehend everything I've seen. *If I'm not crazy*, this would mean she could live in the same world I have experienced, and would be forgiving of the frustrations I caused her. But *if I am*, then she would likely only have a more sorrowful feeling for me than any romantic one.

This brings into question the second option: wishing that I am not crazy. *If I'm already not*, then nothing will change between us. But *if I am*, she could fall in love with me again. However, I do believe I would actually miss my delusions if this were the case."

"Just how stupid are you?!" Griff yelled, pursing his lips through a crack in the next room. "Vote for multiple wishes, and then vote for her to just fall in love with you if that is your end game anyway!"

The witch waved her hand, covering up the hole with stone and silencing Griffith. She pretended that she did not somewhat predict Holt's train of thought, as she assured him that his desires were pure and achievable.

"There is just one more thing. In order to make this happen, I need you to be in a physical setting of desire and value to you. Perhaps the town you were mentioning before would work?"

And so they agreed. The witch would transport Holt off to a waterfall in the town that he loved, to wait upon the wish ritual. She would perform this ritual from a distance, and promised for him to see fast results directly after making his wish. He was told to wait until sunset, and make the wish as the last drop of light disappeared from the reflective waterfall.

Holt Dooley, sat still on a bench at the falls overlook, but his mind was moving like a teeter-totter weighing the two wish options. He felt vulnerable, trying to determine a myriad of outcomes without fidgeting his piece of driftwood. Watching as the pink sunlight made its escape up the waterfall, it reminded him of an hourglass.

His stomach grew nervous, as he wondered if he could mess it up by not timing the wish perfectly. To overcome this possibility, he decided to chant his wish over and over in hopes that one would land with perfect timing.

"I wish for Euna to completely understand all of my experiences," he started.

"I wish for Euna to fully understand all of my experiences."

"I wish Euna would completely comprehend all of my past thoughts and experiences."

Hearing himself talking out loud to nobody, he decided to change up his words again.

"I wish I never went crazy."

That was it, the last words he uttered before no light could be seen reflecting from the waterfall. He sat under branches that hid the sky and isolated him into further darkness.

"Holty! Come back to the tent! It's getting dark and you know I don't like to be alone with all of the creepy crawlies!" said Euna.

Holt fell off the bench and stared at Euna, who was cupping a citronella candle. Her face was tinted gold with the flame's light, and unmistakably he recalled the countenance he fell in love with. He quickly scurried over and grabbed her head and kissed it. One on the forehead, a couple on the cheek, and then just about every square inch of her face.

"What was that for?" she said laughingly.

"I'm just so happy to be with you!" he shouted.

Matching his excitement, she bent her knees as if she were going to jump for joy, leaping to his arms for the biggest hug he could handle. Holding tightly, her feet barely hovered over the ground as he spun her around and then stopped too quickly for comfort. She slung somewhat ungracefully into one of his arms, which was rigid as the limb of a tree, and fell out of his grasp. Looking up at Holt from the dirt, her smile waned to displeasure. She let out a groan as she looked at his body, which displayed no intelligible movement, *frozen in time.*

Euna pulled out Holt's old piece of driftwood from her dress pocket, placing it on the toe of his boot as she sobbed. When the wood left her hand, the color of her hair began to change from black to red. She grew slightly in stature, and freckles began to appear.[143] There Rosaline now sat, in the center of the universe, and the center of nowhere[144]. She sobbed over her loss, but determined to fix this wrongdoing.

---

[143] It seems the driftwood was an ingredient Rosaline used in order to appear as Euna.

[144] "The center of the universe is often labeled as in Idaho, at approximately 47.47159411,-115.92395886, though I'm not sure if this is of any relation.

Holt's Driftwood

CHAPTER 20

(Closure)[145]

If I could go back in time, I would.[146] I didn't know that the driftwood would alert them to his location. When I got back to my seer scale and recounted the meeting which took place to make that decision, I attempted to view Holt, to no avail. I hurried back to the landscape he was once frozen in, and could not find him. If I would have just stayed with him, he might be safe.

Finding Holt's journal, abandoned with his other belongings, I hovered over the nearby cities and landscapes searching for any trace of him. When this hope was exhausted, I traveled back to Griff to craft a new plan of action. One might believe rummaging through Dooley's stuff would be an invasion of privacy, but when the world as we know it stopped in time like it did, humans were

---

[145] As the orator narrated this section of the dialogue, she was audibly upset. Enough so that she switched from third person language to first person, possibly without even realizing it. This is what my transcription reflects.

[146] The identity of the narrator being now obvious, I will elaborate more in the epilogue.

stripped of the rights and social norms they grew accustomed to, next to the animals.

Of course, this is the matter at hand, the reason I have recorded Holt's story; so that we can aid those who are as still as statues -- the ones who no longer sense, think, or have a heartbeat. I'm speaking to anyone who can listen to me. If you are able to hear this, you are a seer. You have been lucky enough to be spared from this monstrous authoritative decision, though your family, friends, and most all of those living in your environment have not had that luxury. Let this feed your response of action, and band together to rise against this. It is time the citizens of our realm had a say.

It is likely that by the time I have distributed this account, I will be harshly reprimanded, imprisoned, or killed. My desire is that someone will carry on my torch, and not let it burn out in vain.

The water still rushes, the wind whistles, and the trees still wave. Let them comfort you if you now lack company.

EPILOGUE

Friends, as I told you from the beginning, I found this audio recording and journal at my doorstep. After listening once, I felt it necessary to gather everyone I could find that had not been "frozen" as she called it, to help piece together what has happened, and make a plan of action to help humanity and our world as a whole. Evidently, not only is the witch an important character in the story, but also the one narrating the audio log. This is one of many aspects of the plot that testify to its accuracy.

I have heard through interactions with some of our assembly, rumors of a flying canoe, a pig carrying a radio, and other apparent artifacts of this story have been attested to. As those who were left unfrozen, or "seers" as we have been called, I feel our duty is to a timely response. Our utmost priority lies in finding the witch called Baba Unaka, and gathering all of the information we can to undo this phenomenon.

CPSIA information can be obtained
at www.ICGtesting.com
Printed in the USA
LVHW102331160522
718952LV00015B/332

9 781662 918254